"I didn't mean t

Gage said, reaching to grip her arms lest she fall into the water. "I just watched you here, with the breeze blowing your dress against your body, your hair tangled and curling over your shoulders, and I had to touch you."

"Touch me?" She felt dazed from the desire blazing from the eyes of the man who held her.

"Only a bit," he said softly, persuasively. "Like this." His head bent and he kissed her, a sweet, seeking union of lips that made her breath catch in her throat. His hands held her, and she leaned forward until she was supported by the firm strength of the man.

"You draw me like a magnet, Lily." He lifted his head and she felt the heat of his gaze, felt the beating of her heart in her throat and knew the wonder of being a woman....

* * *

The Marriage Agreement
Harlequin Historical #699—April 2004

Acclaim for Carolyn Davidson's recent titles

Texas Gold

"Davidson delivers a story fraught with sexual tension."
—*Romantic Times*

Tempting a Texan

"A pleasant bubble-bath read with Carolyn Davidson's
usual fine writing to recommend."
—*Romantic Times*

A Marriage by Chance

"This deftly written novel about loss and recovery
is a skillful handling of the traditional Western,
with the added elements of family conflict
and a moving love story."
—*Romantic Times*

The Tender Stranger

"Davidson wonderfully captures gentleness
in the midst of heart-wrenching challenges,
portraying the extraordinary possibilities that exist
within ordinary marital love."
—*Publishers Weekly*

CAROLYN DAVIDSON

The Marriage Agreement

HARLEQUIN®

TORONTO • NEW YORK • LONDON
AMSTERDAM • PARIS • SYDNEY • HAMBURG
STOCKHOLM • ATHENS • TOKYO • MILAN • MADRID
PRAGUE • WARSAW • BUDAPEST • AUCKLAND

ISBN 0-373-29299-6

THE MARRIAGE AGREEMENT

Copyright © 2004 by Carolyn Davidson

This edition published by arrangement with Harlequin Books S.A.

® and TM are trademarks of the publisher. Trademarks indicated with ® are registered in the United States Patent and Trademark Office, the Canadian Trade Marks Office and in other countries.

Visit us at www.eHarlequin.com

Printed in U.S.A.

Please address questions and book requests to:
Harlequin Reader Service
U.S.: 3010 Walden Ave., P.O. Box 1325, Buffalo, NY 14269
Canadian: P.O. Box 609, Fort Erie, Ont. L2A 5X3

The Marriage Agreement represented the end of a journey for me. I finally wrote the story of Yvonne Devereaux, the third of the Devereaux siblings. She was what my editor and I called A Fallen Woman and, as such, one of those ladies who used to be kept in the closet. I loved Yvonne, found her to be honest, forthright and, above all, loyal to her family.
So what if she made some mistakes in her life?
Don't we all! So this book is dedicated to Lily, to all the Lilys who are a part of our families and who deserve all the love and respect we have to offer. I loved the Devereaux clan, and I hate to leave them, but they've all managed to find their way in this world and in the world of my imagination, so I have no choice.

To Mr. Ed, my own hero,
and manager of all my affairs (yes, even *that* one)
I offer my love and devotion for all time.

Prologue

Mississippi River
North of Memphis
Spring, 1878

The messenger stood in the shadows beneath the over-hang. The deck was deserted, except for the silent man who watched and waited; but waiting and watching was what he did best. It was his job. And he was very good at it.

The tall man who strolled casually toward him did not change direction, yet the messenger sensed he'd been spotted. And that was all right. It was because of Gage Morgan that he'd come to this place. So he watched as Morgan leaned with languid ease against the rail of the steamboat, looking across the muddy waters of the Mississippi toward the faint lights of a house.

Lifting a slim cigar from his jacket pocket, Morgan held it to his mouth and, with a soft scratching sound, set fire to the match he carried. He puffed once on the cigar and the smoke dissipated as it blended with the darkness, leaving only the red glow to remain.

"What news do you have?" His words were soft, barely

carrying to where the messenger waited. Morgan stood as if mesmerized by the water flowing past the ship, as though deep in thought.

"I heard from Washington today. Everything is being put in place. They're leaving it up to you to set the stage, but they want you to know that a lawman in Sand Creek is aware of the situation."

"What would they like me to do about a cover?" His laugh was low, as if his thoughts amused him. "Forget I asked," he said.

"You can go in as a married man who's sent his wife off to keep her safe."

"That won't do it," Morgan argued mildly. "Aren't there any agents available?"

"You don't want much, do you? A woman like that is hard to come by."

"Not if the price is right," Morgan returned mildly.

"Maybe you'd better find one yourself," the messenger suggested, then with barely a whisper, he slipped through the shadows and made his way from his hiding place, leaving Gage Morgan to consider the situation.

What he needed was going to be well nigh impossible to come up with, but he was willing to give it a shot. The cigar flared again briefly and then was extinguished by the water below as it was cast into the muddy depths.

Chapter One

Three aces, fanning before him as he edged the cards apart, was a good beginning, Gage Morgan decided. The chance of the dealer delivering the fourth was slim indeed, but even three of them were worth more than the fifty cents he tossed in the pot to up the ante. This just might be another lucky night. He leaned back in his chair, eyed the pile of coins in the middle of the table and waited.

A haze of smoke hung low over the men who were contributing to his wallet, and Gage wished idly for a wandering breeze to ease the burning of his eyes. Whiskey, cigars and wild women accompanied the dealing of cards, it seemed, no matter where men assembled as poker was played. Tonight promised to be no different than last night or the endless string of midnights he'd spent at just such a table.

He touched his squat glass of whiskey, running his index finger around the rim as he waited for decisions to be made. The five men who circled the table were old hands at this—their faces like stone walls, without a glimmer of emotion visible. And his was the same, he thought idly, should an observer take note. He prided himself on a stoic expression, knew the value of denying himself a gleam of triumph or a frown of consternation.

"More whiskey, mister?" The woman who stood at his elbow looked at his half-empty glass, and her hand brushed his shoulder, catching his attention. He shook his head, an abrupt movement that discouraged her attentiveness to his glass. She moved on to the man directly across the table and Morgan's gaze rested on the red gown she wore.

It clung in all the right places, and the figure beneath the shimmering satin was lush, her hips a bit too slender, perhaps, but the fullness of her bosom was enough to draw every eye in the place. His were no exception.

Allowing his dark gaze to slide upward to her face, he found a wary expression in the eyes that returned his scrutiny. Her mouth was unpainted, a rarity in a riverboat saloon such as this, but her cheeks wore a dusting of some rosy hue. Dark hair hung in a mass of ringlets across her shoulders, halfway to her waist, drawn back from high cheekbones and held in place by silver combs that were incongruous in this place. Real silver, he'd warrant, not cheap imitations that could be purchased for a few cents.

The lady must have an admirer, he decided, some generous man who was willing to pay her price. A three-dollar gold piece would no doubt buy her attentions for a night, perhaps two if she was low on her luck. He felt a twitch in his lower parts, where months of celibacy had obviously rendered him vulnerable to such a female as this one.

Hell, why not? She was obviously available and he was possessed of more money these days than he needed. Lady Luck had been good to him. At least when it came to playing poker. He felt stymied. His other endeavors were not paying forth any recent dividends, and that would not endear him to the men he worked for.

He shot another look at the red dress, then glanced down at the cards he held, and considered his options. "How many, Morgan?'' The dealer held the rest of the deck in his hand, and Gage placed two cards on the table, nudging them toward the man who waited. With a snap of the cardboard, he was dealt two and he touched them with his fingertips, bringing them to rest before him.

The men on either side of him examined their hands in a negligent manner and Gage slid his own newcomers into his hand. The first was a trey and he glanced at it for a moment before he fanned the hand to expose the second. The ace of hearts sent a message of success to his mind, and he paused for only a moment before he tapped the five cards into a neat pile and held them in his palm.

''I'll raise,'' said the fourth player, pushing a three-dollar gold piece toward the pot.

Gage selected a matching coin from those in front of him and met the raise, then hesitated for just a moment. With an idle gesture, he added another glittering coin. Around the table the players watched, their eyes hooded, smoke rising to drift above their heads as they contemplated his move.

''I'm out,'' said one, tossing his hand facedown before him.

''Too rich for me,'' said another, pushing back from the table to stalk toward the bar. The third man shot Gage a measuring look and shook his head.

''It's all yours, far as I'm concerned.''

With a casual sweep of his palm, Gage gathered the pot into a stack before him. A sound from across the table brought his head up quickly, and he rose from his chair. The soft cry of pain he'd heard was repeated as the woman in red struggled with one of the men so recently relieved of his money. Pale beneath the smudge of rouge she wore, her wrist held captive by a disappointed card player, she bit at her lower lip, her eyes darting from one to another of the men, as though she sought rescue.

"Come on, Lily." The man whose big hand encircled her arm seemed intent on hauling her off as if she were the spoils of battle, and Gage knew a moment of profound disgust. That the card player was taking out his losses on the woman seemed to be a likely scenario. He paused in the act of claiming his winnings to speak a quiet protest. Watching a woman being treated as an object of scorn was beyond the pale, and he refused to look the other way in the interest of peace.

"I don't think the lady is interested, fella." His gaze never faltering from the two involved in a silent struggle, Gage filled a leather pouch with the money on the table, stuffed it abruptly in his pocket and pushed his chair away.

"Lily?" Gage spoke the name aloud, and dark eyes turned on him with a silent plea in their depths. "Are you interested in spending time with the gentleman?" Gage asked, allowing an edge of steel to touch the words. He'd never been one to seek out trouble, but when it came calling he didn't doubt his ability to handle any situation that might arise.

The dark curls moved, catching the lamplight overhead as the woman shook her head, a definite denial of her interest in the man who held her in his grasp. It was all Gage needed to see, that one movement that signaled for his help.

He moved quickly, his long legs reaching her in three strides, and the hand he placed on her captor's shoulder dug deeply into muscles that felt the pain of long fingers and abundant strength. Anger etched the face of the man whose attentions were unwanted, and his mouth spewed forth an insult Gage could not abide.

"You can have her," the disgruntled man said, thrusting Lily's wrist from his grasping fingers. "She's nuthin' but a whore, anyway. Not worth arguin' over."

The woman stepped back, her eyes fearful, and Gage

took less than five seconds to deliver a pair of punches that sent the two-hundred-pound man to the floor. In the short silence that followed, two husky employees appeared, and the thoroughly incapacitated suitor was lifted and removed from sight. Around Gage the hum of voices rose again and he shot a look of inquiry at Lily.

She attempted a smile, but the quivering of her lips denied even that small expression of humor. ''Thanks,'' she whispered. ''I wasn't sure how to handle that.''

''You're new in here,'' Gage said. ''When did you come on board?''

Lily moistened her lips, an unconscious gesture Gage decided, since she didn't seem to be interested in attracting him. In fact, he'd be willing to warrant she wasn't interested in drawing any more attention to herself than necessary.

''Yes,'' she said softly. ''I'm new. Mr. Scott hired me this afternoon when y'all docked at Saint Louis.''

Gage took her elbow and steered her toward an open doorway, beyond which the Mississippi River lay, its current carrying the boat southward at a leisurely pace. She allowed his guiding hand, offering no protest as they stepped out on deck and moved to the rail. Slender fingers gripped the gleaming wood, and she bent her head, as if the weight of it were too heavy for her fragile neck to support.

''Are you feeling ill?'' he asked. ''Do you need to sit down?'' And then he eased his arm around her waist as he heard footsteps behind them.

''Lily?'' It was the voice of Ham Scott, the owner of the boat, a man Gage knew to be fair but possessed of a short temper when it came to disturbances in his establishment. ''What's the problem? I thought you understood what was required of you when you came on board.''

She shuddered, lifting her head with a jerk at the man's

accusing words. Gage tightened his hold for a moment on her slender waist, then released her as he turned to face Ham. "I'd already asked the lady for her company, Scott. There was a slight misunderstanding, that's all."

"I don't like brawling in my place, Morgan." His eyes glittered in the moonlight as he allowed his gaze to touch Lily and then focus once more on the man he challenged. "Lily knew she'd be expected to be nice to the gentlemen on board when I hired her on."

Gage smiled. "She's being nice to me, and I can guarantee she won't be wearing bruises, come morning."

Ham hesitated and then nodded shortly. "We'll let it go for now, but she's got work to do for the next hour or so. I can't afford to let my girls run off before midnight. Especially since she turned down a customer already. There's too many men in there wanting drinks served to their tables during the stage show. Lily has to do her job."

Gage nodded. "All right, I understand that." He looked at Lily, and his mouth twisted in a wry smile. "I'll just sit and watch, if you don't mind, though. I'd like her in one piece when her work's over for the night."

"Sounds fair to me," Ham said. And then he shot Lily a measuring look. "Are you sure you've worked a riverboat saloon before?"

She nodded. "I mostly sang, though."

Ham lifted an eyebrow as he considered that statement. "I'll listen to you tomorrow—see how you sound. My singers don't serve drinks, Lily. That might suit you better."

"Thank you, Mr. Scott," she said quietly. Her back was straight, her shoulders square as she walked back into the noisy, smoke-laden saloon, and Ham Scott chuckled beneath his breath.

"Gage Morgan to the rescue," he murmured. "That white hat looks good on you, Morgan. Problem now is you're stuck with paying for a woman for the night. Lily's been getting the eye from half a dozen fellas in there. She'll bring a pretty price.''

''I'm not averse to paying for what I get,'' Gage said softly. He pushed away from the rail and slid a hand into his trouser pocket. ''Now, I think I need to keep an eye on my investment.'' He drew a five-dollar gold piece from his pocket and flipped it in the air. ''This should cover Lily's company till morning, I'd think.''

And then he halted in his tracks, watching as Ham snatched the coin from midair and pocketed it. ''Tell her you've already paid in full for whatever strikes your fancy,'' he said. ''From what she told me, she's been around for a while. You oughta get your money's worth.'' He grinned. ''Her name's Devereaux. Lily Devereaux. These French women are supposed to be good at what they do.''

Gage knew a moment of disgust at the words, but a bland expression covered his thoughts as he strode in Lily's wake. A table at the rear, farthest from the low stage, was empty and he settled there, aware that he was the focus of more than one man's attention. Lily stood at the bar, waiting for a nod from customers who needed a refill, and her eyes drifted across the crowd until they met his.

He lifted his index finger and nodded at her, then watched as she made her way through the tables to where he waited. ''What can I get you?'' she asked, standing across the width of the table. Her voice was husky, as if she held back tears, and Gage felt a moment of pity, laced with an awakening in his nether parts.

''Just a whiskey, Lily. I'll wait here till you finish working, and then we'll go to my stateroom.''

She hesitated only a few seconds, and then nodded, turning away. Gage watched as she walked across the floor, noticed the eyes of those who followed her progress and felt a surge of possessiveness that gave him pause. He'd managed to stick himself with a woman's company for the night—not that it would be any great sacrifice to spend a few hours with Lily. He was allowed to be jealous of her time over the next hour or so. He'd already paid the price.

Her feet hurt, her face ached from forcing a smile into place and keeping it there, and for Lily Devereaux, it seemed that she'd reached the end of her rope. If not for the man called Morgan, she'd even now be fighting off the filthy hands of the man who'd been intent on dragging her from the saloon earlier. And no doubt Mr. Scott would have allowed it, rather than cause a disturbance.

It seemed that Morgan had no such qualms in that direction. His two-fisted attack had delivered her from the disgruntled loser at the poker game, and placed her smack-dab in his debt. It seemed she was about to discover just how far she was willing to go in order to survive.

There was little doubt in her mind that the man called Morgan would expect full payment for the rescue he'd pulled off. The memory of his scent clung in her mind, that faint odor of smoke that was a part of this room, the masculine smell of some sort of shaving soap, and the aroma of a male creature bent on seeking out a woman. She had no doubt that she would receive his full attention once her work in the saloon came to an end, when the last drink had been served and the last table wiped with a dingy cloth.

Even now his gaze followed her and she knew the heat of masculine appraisal bent on her form. The dress was snug, her shoes too small. Apparently the last woman to work this room hadn't had much of a bosom. Lily's own abundant curves were well-nigh overflowing her low neckline, and she concentrated on ignoring the men whose eyes were drawn to a figure her mama had described as ample.

Men like their wives to be modest and their charms to be viewed only by their husbands. A man only marries a woman he respects. Mama's words that rang in her head had proved to be true in the end. The past two years spent on her own had provided Lily with enough shame to last her a lifetime. The Union soldier who'd bargained with her, torch held in his hand, the flame reflected in his eyes as he offered her the choice that was really no choice at all, had kept his word—to a point.

She shook her head, as if that small movement would dismiss the past from her mind. "Take those men in the corner their drinks," the barkeep said from behind her. She turned to the glossy walnut bar, where rows of bottles caught the light from kerosene lanterns hanging from the ceiling. "Two bits each, Lily." Handing her the rough wooden tray, he nodded to where three men huddled around a small table.

Making her way through the tables, ignoring the grasping hands that reached to touch her dress, she focused instead on the man who had effected a rescue and was even now watching her from the table in the rear. Smoke-gray eyes seemed darker in the gloom of the saloon, lights dimming as the lead singer stepped forth from the wings to take her place on center stage.

The men's raucous voices stilled, and all eyes were upon May Kettering, the tall, blond beauty whose voice rivaled that of an opera singer Lily had heard in New York City. The woman was statuesque, voluptuous, and knew the power she wielded over her audience. Following her into the spotlight would be like wandering into an arena after the lions had devoured the Christians, Lily decided. Definitely an anticlimax, no matter how well she could carry a tune.

She listened from the side of the saloon as May sang, knew that the men listening had no idea of the meaning of the words that soared from the woman's throat. And yet, there was something about the music that spoke to the soul, and even those who had never seen or heard of an opera were touched by the magnificence of the music.

A burst of applause greeted May's final note, and she nodded at the piano player, a man whose talents were far beyond what one usually found in a place such as this. A saloon was still a saloon, no matter where it was, and although a riverboat might boast a decent piano player, this one was beyond decent. May paused, then lifted her head as the music began, and her voice lifted in song, this time in English, the words of love and sorrow and an aching heart.

For a moment, silence greeted her final notes and then, as she swept from the stage in a swirl of skirts, the men exploded with applause and whistles. "Can you sing like that?" Ham stood beside her, had managed to approach without gaining her notice, and Lily glanced at him with a quick shake of her head.

"Not even a little bit," she admitted. "My voice is pleasant, and I sing ballads mostly, but I'll look like a schoolgirl next to May."

"Not in that dress you won't," Ham retorted, eyeing her with a grin. "Honey, you don't look like any girl I ever met in school."

She felt a blush rise to cover her cheeks, and glanced to where Morgan sat, watching from narrowed eyes. "How long before I can leave?" she asked.

"Another half hour or so," Ham told her. "I'll let you go early tonight, since Morgan paid in advance."

She inhaled sharply. "What do you mean? Who did he pay?"

"Me, sweetheart. And for what he handed over for your time, you'd do well to keep the man happy for the whole night."

She met Ham's gaze. "And if I don't measure up? What then?"

"Then you don't get to sing for me tomorrow, and I'll have to put out the word that your services are available after the saloon closes at night."

"That's blackmail," Lily said quietly. "I didn't hire on as a whore, Mr. Scott."

"And who are you going to complain to, Miss Devereaux?" he retorted quickly. "I own this boat, and what I say goes. We won't be docking anywhere for another couple of days. I'd say it would behoove you to measure up to Mr. Morgan's expectations."

Lily stalked toward the bar, blindly making her way on feet that protested, fearful of tripping and falling over the multitude of men who managed to block her way with outthrust hands and vile suggestions. Tears threatened to fall as she reached the relative safety of the walnut bar, and she leaned against it, barely able to conceal the trembling of her hands as the bartender, a man named John, pushed a loaded tray in her direction.

"That table by the door, Lily," he said quietly. "Are you all right, honey?" he asked, not releasing his hold on the heavy tray as she would have lifted it.

"No, but I doubt it's going to get any better," she said harshly.

"Uh-oh," the barkeep said softly. "Here comes trouble."

"I'll give you a hand with that, Lily." Gage Morgan stood behind her, and the barkeep met the man's gaze with a look of query.

"Lily don't need any trouble, Mr. Morgan," John said quietly.

"I'm not going to give her any," Morgan returned. "Just thought I'd lend a hand."

His warmth behind her was a revelation, Lily decided.

Though they stood inches apart, the heat from his big body touched her from nape to knees, and she resisted the urge to lean against him for just a moment. Wouldn't *that* bring every eye in the place in her direction?

Morgan's hands were strong, his fingers long and he lifted the tray without a trace of effort, then nodded at Lily to lead the way to their destination. The men whose drinks he carried watched in bafflement as the duo neared their table, and then Lily smiled and sorted out each drink with its intended owner.

"That's two bits each," she said pleasantly, and smiled nicely as the men responded quickly, placing their cash on the tray, three of them adding a bit extra for her. Morgan stepped aside and nodded at her, ushering her back to the bar with a small ceremony that was the center of attention in the smoky room.

"Thank you," she whispered as he placed the empty tray on the bar. She transferred the cash to John's hand and tucked the extra coins into her bodice. A choked sound from Morgan brought her eyes in his direction and as she watched, his gaze fastened there. Not only was the dress too small, but the neckline was lower than anything she'd ever worn, and her breasts were in dire straits, almost overflowing the red fabric. She tugged at the ruched edging that rimmed the sweetheart neckline, to no avail, for it was already stretched almost beyond bearing.

Morgan cleared his throat and faced the bar. "Give me a shot of whiskey, straight up," he told John, his voice strained.

John grinned. "Quite a woman, ain't she?" he asked, pushing the glass across the bar and into Morgan's grip.

"More than most," Morgan said bluntly. "And certainly more than these clowns deserve to have delivering their drinks."

"I think I mis-spoke myself," John said quietly. "She's

a lady, Morgan. I recognized that right off, first time she opened her mouth this afternoon.''

Morgan lifted his shot glass and drank deeply, downing the whiskey as if it were bad-tasting medicine and he was in dire need of a cure. And then he glanced again at Lily and his gaze touched her face and hair, his eyes a darker gray than she'd first thought. He pushed the glass back toward the bartender and shook his head as John would have refilled it from a bottle behind the bar.

Lily listened to the two men, her eyes traveling from one to the other as they discussed her attributes and decreed her a step above the position she held here. It was almost too much for her patience to bear, she decided, that these two should speak of her as if she could not hear their opinions, and certainly should not be concerned with them.

"I'm not a lady, Mr. Morgan," she said finally. "No lady ever dressed like this or served drinks in a saloon."

"Ah," he said softly, touching his brow with his index finger, as if he saluted her. "But I suspect that at one time you were a most respectable woman, Lily. And I think that you still carry yourself as a lady, no matter what you're wearing or what your job is."

"I'm not very good at some things," she said boldly. "You may be sorry you paid Ham Scott for my time." She felt, as she spoke, the warm flush of crimson that touched her cheeks and proclaimed her embarrassment.

Morgan smiled, a slow, gradually widening movement of lips and teeth that made his eyes narrow and gleam in the light of the kerosene lanterns overhead. "I doubt I'll be disappointed in you, Miss Lily," he murmured, and she felt the heat of his gaze touch her breasts once more, as if he could make out the outline of the coins she'd stored there during the evening.

Another table of men beckoned her and she left Morgan where he stood, aware that he turned his back to the bar and leaned his elbows on it as he watched her cross the floor. For some reason, the men she passed by kept their hands to themselves and she heard soft murmurs from behind her as she passed by.

"Morgan...handy with a gun," one man whispered.

"Wouldn't take kindly..." another said, then spoke in an undertone as she moved past his table.

It seemed that Gage Morgan's interest in her was bearing fruit tonight, and she could not help but be relieved by the changed attitude of those who ordered drinks during the next half hour. When Ham Scott stepped up to the bar and nodded at her, she lifted her eyebrow in question.

"I reckon you've done your share for the night," Ham said easily and then glanced at Morgan. "She's got work to do tomorrow," he said lightly. "Including singin' for me in the morning."

"I'll see to it she gets a good night's sleep," Morgan said, moving to take Lily's elbow in his grasp. "Come on, Lily," he murmured in an undertone, leading her to where an open doorway beckoned.

She stepped before him as they skirted tables, and then beside him as they paused to look out on the river. "I don't know where your room is," she said. "And I'll need to go to my bunk first to get my things."

"What things?" Gage asked, his hand tightening as if he were unwilling to allow her out of his sight.

"My nightgown, for one," she said, and was silenced by his low chuckle.

"You won't need it, Lily."

"I need my hairbrush and face cream," she told him, breathless as she considered his words. "I can't go to bed without washing my face."

"All right," he said, allowing her this small victory that wasn't really any triumph at all, she decided. Only a stop-gap until she should face him in his stateroom and be required to deliver whatever he deemed to be his due.

"How much did you pay for me?" she asked as she turned away from the saloon, leaving behind the music of the piano and the catcalls that followed their exit.

"Does it matter?" He slid his hand down and held her fingers in his palm.

She shrugged. "I suppose not. I probably won't come up to what you expect anyway. I'm not really in the business, Mr. Morgan."

"I already figured that out, Miss Devereaux." He squeezed her fingers a bit and she knew a moment of relief, whether from his reply or the touch of his hand holding hers securely in its depth.

"How did you know my name?" she asked.

"Ham told me."

"When?" She halted outside a door and inserted a small key in the lock.

"After you went back inside, earlier." He waited there as she stepped into the room and gathered her things in the darkness, the space she shared with two other women so small she had memorized the location of each item she owned. All of them fit on the narrow bunk she was to have slept in tonight, and for a moment she rued the circumstances that had so changed her destination for the next few hours.

"All right," she said, emerging into the moonlight. "I think I have everything I need."

Morgan looked down at the armful she clutched to her breasts. His smile was gentle, as if he teased her. "Brought the nightgown anyway, I see."

She nodded, unable to speak aloud, so rapid was the beating of her heart as she faced the thought of earning her keep in a way she'd thought behind her forever. The face of the Yankee colonel appeared before her again, and overlapped that of Gage Morgan, just for a moment. She blinked, and he was gone, but his memory was like a burning ember in her mind.

"I don't know what made you think I was going to marry you, Yvonne," he'd said with a laugh of derision. *"I thought you were smarter than that. A man marries a woman of his own class, not a Southern belle who can't even speak proper English."*

Forever she would rue the moment she'd crushed his skull with a poker from the fireplace. The memory was alive in her dreams nightly, and now she was paying the price for the rage that had beset her two years ago in New York City.

She closed her eyes, and felt Morgan's hand touch her cheek. "Are you all right?" he asked, his gaze shuttered. And then he smiled, a mere movement of his lips. "I didn't mean to upset you, Lily. I understand the bit about the nightgown."

She opened her eyes and focused on the man's face. No longer did he bear any resemblance to the Yankee. Even his speech was softer, bearing a trace of the South in its whispered vowels. "It's all right," she said, forcing her lips to curve in a smile. "I brought a dressing gown to wear in the morning when I travel back to my room."

Morgan's eyes narrowed on her and she caught a glimpse of some dark emotion in his gaze. "I may have a hard time letting you go, come morning," he warned quietly. "In fact, I may just keep you for myself while I'm traveling south."

"Can you afford me?" she asked, turning as he guided her toward a narrow stairway leading to the upper deck. They climbed the stairs and she heard him murmur a soft phrase that evaded her.

Halting her at the top of the flight of stairs, he drew her close and bent his head to touch his lips to her forehead.

"I can afford you," he said quietly, and she sensed an assurance in his voice that brought her once more to a state of near panic.

"Will Ham—"

Morgan stilled her by a simple act. Bending his head a bit farther, he touched his mouth to hers and held her immobile, one large hand cradling her head, the other firm against her back. She felt the heat of him, the hard, damp kiss of a man who would not be denied, and though she trembled in his embrace, she knew a moment of anticipation so great it threatened to overwhelm her.

Chapter Two

Lily stepped into the stateroom and paused, the lack of lighting in the small area halting her progress. Behind her, Morgan closed the door and she caught her breath, aware of his body brushing against her back, his hand touching her shoulder as he guided her forward into the darkness.

"I can't see," she whispered. "Are you going to light a lamp?"

He stepped to one side, and she heard the rasping sound of a match and then blinked as it flared and lit the space between them. His face was all harsh planes and angles, his eyes dark, and she trembled as he bent to apply the flickering flame to the lamp on a shelf by the door.

"All right?" he asked, turning again to face her. The light was too bright, she thought as she looked around her. The stateroom was starkly simple; nothing in the small room seemed welcoming. A wide bunk against the wall was flanked by a chair, where an open valise lay. Beside it was a table, upon which a pitcher and bowl were placed, along with a neatly folded towel and the utensils necessary for shaving. In mere seconds she'd surveyed her surroundings, and then glanced up at him, aware that she hadn't answered his soft question.

"Yes, I'm fine," she said quietly, even as her heart thumped unmercifully in her breast, and her fingers clung damply to the articles of clothing and grooming she held.

"I'll take those," he offered, holding out his hand, and she stared dumbly at his open palm, then shook her head.

"No, just tell me where I can change," she told him, and realized as she spoke those words that there was not even the benefit of a screen for her privacy.

Morgan smiled, his gleaming eyes sweeping her length. "Right here will do," he said, lifting one hand to touch the bodice of her dress. His fingers were long, elegant and tanned, and she was reminded of their dexterity as they'd handled the cards earlier. Now she knew a moment of panic as they lingered just above the line of cleavage where her breasts strained the fabric of the red gown...then brushed against her skin, as if he must test the texture.

His murmur was soft, inviting. "Would you like me to give you a hand?"

"No." She shook her head in an abrupt movement, stepping back, her flesh tingling where his fingertips had rested. "I'll do it," she added hastily, aware that a five-dollar gold piece was a high price to pay for an evening with a woman whose value was yet to be determined.

"All right." Agreeably, he turned and propped a shoulder against the door jamb, his gaze focused on her in a lazy manner. His eyes seemed darker, she thought, glistening in the lamp's glow, and with indolent ease they passed over her, lingering on the curve of her breasts, and then settling on the line of her hips. Heat rose to color her cheeks, and its warmth radiated from her skin.

"Lily?" Her name had never sounded so soft, had never whispered against her ears with such a seductive murmur as he repeated his offer. "Shall I help you?" His lids barely masked the glitter of passion as he watched her, and she thought for a moment that he surely possessed some

eerie power, perhaps the ability to see beneath her clothing.
Her breasts were taut and tingling, her legs trembled, and
she prayed silently for the strength to perform this denial
of all she'd been raised to believe in.

With a sound of dismay, uttered in a barely audible
whisper, she turned from him, reaching behind her back.
The task of undoing the fastenings that held her dress together was hampered by the trembling of her fingers. He
touched her shoulder gently, halting her efforts.

"Begin with your hair, Lily," he said softly. "Let it
loose. Please."

"My hair?" Obediently, she lifted her hands to touch
the dark curls, her fingers curving to pull the silver combs
from place. The heavy fall of waves caressed her shoulders
and she turned back to face him. His eyes narrowed, as if
drawn to the unruly tresses and he gently grasped a curl,
allowing it to wrap the length of his index finger. His gaze
settled there for a long moment, as though the texture and
weight of that lone bit of waving hair held some sort of
appeal.

Gray eyes silvered as his hand abandoned that single
curl and instead rose to fit his palm to the curve of her
neck. Long fingers moved upward, tunneling through her
hair, and the heat of his hand was like a branding iron on
her scalp. Without warning, his head lowered and his
mouth touched hers, opening to suckle the plump line of
her lower lip. A warning growl made her aware of danger
just as his other arm circled her waist and snagged her
against his length.

The kiss took on a more seductive angle, his head tilting
as he sought to invade the soft tissues behind her lips. A
harsh sound in his throat gave her warning that Gage Morgan was not to be denied, and she shrank from him and
the force of his desire.

Tears spilled from her eyes to flow unchecked down her

cheeks, and he hesitated. Lips that had demanded her sub-
mission softened, opening a bit, damp and warm against
her mouth. "I won't hurt you, Lily," he murmured. His
touch on her nape became a caress, yet she trembled in his
embrace, her breath a soft gasp.

Her scent rose to tempt him, an aroma of flowers
blended with that of woman, and he inhaled it, recognizing
the moment as one that would dictate the whole of their
relationship. She was warm against him, yet she shivered,
and he became aware that his attraction to her was not
mutual. The woman he held in his arms was compliant to
his touch, but her murmured cry denied the passion he'd
hoped to arouse within her body.

"Well, hell." Morgan uttered the curse even as he heard
her almost silent sob, knew a moment's remorse as she
cringed from his touch, and then opened his eyes to see
twin trails of dampness on her cheeks. A frown marred his
brow as he took her measure.

"Lily…" He hesitated, and then shook his head. "I'm
sorry." The words seemed not enough of an apology he
decided as he lifted a hand to touch her cheek. "I really
planned to be a gentleman. I'm not generally so heavy-
handed when I spend time with a woman." It had been
too damn long, he thought. Too many months without a
woman's touch.

His palm spread wide across her back, and his fingers
caressed her through the satin dress she wore. Bending to
her again, his mouth touched her forehead, then brushed a
path to her cheek. "Can I start over?" he asked. And then,
without waiting for her answer, he turned her within his
embrace and worked slowly at the fastenings of her dress.

"How did you get into this thing?" he mused, his fingers clumsy at the task.

"One of the girls helped," she said, and shivered anew

as his hands found bare skin just below her waistline. "Please, can you blow out the lamp?"

His words held a tinge of amusement. "Has no one ever told you that some things are better accomplished in the light?" Turning her to face him, he smiled and looked down to where her hands gripped the red satin over the contours of her breasts. "Am I not going to be allowed to look?"

Lily bit her lip, tasting the blood, aware that he was more patient than she had a right to expect. "I told you I'm not very good at this," she whispered. "I'm not worth five dollars, I fear."

His head tilted to one side and his smile vanished, as though he saw something within her that held him immobile, his eyes darkening. His words were dry and a bit cynical, but spoken carefully. "How many men have bought your favors, Lily? A hundred? Fifty, maybe?" He paused and she swallowed, the lump in her throat almost smothering the laugh that denied his suggestion.

"Am I the first?" he asked, the words so quiet she strained to hear them.

"No." And he wasn't, not if she were to be honest. The Yankee colonel had paid the price for her compliance five years ago, and made a whore of her in the process. When he took her from her home.

"But you haven't done this often, have you?" he persisted, his hands holding her firmly in his grasp.

She shook her head. "No." Then she tilted her head back to offer him a look of resolve. "But I expect it's something I'll learn, Mr. Morgan."

He sighed and shook his head, a strangely sad emotion washing over him. Her scent rose again to tempt him, that of a woman whose skin was clean, almost a rarity in her profession. He denied the stirring in his groin, turning his back on the thought of taking this female to his bed, and shook his head.

"But not tonight, Lily," he said. "I won't take a woman who weeps at my touch."

"If Ham Scott finds out—" She broke off and her teeth touched the spot where blood had begun to dry.

"He won't," Morgan said, his finger nudging her lip. "Don't do that, Lily. You've already made it bleed." He looked closer and his eyes darkened. "Or did I do that to you?"

And if he had, would it matter? she wondered silently. But her head moved, offering a denial of his concern.

His hands were warm, resting on her back, and his words offered a reprieve. "I'll turn my back and you can get into your nightgown," he told her. And true to his word, he turned in a half circle and faced the door.

With swift movements, Lily allowed the satin dress to slide to the floor, then snatched at her nightgown and pulled it over her head. Beneath the dress, she wore sleek satin drawers that matched the dress and in a moment they were folded and placed on the bed.

"Now what, Morgan?" she asked. "I have six bits if you want part of your money back. In fact I have a dollar in my bag, back in my room."

"Turn around and look at me," he said roughly. "And don't mention money again." He looked down at her hand where she held the tips she'd received in the saloon, taken now from the bodice of the dress. "Do you think I'd take it from you?" he asked, his jaw taut.

She shook her head. "I suppose not. But then, I don't really know you, do I?"

"Not as well as you will by morning," he said, and buffered the words with a grin. "I've never bought a woman's favors before, Lily. I think I'm grateful to you for not allowing me to spoil my record."

"Then what do you expect for your five dollars?"

"I think I want to know who Lily Devereaux is," he answered. ":Where she comes from—and maybe even more, where she's going."

Lily dropped her gaze and laughed, a mirthless sound. "Lily Devereaux only exists on this boat," she said. "She's a brand-new person, Morgan."

"And what is that supposed to mean?" His words were soft, as if he realized she would respond to his coaxing quicker than to a harsh demand.

Lily wrapped her arms tightly around her waist, and then dropped them quickly as Morgan's eyes took note of the curves of her breasts as they were supported by her forearms. "Don't look at me like that," she said, warming as a flush of embarrassment rose to tinge her face with color.

"For five dollars, I should be able to look, Lily," he told her patiently. "I've already promised not to take more from you than you'll give me freely."

"If I told you—" She broke off abruptly and turned her head aside.

"Told me what?" he asked.

A desperate longing to gain some small bit of respect from the man drove her to offer a small bit of knowledge into his hands. "I'm not what you think I am, not a woman who works on her back for a living."

"I already figured that out," Morgan said. And with those words spoken, an inkling of a bold move, a rash decision, filled his mind. "I don't know what you are, Lily, but I'd lay odds that you don't belong on a riverboat, serving trash like the man who touched you earlier." He motioned toward the bunk. "Go on. Crawl between the sheets." He walked behind her, watching as she bent to pull back the top sheet and then retrieved the pillows. Her glance at him merited a small smile.

"Don't worry. I'll stay right here for now."

Her curves were nicely traced by the taut lines of her nightgown as she leaned forward on one knee, drawing his gaze. Morgan caught his breath, almost ruing his vow.

Turning to face him, she settled on the edge of the mattress and he nodded, the demand implicit. Her feet slid beneath the top sheet and she drew it up to her waist, and then eased her way to the pillows. Morgan stepped closer and lowered himself to sit beside her.

"Now, unless you want me to change my mind, lady, I want you to tell me about Lily Devereaux." He waited, his gaze unmoving as he met her dark eyes. She swallowed, a visible movement of throat and lower jaw, and then lifted her hands in a helpless gesture.

"I don't know what you'd like to know, Morgan. I'm from the South...." She hesitated and he smiled, a lazy arrangement of lips that expressed amusement.

"I figured that out right off, honey," he told her. "Now tell me something I didn't know. Like who's out there looking for you."

She paled beneath his gaze and he felt a sense of triumph. He was, it seemed, on target with his suspicions. The lady was on the run. "Lily?" As she hesitated, his hands smoothed the sheet and toyed with the hemmed edge.

"No one's looking for me," she told him harshly. "I went north after the war was over and worked for a while. And then I found I wasn't suited for the cold weather and decided to head back toward home."

"And where is that?" he asked idly, noting her subtle movement as she edged away from him. One hand shot out and grasped her wrist, holding her firmly, but with a gentle strength.

"South of here," she quibbled. "I'm not saying more than that, Morgan."

"How did you get north?" he asked. "Must have been a long walk, honey."

"I rode on a horse, then in a buggy. Finally on a train." Her jaw set grimly as if she had been pushed far enough for one night, and Morgan relented.

"One more question," he said. "But I want the truth, Lily. Were you with a man?"

She hesitated, and that small pause told him what he wanted to know. And then her chin lifted and a spark of defiance lit her eyes. "And if I was?" she asked.

Morgan shook his head. "It doesn't matter," he said. "I just wanted to know if you'd be honest with me." But it did matter, he thought. More than he'd realized it would. Lily Devereaux had secrets, but his curiosity was aroused—beyond the point of wanting to peer into her past, to the brink of an uneasy desire to discover her hidden reasons. Surely, the woman had known the risks she took by working on the riverboat. Something, or someone, had driven her to this desperate situation.

It was a puzzle. And Gage Morgan was a man who thrived on solving just such a conundrum. With a sigh he motioned to her to move to the back of the bunk. She did, watching him with eyes that shone with a trace of moisture.

"I'm only going to sleep beside you," he told her. And then he shed his boots and shirt and lay down beside her, atop the sheet. It was to his credit that he waited until she slid into slumber before he gathered her in his arms and held her close.

Lily awoke with a start, aware of a weight across her waist, and the warm, solid bulk of a man beside her. She held her breath, frantic as she sidled from beneath the heavy arm that held her prisoner.

It tightened its grip and the man who owned it murmured her name. "Lily. Just lie still. You're all right."

Morgan. She breathed his name aloud then and felt disappointment creep into her heart. "You promised—"

"I promised not to hurt you, Lily," his sleep-roughened voice said, reminding her of his words. "Are you wearing any bruises?" The arm holding her shifted, and she felt his fingertips trailing warmth across her skin as they traveled to her hand and then warmed her through the fine cotton of her gown, moving up toward her shoulder.

The fact that a thin layer of fabric hid her from his gaze seemed immaterial, she decided. Morgan knew his way around a woman's body, knew the effect his touch was having on her flesh. She'd known the feel of a man's hands, but that memory was far removed from the reality of Gage Morgan's whispering caress.

"It's morning," she whispered.

"So it is." He yawned, and she turned her head to watch as his mouth released the sigh. His gaze cut to meet hers and a crimson streak edged his cheekbones. Beneath the languid glance he offered, she sensed the taut control he held over his body. "I told you I was going to sleep in the same bed, Lily," he reminded her. "In case Ham Scott asks me, I can tell him truthfully that I held you in my arms all night long." His grin was quick. "After you went to sleep," he added slyly.

"Please let me up," she said, aware that she was at his mercy. And then he cupped her chin and turned her head fully toward him.

"You'll spend your nights here, Lily. Until we get to the Gulf, you'll be in my bed."

She shook her head in bewilderment. "Why? Why on earth would you want me in your stateroom, Morgan? I doubt I'll be any good to you."

His shrug was diffident, and she felt the movement of his shoulder beside her. "I don't know," he admitted. "Maybe I don't want anyone else to have you. Sort of a dog in the manger thing, I suspect.'' Yet, it seemed there was more to it than that, and the fine hair on the back of her neck lifted as a chill passed over her.

And then he laughed softly. ''Although I'm not sure that old saw applies in this case. Maybe I'm just not willing to share, even if you're not ready to give me what I've paid for.''

She flexed her hands into fists and clenched her jaw. ''I pay my debts, Morgan. If you want—''

He rose over her, shifting so quickly she was taken by surprise. His arms pinned her to the mattress, his big body poised above her threateningly, and she felt like a hunter's prey as she looked into his face. His mouth was twisted, his eyes harsh with a look she could not define.

''You don't owe me a debt,'' he said, grinding out the words quietly. ''I told you I wouldn't ask for anything from you, and that still goes.'' His mouth softened as he scanned her features, and she thought for a moment he might have set aside his anger, if indeed that was the emotion that had gripped him.

Then, against her body, she felt the unmistakable ridge of his desire and she shrank from it, wishing with all her heart she had not prodded him into challenging her.

''This is all I'll ask of you,'' he said, bending to her, touching her lips with his, brushing across the width of her mouth, gently taking that which she could not deny him. ''Just a kiss,'' he murmured. ''Probably the most expensive kiss I've ever enjoyed.''

''And tonight?'' she asked, fearful of his answer. If he tired of her reluctance and turned her loose, freed her from his protection, she was fearful of what the night hours might hold. On the other hand, if he paid again for her time, if he expected her to sleep in his bed, she might find herself exposed to an even greater danger.

Morgan was a man she could imagine as a lover. She

who had vowed never again to allow a man's hands on her body, felt a softening toward the male creature who loomed over her.

"I already made it clear, I thought. You'll sleep here tonight," he said, lifting his weight from her, then bending his head to steal another kiss, one she gave with but a moment's hesitation. And then she rolled from the bunk, snatching at her dressing gown quickly, pulling it on and tying it firmly at her waist.

Her hands busied themselves with her brush, taming the dark hair that formed a riot of untamed curls around her face, spilling over her shoulders. He watched, sprawled in the bunk, his bare feet crossed at the ankles, his gaze unswerving. And then as she gathered her things together, he rose, taking the red satin dress from her hands and folding it.

"I'll just keep this for now," he said. "I think we'll ask Ham to find you something else to wear today."

"I'll be in trouble if I show up without that dress," Lily warned him. "I need it to wear when I sing for him this morning."

Morgan shook his head. "No, you don't. Wear whatever you had on yesterday, before he stuck you into this thing."

She shot him a glance of disbelief. "I thought you liked it on me."

"I do. But I don't think I like every other man on board looking at you wearing it."

"You can't call the shots with him," she said. "He's not a soft touch."

"Let me worry about that. You just get yourself in my room tonight when you've finished the last show."

Her chin lifted defiantly. "I don't know that you can afford to buy me, Morgan. I'm not even sure you'll want to after a couple of days. I'm afraid you won't be getting the best part of this bargain."

His teeth were white and even when he smiled, his eyes holding a determination she would not dispute. "I'll get what I want," he said. "I always do."

The door opened with a creak and she slipped through the opening into the narrow passageway, to where the cabin she shared held a modicum of safety. Inside, the two occupants slept, her own bunk untouched. In a matter of minutes she'd donned her clothing and slipped into her shoes. The women slept undisturbed, and she left as quietly as she'd come.

"Lily?" Ham Scott stood before her, his eyes registering his displeasure with her appearance as she left the area where breakfast was being served. "You lose your red dress during the night?" he asked.

"Mr. Morgan wouldn't let me take it with me this morning," she told him.

Ham waved a hand, dismissing her words. "You'll have to retrieve it before you go to work tonight." He turned aside and issued a command she'd expected. "Come on inside. I want you to sing for me."

May Kettering stood on the stage, dressed in a simple cotton frock, and her gaze moved over Lily in a lazy survey as she sang the final bars of a song. "Thanks," she murmured to the piano player. "You've got it down pat, Charlie." And then she lifted her hand and beckoned to Lily. "Come on up here, honey."

Ham stood aside as Lily climbed the three steps to the stage and approached the woman. "I enjoyed your singing last evening," she said quietly. "I fear I don't have much talent compared to your ability."

May lifted an eyebrow. "We all have talent of one sort or another, Lily. I'd like to hear what you've got to offer." Her nod at the piano player was barely perceptible, then she looked back at Lily and made a suggestion.

"Do you know 'I Dream of Jeannie'?" she asked. She hummed a few notes, and then sang a line of lyrics. "'I dream of Jeannie with the light brown hair—borne like a vapor on the summer air—'"

"I know it," Lily said quickly. Singing ballads was not new to her, for her voice was more suited to their simple melodies.

Charlie allowed his fingers to move leisurely across the keys, his chords giving Lily the key he'd chosen. She focused on May, aware that her salvation lay in the woman's influence on Ham Scott. Untrained, yet melodic, her voice rose in the first notes of the song May had chosen. It was guaranteed to make any wanderer homesick, she thought, and she was no exception.

May smiled, her mouth quirking with approval. "You'll do, honey," she said as the last note faded. "Stephen Foster is your style."

Ham walked to the edge of the stage and cast a glowering look at his star performer. "That's not what I had in mind for her, May. I wanted a contrast to your way of singing. You know, lifting her dress and showing her legs some. A fast song with words the men in the crowd will get a kick out of."

May snorted, a strangely inelegant sound coming from such a woman, Lily thought. "You don't know diddly about what men want from a singer, Scott. Lily has a body that'll show up well in most anything she wears. And keeping them guessing about her legs will have them on the edges of their seats."

"Well, she's not wearin' that rag," Ham said bluntly. "I want her in the red satin."

"No." It was a softly spoken denial, yet held a definite threat should it be ignored. "She won't be wearing it again." Morgan shoved away from the doorway and approached Ham, the red satin crumpled in his hand. "We're docking somewhere today, aren't we?"

Ham nodded, his look at Morgan bordering on anger. Yet he held his tongue, as though he dared not argue with the man who faced him.

"When the boat stops later this morning, I'll find something for Lily to wear." The glance he shot in her direction was eloquent, and Lily was silent. "She needs to wear something that makes a man wish he owned her, but at the same time establishes her unavailability to those in the crowd."

Ham's eyes narrowed and he held up a hand in protest. "See here, Morgan. I'm not investing money in the girl so's she can look like the picture on a box of candy and be just about as touchable. These men are willing to pay for the women they want."

Morgan straightened from his relaxed stance and tucked one hand in his trouser pocket. "I'm buying her company for the rest of the trip downriver," he said mildly. At Ham's grunt of derision, Morgan smiled and showed the edges of straight, white teeth. He resembled a wolf about to attack, Lily decided, and apparently Ham thought along a similar vein.

"Long as you've got hard, cold cash, she's yours," the man said after a moment. "But you'll pay a high price, Morgan. I've had several offers already."

"This isn't the place for this discussion," Morgan told him, his voice a low, menacing growl. And then he looked once more at Lily. "I think the lady needs to voice an opinion on the matter."

She looked down at the floor, wishing herself a million miles away, and was relieved to feel May's arm around her shoulders. "Y'all need to leave the girl alone," May said with a decided lilt in her voice. "She's got more important things to think about right now. We've got music to work on.''

She waved long, graceful fingers in a languid movement at the two men and laughed, a dark, smoky sound. ''Go on now. Out with the pair of you. You can settle your business somewhere else.''

Morgan nodded, his final look in Lily's direction one of approval, she thought. At least his eyes warmed as they focused on her face, and she thought a small smile tilted his lips for just a moment.

''He's smitten,'' May said bluntly. ''You must have given him quite a night of—''

''No.'' The single word was a denial of May's assumption, spoken softly but firmly as Lily met the other woman's gaze. ''I gave him nothing. Nothing but conversation and my company in his room until morning.''

May looked dubious, but laughed aloud. ''Well, keeping him dangling seems to be working, sweetheart. Just don't let it go to your head. One of these days, or nights, he'll expect payment for his protection of you.'' She smiled and bent her head, the better to speak in Lily's ear.

''I've never heard of Gage Morgan *buying* a woman's favors. You're a first.''

''You know him?'' Lily's eyes widened as she watched May's smile. The woman's dark eyes flashed with humor, and she smiled openly, yet Lily would lay odds that they held an abundance of secrets.

''He's been on the riverboat before, a couple of times in the past months.''

''Is he only a gambler? Or does he have another occupation?''

May shrugged idly. ''Who knows? He gambles, but I have a notion he doesn't need to, not for his spending money anyway. The girls would give their eye teeth to have him pay them a little notice, but he's not that way.''

Lily nodded, her thoughts spinning as she considered May's remarks. The man was not poor, of that there was no doubt. And yet he seemed to her to be more ambitious than his occupation would indicate. "Maybe he comes from well-to-do people," Lily surmised.

"Well, it doesn't matter much right now," May said flatly. "This morning we've got a program to work up for you. Ham won't let you sing center stage if the audience doesn't take to you." She motioned to Charlie, who had strolled back into the saloon from the deck outside.

"Let's try a couple of ballads, Charlie. How about 'Swanee River'? Do you know that one, Lily?"

"I think so." In fact, it was a song she'd heard from childhood, one her mother had sung to her. "Let me try it."

May stalked her, pacing in a circle as she sang, and Lily finally closed her eyes, the better to concentrate on the words that appeared in her mind as Charlie's talented fingers moved up and down the keyboard. "Now let's try 'A Soldier's Farewell,'" May said, and Charlie obligingly changed keys and began a short introduction.

Lily recalled the words as she waited for her cue to begin and then the music became merely a backdrop for her voice as Charlie played chords that supported the music she created.

"Lift one hand a bit. That's it," May said quietly. "Now touch the skin beneath your eye with the tips of your fingers. Just a whisper of movement, as if you might have shed a tear."

Lily's eyes flew open and she felt her throat thicken as the melody soared. A lace-edged handkerchief in her pocket was in her hand then, and the gesture she obediently performed bore fruit as a lone tear slid from each eye.

"You'll have them cheering and standing on their feet, honey," May said. "Just keep that innocent look on your face, and don't meet their eyes. Keep lookin' over their heads as if you're watching for some handsome stranger to come in the door.''

And well she might be, Lily thought. Although Gage Morgan was no longer a stranger. She'd spent the night with him, slept in his arms, if his word could be believed. And if she were to be completely honest, she had to acknowledge she bore no memory of those hours, as if she had been aware of the safety he offered.

''Well,'' May said after a moment, ''I think Ham Scott would be a fool to waste you on serving beer.''

''I'm no fool,'' the man said from the doorway. ''We'll give you a shot at it tonight, Lily. It'll be sink or swim.''

Behind him, Morgan watched and then turned aside.

Chapter Three

The applause soared to the ceiling of the saloon and Lily bent her head in response, then stood upright to face the men before her. Breathless as she heard the whistles and stomping feet of the men who cheered her performance, she relished the moment of undiluted pleasure.

Standing with his back to the bar, Gage Morgan watched, a half smile twisting his lips, his eyes glittering in the light of kerosene lanterns. His presence drew her, and with a degree of reluctance, Lily looked his way, flicking a glance at the dark-haired man who viewed her with a gaze that laid claim to her.

And after all, Lily thought grimly, he had the right. He'd bought her company for the duration of the trip down the river, and had already given Ham seven more five-dollar gold pieces to complete the purchase. She'd watched as the money changed hands, and then turned aside, feeling like so much merchandise being traded over the counter in a general store.

Or perhaps as if she'd been rented out by a madam in one of the establishments men patronized in every town between New York City and San Francisco. In any event, it was a case of being bought and sold, and the humiliation of it clung to her like wet feathers from a plucked chicken.

She looked out over the men gathered before the stage and allowed a small smile to touch her lips, then backed from their view to stand behind the gaudy velvet curtain that hid the wings of the stage. May touched her shoulder, a gentle brush of her fingers, and the words she spoke were like balm to Lily's hurt pride.

"I told you they'd love you, didn't I? Morgan picked out just the right dress for you to wear, honey." May's fingers tugged lightly at the soft, turquoise fabric, and her knowing eyes swept over Lily's slender form. "You had them in the palm of your hand when you sang that last song," she told her. "Men away from home, no matter how hard and callused they might be, are always suckers for that kind of music."

"Ham said he wants me to split this skirt and let my legs show when I walk," Lily told her. That his exact words had been a bit more specific was a humiliation in itself, she thought. *Men like legs. The longer, the better.* His gaze sliding to encompass her entire body had reminded Lily that Ham was, in effect, the man who'd sold her to Morgan, as if he owned her, body and soul.

"Ignore him," May advised her with a smile. "I'll remind him how much the men liked you, just the way you look right now. He won't argue with me."

And that was the truth, Lily decided. Whether or not May was occupying Ham's cabin was none of her business, but obviously the woman had influence.

"Now," May said briskly, "you need to find someplace to put your feet up for an hour. Your next show is at eight." She shot a quick look at Morgan and earned a lifted brow as he smiled at her. "Try Morgan's cabin. Ham won't bother you there."

"No," Lily agreed. "But Morgan might. And I'd just

as soon not have to get that close to him till I have to.''
Memories of the previous night had huddled in the back
of her mind all day long. The thought of what Morgan
might demand of her once the last show was finished was
uppermost in her mind, and the further she could stay from
him, the better she'd like it, for now.

May seemed to sense her disquiet. ''He won't bother
you between shows,'' she told her. ''That's almost a guarantee. Do you have a key to his cabin?''

Lily shook her head. ''No. I'll have to ask him to let me
in, I suppose.''

''Well, you can't go back to your old bunk,'' May said
flatly. ''Ham's already given it to the woman he hired to
help with the cooking. She was stuck in the galley cabin
with Hank, and more than ready to share a room with
women.'' She touched Lily's shoulder, urging her from the
wings. ''I'm on,'' she said, and tugged at her dress, then
patted her hair as she prepared to take the stage.

The three steps that led downward to the saloon floor
were in shadow, and Lily used the wall for balance as she
touched the first tread. A hand settled on her elbow and
without looking up, she recognized Morgan's scent and the
firm grip of his fingers. Her whisper of thanks was swallowed by the roar of the men as May strolled out onto the
stage.

''Come on,'' Morgan said quietly. ''You look like you
need to put your feet up.''

Lily shot him an amused look. ''You must have been
talking to May. That's almost a direct quote,'' she said.
Her feet ached. The pair of shoes Ham had tossed in her
direction apparently had belonged to the same woman
who'd worn the red dress and the other shoes. They were
a size too small, and Lily's toes felt numbed from the pressure.

Edging along the wall, Lily headed for the door to the

port side of the boat, Morgan close behind her. The fresh air was a relief after the smoky atmosphere in the saloon, and she inhaled deeply as she walked to the rail. Her hands touched the smooth wood and clutched it as she looked down into the water.

Muddy brown, the Mississippi was anything but a beautiful river. She'd decided that at first glance, and her assessment had not altered over the past two days. Beside her Morgan was silent, his hand sliding from her elbow to rest on her shoulder, his arm bending to tug her closer to his side. She allowed it. Indeed, she had no choice, she thought, her mouth twisting as she relaxed against him.

"Ready to lie down for a bit?" he asked, his head bending, allowing his lips to nuzzle her temple.

"Where will you be?" she asked, tilting her head to peer up at him in the darkness.

He was silent for a moment and then he laughed, a dark, edgy sound that brought gooseflesh to her upper arms. "Now, where do you think I'll be? It's my cabin, Lily."

"Why don't you go and play poker?" Her voice sounded waspish, she thought, and not for a moment did she rue the tone.

"Not tonight." And that seemed to be his final word on the subject, for he turned her and nudged her in the direction of his cabin.

He left the lamp unlit, and she stood just inside the door until he crossed before her to the single, small porthole that looked out on the water. A curtain hung over it, and he drew it back, allowing the stars to filter a faint glow into the room. "We don't need the lamp, do we?" he asked, turning back toward her.

"I don't," she answered shortly. "I'm going to take off these miserable shoes and give my feet a rest." She crossed the room and felt for the end of the bed, then settled there, lifting one foot, then the other to remove her shoes.

"Wanna take off your dress?" He spoke in a low, lazy drawl, a touch of the South turning his words into a smoky invitation.

"No, thanks." She tucked the pillow under her head and settled close to the edge of the bunk, wishing fervently that he would leave her alone. It was not to be.

"Move over just a little," he said, and then bent to pick up her feet and shift her toward the center of the quilt. His body blocked the light from the porthole as he lowered himself to sit beside her. With an easy movement, he circled her ankles and brought her feet to rest in his lap.

"Morgan?" Her knees bent as she attempted to move from his grasp, but his fingers tightened and he shushed her with a soft, hissing sound.

"I'm not going to hurt you, Lily. If I were going to give you trouble, I'd have done it last night. Just lie there and think lovely thoughts. I'm going to help you relax."

And he did. His hands worked magic as she obeyed his dictates, fingers rubbing her toes, his palm massaging the arch of each foot, and never once did those big, warm hands stray above her ankles. She closed her eyes, the pleasure of being tended in such a way touching her heart in a way she'd almost forgotten.

"What are you thinking, Lily?" he asked quietly.

"You'll laugh," she answered, and then chuckled herself as she considered her answer. "I was thinking of when I was very young and my mother used to bathe me at night and then cut my toenails and tut-tut over the calluses on my feet. I used to go barefoot whenever I had the chance, and she told me time and again that ladies always wore shoes."

"You had a happy home?" His voice was dark, blending with the shadows in the room, soothing her, luring her into a state of relaxation she had not enjoyed in over a year. She nodded, even though she knew he could not see the movement of her head.

"A wonderful home," she said after a moment. "My brothers used to tease me unmercifully, but I knew they adored me. My father—" Her voice broke and she swallowed the emotion welling up within her. "He put me up on a horse when I was two years old. Mama scolded him and made a fuss, but I loved it."

"Where did you live?" he asked in that same, soothing tone.

She roused from her reverie and drew one foot from his hands. "Far away from reality, I fear. Someplace I can never go again."

"Reality?" He lifted her foot again and held it with a firm grip. "Hold still, Lily," he said. "Just take it easy for a few more minutes. You'll be wishing you had when you put those shoes back on."

"Probably." It wasn't worth fussing over, not when his hands were so warm and firm against the bones and muscles they tended.

"We're going to get you a new pair when we dock next," he said. And as if that were the final word on the matter, he changed the subject.

"Had you planned on going all the way down the river?" he asked, his words an idle query, as if it were of little account in the general scheme of things.

She held her breath and thought with frantic haste. If she told him she'd planned on leaving the boat once it neared the homestead in Louisiana, he might protest, might even tell Ham that his employee was planning to run off. On the other hand, she'd never had an easy time telling falsehoods. Her mama had always said she couldn't lie worth a tinker's damn, whatever that meant.

"Well, I suspect you're not going to tell me your plans,

are you, Lily?'' His hand slid up from her ankle to curl around the back of her calf.

''Don't,'' she whispered. ''Please, Morgan.''

''Are you going to stay on the boat to the end of the ride?'' he asked again, his fingers gentle as they kneaded the firm flesh beneath the stockings she wore.

''No.''

''Where will you go?''

His fingers worked unceasingly at her muscles, but they'd moved back to her foot, and she breathed a sigh of relief. ''I don't know for certain,'' she said after a moment.

''Home?''

''I want to, but I'm afraid it's too late for that.''

''Not if your folks are worried about you, Lily. It's never too late to go home when the people you love are there.''

She laughed softly. ''Listen to the man. When was the last time you saw your family? What about the people you love, Morgan?''

''I don't have anyone to go home to,'' he said. ''Not anymore.''

''A loner?''

''No, I've had to live in close quarters with other men sometimes. But not lately.''

''Not with a woman?'' The darkness made her bold, and she waited in silence for his answer. If she'd expected some revelation of the man's past, she was in for a disappointment, for he simply lowered her feet to the mattress and rose from the bed.

''I'll come back and rap on the door ten minutes before you go on stage again,'' he said, and now his voice was cool, remote, as if he'd withdrawn from her. His footsteps were quiet as he crossed the few feet of floor to the door, and then he was gone.

Lily looked at the circle of light, beyond which the stars glittered in a dark sky. He was different, nothing like the men she'd known before now. Perhaps somewhat like her brother Roan, she thought, that strong, silent man who had gone to fight on the other side during the great conflict. He'd worn a blue uniform, and almost broke his mother's heart in the process.

Her eyes closed as she considered the place where she'd been born and raised, and the words, "River Bend," vibrated in her mind. Pictures of the big, white plantation house, the fields filled with those who worked them, and the horses her father took such pride in raising, blended into a kaleidoscope of color behind her closed eyelids.

Lily sang four songs, with barely a pause between them, before she left the stage. Ham met her in the wings and his brow furrowed as he scanned her dress. "I didn't think they'd take to you in that outfit," he said gruffly. "I'll have to admit Morgan was right. The dress fits the music all right."

"Thank you," Lily said. She looked down at the simple lines of the gown, and brushed the skirt, relishing the fine fabric. "It's the nicest thing I've worn in quite some time," she told Ham.

"Morgan told me he bought another one, too. Said it's cream-colored with lace and a wide ruffle across the shoulders. Shows a little more skin."

Lily nodded. "I haven't tried it on yet. But it's the same size. It ought to fit."

Ham's grin was knowing, and his head tilted to one side as he met her gaze, and then surveyed her with eyes that seemed to note every square inch of her body. "I suspect Morgan's pretty familiar with your—"

"That's enough." The words were low, spoken in a graveled tone that brought Ham up short. Morgan was cutting the man no slack, Lily decided, and for that she could only be thankful.

"You want something to drink?" he asked Lily. "You'll be on stage again in ten minutes, won't you?"

She nodded and followed him down into the saloon, then sat at a table near the wall as he walked to the bar. The glass he offered her was cool, the taste that of lemon, with but a tinge of something stronger.

"I don't drink," she said, after the first swallow.

"There's not much in it," he said. "Just enough to relax you a little. Ham had you pretty strung out back there."

"He's not happy with your interest in me," she told him, sipping again from the glass.

"That's too damn bad." Morgan sat beside her, his arm casually draped over the back of her chair. It was an unmistakable signal, one she knew to be deliberate, and the men who watched with furtive glances recognized it as such. "Don't look so worried," he murmured, lifting her glass and handing it to her again. "Drink a bit more. Your throat will feel better with a little gin to relax it."

And as she stepped onto the stage just minutes later, she recognized the wisdom of his words. The music surrounded her, the piano player watching her, his smile approving as she sang the first notes. She was silent between songs, unwilling to speak to those watching her. May had an inexhaustible supply of stories she told the men between her numbers, and her quick wit, along with the quality of her music, had made her a favorite of the customers.

Yet when Lily sang tonight, she'd seen a softening of the men's faces as they watched her, noted their attention drawn to her by the time she'd completed the first few bars of the opening song. Perhaps it was the dress, she thought, its lines subdued and ladylike. Or maybe the music. Perhaps May had been right. Simplicity seemed to work.

Three complete shows made up the evening's entertainment, with a trio of dancing girls bringing the men to their feet. The girls were snatched up as they left the stage, and with much laughing and suggestive jokes filling the air, the scantily dressed women had their hands full fending off their admirers.

A table at the back held five or six poker players, men who rode the river in hopes of making their fortune with a deck of cards. But Morgan, true to his word, did not join them tonight. In fact, he barely took his gaze from Lily, and when she finally received a nod of dismissal from Ham, Morgan followed her from the saloon and out onto the deck.

"Ready for bed?" he asked, sliding his arm around her waist and drawing her close.

She felt her throat thicken, and the words would not pass her lips. Nodding, a small single movement of her head, she looked up at him and drew away.

"Don't, Lily," he said, tightening his grasp. "If Ham is watching, we want him to think you're earning your money, don't we?"

"I don't care what Ham thinks," she said, the words fierce, as if she dared the other man to challenge her.

"I do." Morgan steered her toward his cabin, and she waited while he opened the door. As if it were a replay of the previous night, she stood aside while he lit the lamp, and he closed the curtain they'd left open earlier. He watched her closely, then opened the door, hesitating on the threshold.

"Go to bed, Lily. I'll be back shortly."

She awoke with his arm around her, his body beneath the sheet behind her, and her mind searched for a memory, but there was none to be had. Her gown was tucked neatly around her, just as she'd arranged it when she'd crawled between the sheets, and his fingers were circumspectly splayed at her waist. Though why that should be considered safe territory she did not know—only that a few inches up or down would have made a difference. The thought of that wide palm touching her breasts or belly made her shiver.

"Awake?" he asked, his early-morning voice sounding rusty in her ear.

"Yes."

"Ready to get up?"

Lily nodded and then fortified her silent reply. "Yes."

"You don't want to snuggle a little?" She thought he sounded amused.

"No."

"All right." He rolled out of the bed and rose in a smooth easy movement, leaving her to clutch the sheet as she turned her head to watch him. "Unless you want to be mightily embarrassed, you'd better look at the wall, Lily," he told her bluntly.

She turned away, her quick glance making her aware of his masculine form. She'd seen men in various stages of undress during her growing-up years. Her brothers weren't known for being especially modest, but never had she been in such close proximity to a fully aroused male. Unless she counted the colonel who'd used and abused her with such uncaring deeds.

The cabin door closed and Lily released the breath she'd held.

The woman was getting to him, filling his thoughts. She'd drawn him from the first, and he was wary of her appeal, that womanly aura that lured him. Perhaps even at the risk of losing focus on the job at hand.

There was no doubt that Lily Devereaux was unique, a puzzle he yearned to unravel. She was both worldly-wise and innocent, and how that could be only added to the conundrum. Somewhere, she'd gotten on the wrong track and been hurt. She was wary, and with good reason, Morgan thought wryly. He'd made no bones about how he felt, yet he was behaving in a manner most unlike him, allowing her to call the shots in the tug-of-war they'd put into motion.

Spending two nights with a woman and never touching her was new to him. Women were among his favorite things in the world. And he'd treated them as such. *Things*. With that thought, he walked to the side of the boat and leaned against the sturdy railing. All except for one notable example, and his lips curved as he recalled the one woman he might have loved.

She'd been unavailable to him, and sometimes he thought she feared him. Or maybe she'd been unknowingly attracted to that part of him that he held inviolate. That deep, dark measure of his inner being that he revealed to no one. He knew his own strength, had learned to conceal his feelings beneath a facade of cool, unswerving devotion to duty.

And then he walked away from the one woman who might have pierced that armor he wore. Until he'd seen Lily Devereaux two nights ago, he'd thought himself immune to feminine charms. He'd been able to admire the women he met, had on occasion accepted their advances and even the favors they offered. But they'd meant nothing to him, had not stirred his emotions.

Lily was different. Not what he'd expected when first he'd seen her. Certainly not what he'd planned to find when he took her to his cabin. But, maybe, after all, exactly what he needed right now. Depending on how desperate she was.

"You're up early." Ham stood beside him and Morgan silently cursed his careless behavior.

"Never let a man creep up on you," his superior officers had said, drumming the advice into him during his training.

And had it not been for thoughts of Lily, he'd have heard Ham's approach. Now he turned to him in a casual manner.

"I wondered if we were stopping today."

"Tomorrow. We'll be in Memphis in the morning."

"I thought I'd look around a while," Morgan said. "Maybe take Lily shopping."

"Not tomorrow. May's got plans to sing a couple of duets with Lily. They're gonna practice in the morning."

Morgan swallowed the words that threatened to spill from his lips. Lily was paid little enough for the work she did. Her time in the mornings should be her own. Better instincts kept him silent though. Until he considered his options, and looked at Lily with his job in mind, he needed to play his hand with care.

Once he left the riverboat, Lily would be on her own again, with no one to protect her, should he leave her behind. It would be in her best interests if Ham found her to be indispensable. Or at least a real asset to him.

He shrugged, looking back out on the river. "No matter. I can find what I want for her without her along."

"You're kinda stuck on the girl, Morgan," Ham said quietly. "You don't generally pay much mind to the women. At least you haven't the other times you've traveled on my boat."

Morgan's jaw tensed as he considered the man's observation. "She's worth spending time with," he said finally, unable to admit, even to himself, what was so dratted appealing about the woman.

"Well, she's pretty enough, with those big, dark eyes and that mop of curls," Ham said with a grin. "And the men can't take their eyes off her figure. She's made a hit."

"Well, if she doesn't get some shoes that fit, she'll be singing from a chair," Morgan said sharply.

Ham shrugged idly. "If she can't wear what I provide she'll have to buy her own." He lit a cigar and squinted through the smoke. "Unless you're planning on going out to get them for her." He grinned as he considered the lit end of his cigar. "Got it bad, don't you, Morgan?"

He swaggered a bit as he strolled away, and Gage held his tongue. The only way he'd be buying shoes for the girl was if he could take her with him. He'd see to it that her practicing with May took place early on in the day tomorrow, before breakfast if necessary. One way or another, he'd find her a pair of shoes that fit.

"I've never sung before breakfast in my life," May said gruffly, slanting a glance at the man who watched her walk up onto the stage.

"I'm making it worth your while," Morgan said.

May grinned widely. "Any woman would warble her heart out for the promise of a shopping spree."

"Uh-uh," Morgan admonished her. "One dress is all I promised you. Just one, May."

"When you're as hard up for money as I am, one dress sounds like a winner," she said smugly.

His brows raised, signifying his doubt, and May laughed aloud. "I can tell you're not a true believer, Morgan."

"I'll never believe you're down to your last nickel," he said. "You'll always hold some in reserve, kinda like the rainy-day theory."

"Where's your woman?" May asked, darting a look toward the doorway. "We have a piano player and half a duet here. All we need is the star of the show."

Charlie's fingers chorded softly, and a ring of smoke rose over his head as he played. He'd offered no protest at Morgan's request to play at such an ungodly hour and watched the same doorway that held May's attention.

The woman who appeared there had the benefit of sunlight behind her, the red streaks of dawn having given way to early-morning gold. Her dress formed a lissome silhouette around her as she hesitated, as if gauging her welcome. "Am I late?" she asked, shooting a shuttered glance at Morgan.

He made a pretense of looking at his pocket watch and shook his head. "Right on time, actually, honey," he murmured, favoring her with a slow smile.

She walked toward the stage and looked up at May. "I appreciate you getting up so early for this. Morgan said we'd be going shopping after breakfast."

"Sure are," May told her. "You and I are gonna get all decked out with new outfits, sweetie." She looked down at Lily's feet. "And new shoes, too."

Charlie's fingers ended their wandering and he nodded at May. "Let's get goin'," he told her. "Breakfast is waiting."

The shops were filled with gowns and all the underpinnings that went with them. The shoemaker found just the right shoes to match Lily's dress. With a brusque nod, Morgan announced his approval and followed the women from the cobbler's shop, boxes in hand.

"Do you think we've pushed him far enough?" May asked in an undertone, bending to speak in Lily's ear.

"I heard that," Morgan told her dryly. "If we don't get back to the boat right soon, neither one of you will have a job, and I'll have lost all my belongings. I don't think Ham will wait much longer for us."

The thought of escaping the steamboat was like a beacon before her, but Lily could not imagine Morgan's anger should she run from him. He'd be obliged to chase her down. And find her he would, of that there was no doubt. He'd paid for her time, and like it or not, she was committed to fulfilling her part of the bargain. With a sigh, she took his right arm, even as May clung to his left elbow, heading back to the dock.

Ham stood at the top of the gangplank, grinning through the smoke of his cigar as they approached. "Well, well. Don't you look like a fancy man, with one lady on each arm, Morgan. Thought maybe the three of you had decided to head for the hills."

"You knew better," Morgan said, leading the women aboard with care, one at a time, lest they lose their footing on the sloping boards. He handed each her parcels. "Here you go, ladies." With a tip of his hat, he watched them head for their cabins and turned back to Ham.

"You ready to leave?"

Ham nodded. "Just waiting for you and your lady friends to show up." He leaned an elbow on the ship's railing. "You win much at the poker tables on this trip downriver, Morgan?"

Morgan shrugged. "No more than usual. Why?"

"Just wondered if you're makin' a living at it. Playing poker is a pretty chancy way to earn your way in life, as far as I can see."

"I make enough to get along," Morgan told him, his voice soft but containing a thread of steel that forbade any further discussion.

Ham shot him a speculative look. "I've heard that you're working for someone else."

"And where did you hear that?" His senses alert, Morgan slid one hand into his pocket and tilted his hat a bit with the other. "You been checking up on me, Ham?"

A quick shake of his head denoted Ham's denial of such a thing. "Just something that's been whispered about over the past day or so. Thought you might like to hear the rumor."

"Well, you can squelch it right now," Morgan told him as he strolled away. "I work on my own. I don't answer to anyone but Gage Morgan."

And wasn't that the biggest lie he'd ever told with a straight face.

Chapter Four

The lines were being readied to cast off from the dock as Morgan neared the front of the boat and he gripped the rail tightly, his mind already on the coming evening. A vision of dark curls and even darker eyes swam in his mind and he shook it off. His eyelids flickered, his gaze narrowed, and there before him hung a drawing of the very woman he'd so determinedly cast from his thoughts.

The post was tall, its surface bearing several printed notices, one of them for a stage show in town, another for a man wanted for bank robbery. The third bore a very well-done likeness of Lily Devereaux, and above it were emblazoned the words: Wanted for Attempted Murder and Robbery.

Morgan blinked, sure that for that fraction of a moment his eyes were playing tricks on him. And then dead certain that they were not as he focused again on the poster. Someone who thought Lily's name was Yvonne Devereaux had offered a five-thousand-dollar reward for her capture.

With one swift movement Morgan was atop the railing, and from there leaped to stand on the dock. He looked up at the poster and snatched it from the nails holding it in place. With a glance toward the gangplank, where Ham was no longer in sight, he folded the paper in quarters and stuck it in his pocket. Then, in a casual manner, he sauntered to where the lines were being cast ashore.

"Hold on a second there," he called in a jovial tone. And as the accommodating deckhand watched, Morgan crossed the narrow stretch of water to stand on the deck. Offering the obliging fellow a small salute with his index finger, he strolled away, toward his cabin.

The woman is a fraud. All the way around. She's lied to me.

His fist raised to pound on the door of his cabin, and then as it would have met the wood, he dropped it to his side. "It's my damn cabin," he muttered. "I shouldn't have to knock on my own door."

The handle turned readily and he stood on the threshold. Before him Lily watched, wide-eyed, her hands holding up the shoes he'd bought with his hard-earned money. Probably gloating over making a fool of him.

He crossed the threshold and closed the door, leaning against it as he lifted one hand to remove his hat. The shoes were lowered, a pair held by either hand until they dangled at her sides, and Lily's eyes closed tightly, then reopened, their surface glossy.

"Going to try tears on me?" Morgan asked softly. "It won't work, *Lily*."

"I don't know what you mean," she said, her words so quiet they might have been whispered.

He lifted a brow and tossed his hat toward the bed. She jumped as it sailed past her to land on the mattress, and he noted the visible shiver that traveled her length.

"Don't you?" He reached in his pocket for the folded poster and held it toward her. "Don't lie to me, Lily. Are you sure you don't know what I'm talking about?"

She shook her head, and the shoes dropped to the floor.

The sound was sharp in the silence, and she looked down to where they lay, then bent to retrieve them.

"Leave them," Morgan said sharply, and watched as she obeyed, straightening again to stand quietly as he approached. His hand was steady as he lifted it to brush her cheek, and he smiled as she flinched from his touch.

"Are you afraid of me now?" he asked. The poster drew her eyes like a magnet and her mouth trembled as she spoke.

"What is it? What have you done?"

"What have I done?" he asked. "I think the question might be what have *you* done?"

Her chin lifted and two tears left shiny streaks down the length of her cheeks. "All right, what have *I* done?" she asked.

"Lied to me," he said, almost tonelessly. "You lied to me, Lily."

She shook her head. "No. I didn't lie. I just didn't tell you everything."

"*Everything?* All you told me was a pack of lies, Miss Devereaux. Apparently beginning with your name—" he made a show of opening the poster and reading it aloud "—*Yvonne* Devereaux, it says here." His eyes lifted to meet her gaze. "And ending with your attempted murder of someone in New York."

"It wasn't an attempted murder," she whispered. "I killed him."

He looked back at the poster. "Not according to this. You robbed him and tried real hard to put him six feet under, but the man is alive, lady. And he's after your hide."

"He's dead," she wailed, and then covered her mouth with one hand as if she could somehow stifle the words that resounded between them.

Morgan snatched at her hand, his fingers gripping her wrist as he drew her up to her tiptoes and pulled her against himself. "Shut up. Just shut the hell up, and for once in your life, tell the truth."

Her knees sagged and he circled her with his other arm, the poster falling to the floor at his side. "Talk to me, Lily, or Yvonne, or whatever the hell your name is. Who did you think you'd killed?"

"Stanley Weston," she gasped. "The Yankee colonel who took me with him when he left our plantation."

"When he left your plantation." Morgan repeated her words aloud, then watched her skin turn pale, as her eyes closed and her head rolled back. "Damn you, don't you dare faint now." He shook her once, a violent movement that snapped her eyes open. They were black, so dark he could not see the division between the pupil and the color surrounding it. "Do you hear me?" he whispered.

She nodded. "I hear you." She stiffened in his grasp and with a tremendous effort, her legs held her upright and she caught her breath. "I hear you," she repeated.

"From the beginning now," Morgan said through gritted teeth. "Who are you?"

"Lily. I'm Lily Devereaux."

His hands moved to her shoulders and his grip tightened. "One more time. The truth this time, *Lily*."

"Yvonne Devereaux died when I left New York," she whispered. "I became Lily. I've told you that already."

"That's not quite the way I recall it, but we'll take your word for it for now, and call you Lily. After you left New York—hell, before you left New York. Did you try to kill a man?"

"I hit him with a poker. I saw him fall to the floor, and there was blood all over the place."

"And so you robbed him?"

She shook her head. "No, I never took anything from anyone. I ran. I left in a pouring rain and walked until I found a place to stay for the night."

"Where?" he asked, feeling her pain even as he strove to inure himself to the emotions she brought to life within him. "Where did you go?"

Her eyes were listless, as if they beheld a time so fraught with peril, so frightening she could not bring herself to deal with it. "To a pawn shop. I had a brooch from my mother and the dealer gave me cash for it." She inhaled, a deep breath that seemed to give her strength. "I stayed that night in a hotel, a place where there were men sleeping in the hallways, because they didn't have enough money to pay for a bed."

"And you had a bed?"

"A man felt sorry for me and gave me his. He spent the night sleeping in the hallway."

"And from there?" Morgan asked, noting the flicker of awareness that told him she heard his query. "Where did you go from there, Lily?"

"I took a train west, toward Chicago."

His voice was a low growl as he repeated the query that was uppermost in his mind. "What did you take from Weston?"

Her eyes focused on him and once more she stiffened, trembling in his grasp. "I took nothing from him. I thought I'd killed him, and I ran."

"Well, according to this poster, you're accused of robbery." He watched her closely, saw the ashen cast to her features and felt a moment's pity for her.

"Why did you hit him, Lily?" Morgan lowered her to sit on the edge of the bed and she shot him a grateful glance.

"Thank you," she whispered, placing her feet carefully

side by side, her hands folded neatly in her lap. "He offered me a house to live in."

"And you took offense at that?"

She shook her head. "No, I was angry because he'd promised to marry me when we left the plantation, and when we got to New York he kept putting me off and he…"

"He what, Lily? What did he do?" And even before she spoke the words, Morgan knew the story she would tell.

"He said he'd never marry a girl who couldn't even speak proper English. He was already engaged to a society woman in the city, but he'd like to keep me as his *mistress.*" As though the word were poison, she spat it from her lips, and then bowed her head.

"Proper English? He said that?" And for the past days Morgan had enjoyed the soft phrases that slipped past her lips, the slurring of letters that proclaimed her heritage. "The man was a fool," he said harshly, then knelt at her feet. It was time to make a major decision here, and not much leeway to do it in.

"Can you bring yourself to trust me? Will you do as I ask you?" As the query penetrated her mind, he watched, noted the expression of confusion that painted her features, and then the hope that dawned in her dark eyes.

"I don't know what to do," she murmured. Her hands gripped together and her knuckles turned white as he watched them tighten. "I thought he was dead."

"Lily." He spoke her name once, then again. "Lily, listen to me." His thoughts moved quickly, past this day to tomorrow and the next, to the multitude of Wanted posters that would be cluttering towns from Chicago to New Orleans and back. "You can't be known as Lily Devereaux any longer. Not if you don't want to be found."

"But that's my name," she said.

"If you pretend to be my wife, you can become Lily Morgan."

She looked up and met his gaze, her eyes narrowing with suspicion. "And then what? Pretend for the rest of my life?"

"I can use you as my wife. You'll make a good cover for me."

"A good cover for what? What are you, Morgan? Some sort of a crook?"

He shook his head. "No, far from it. But right now I need to get back on the job, and with you along as my bride, I'll fit the image I need to portray."

Her shoulders squared and her spine stiffened as she gathered herself, a visible process he recognized. "Let me get this straight," she began. "You're willing to believe me now, but you didn't before? And now I find you've been holding out on me." Her voice rose. "And you accused me of lying, of hiding the truth."

"You *were* lying to me," he said patiently. And then one hand touched her mouth, stilling her protest. "Let me change that. You weren't being entirely honest, let's say." He spoke quietly and slowly, knowing that his movements from this point onward hinged on her reply. "If I tell you what you need to know, will you help me?"

"Do I have a choice?"

"We always have a choice, Lily. I told you that before. Remember?"

"That was about going home again," she reminded him. "This is something altogether different. What if your plans cause me to break the law? Is there a law against posing as someone's wife?" She looked so honestly befuddled Morgan was tempted to laugh. He took pity on her innocence.

"I don't think they can put you in jail for posing as my

wife. But they sure as hell can toss you in prison for trying to kill some dandy up in New York.''

''Well, maybe I deserve it. I meant to kill him. I thought he was dead.'' she said.

He shook his head. ''Oh, Lily. If you could only hear yourself. The man is after you, sweetheart. He's going to hunt you down. And then he's going to gnaw on your bones.''

She shivered again, but her chin jutted forward as her eyes narrowed a warning. ''He'll have to catch me first.''

''He'll catch you all right,'' he told her agreeably. ''Unless you listen to me.''

''Any guarantees, Morgan?'' she asked.

He shook his head. ''None. Except that I'll take care of you to the best of my ability. I won't ask any more from you than I'm willing to give you.''

She shook her head..''Like what? What are you talking about? What are you going to ask of me?''

He spoke slowly, with a degree of patience he hadn't known he possessed. ''I'm asking you to pose as my wife, Lily. I'm asking you to help me with a job I'm in the midst of. And I'm asking you to trust me.'' He eyed her cautiously. ''Can you do all of that?''

She looked at him as if he were holding the only life preserver available and she was the sorry creature about to go under for the third time. And then with a deep sigh, she gave her answer. ''I can trust you, I think. And I'll help you with the job you're in the midst of.

''But I won't pose as your wife.''

He hung his head, a smile lurking at the corner of his lips. ''You won't pose as my wife? Is that what you said?''

She nodded firmly. ''If I didn't trust you already, Morgan, I wouldn't be in this room with you. As to the job you're doing, it can't be much more dangerous than me running for my life from whoever's after me.''

He had his doubts about that theory, but decided to hear her out. ''So? That doesn't tell me why you turned me down on the wife part.''

''I listened to one man promise me he'd marry me. Then he dragged me the length of the country, only to admit he'd fed me a string of lies, and I'd fallen for them, hook, line and sinker. The next time I run off with a man, he'll marry me first, or I won't go.''

''You want me to marry you?'' He was proud of his even tone. The woman couldn't know how hard his heart was pumping at her declaration. With all her shenanigans, he'd have her in the palm of his hand. He could settle with her once the job was done.

She nodded firmly. ''I really don't want a husband, Morgan, but you'll do, since I don't have anyone else lined up for the position. But with one stipulation. Someday when everything is all cleared up, when you've finished with me, I want you to take me home. I want my family to think I've pulled myself out of the gutter, and having you on my arm just might accomplish that.''

The girl didn't know what she was getting into, and he wasn't about to set her straight. He cleared his throat and lifted her from her seat on the edge of his bed. ''A couple of things here, Lily. As far as I'm concerned, you've never been in the gutter, so we won't talk about that again. I'll need to hear the whole story one of these days, but not right now.

''In the second place, I'll marry you. But know one thing, Lily. You'll be a real wife to me.'' He caught her chin in his palm, and lifted her face, watching as his words penetrated her mind. ''You've got it right, lady. You'll be in my bed, and I won't be put off on that point.''

"You want to do *that* with me?" she asked quietly.

He could no longer contain his amusement with her na-ive assumptions. The grin escaped, and with it a soft chuckle. "Doing *that* isn't an unpleasant thing for two adults to do together, sweetheart." His thumb rubbed her jawline reflectively as he watched a flush rise to cover her face. "Trust me on this, Lily. I won't ever hurt you, and I won't leap on you like a damn bull just because we speak those words in front of a parson."

She bit nervously at her upper lip and he rubbed at it with that same thumb. "Don't do that. Just listen to me."

"I've heard what you have to say, Morgan. And I'm agreeing. I'll go with you, and I'll sleep in your bed. But I'll never be convinced that you can accomplish the thing we're talking about without me being the one—"

"Enough," he said softly. "We'll get to all of that later. For now, let's make some plans. But first—" He released her chin from his grasp and bent his head to touch her lips with his. He couldn't resist, and to his astonishment he wasn't about to try.

"Is this part of the other thing?" she asked dubiously.

He shook his head. "No, this is just called sealing a pact between partners." And then before she could move away, he brushed against her mouth again, his lips soft and per-suasive against hers. Carefully, tenderly, he caressed her, his hands curving around her face, then sliding down to rest against her back, his fingers tracing the slender curves of waist and hips. Then, bringing his palms to rest against her rib cage, he deepened the kiss, touching and tasting the fullness of her lips with his tongue.

She inhaled as he left her mouth still wanting, his ca-resses moving to explore her throat, and from there to seek out the soft flesh that tempted him. There, beneath her ear, and again to where her blood pumped down the side of her throat. And finally to where her breasts curved above the lace at her neckline. He spent a multitude of kisses on the firmness he found there, finding her unspoken response to be more seductive than he could have imagined.

"Morgan?" It was a gasp of reaction he'd waited for and he lifted his head to smile at her.

"It's only a kiss, Lily. Only a kiss."

She blinked and he set her aside, willing to wait until the time was right. Lily would be his. That lush body, the curls that spilled over her shoulders, the tempting lips that held a trembling smile—all would be his. And soon.

"You have that confused look about you, Lily." May watched her from heavy-lidded eyes and Lily sensed a hidden meaning in the woman's words. "Like you're trying to figure out which way to jump."

"Jump? I'm not sure what you're talking about, May."

"About whatever it is Morgan has planned for you. He's no dummy. He'll use you for his own purposes, honey. Watch your step."

"You don't trust him?" Lily asked, fingering the sheet music Charlie had offered for her perusal.

"The question is, do you?" May took one of Lily's spiral curls on the tip of her index finger and stretched it out to its full length, then released it, smiling as it resumed its original place. "He's taken with you, that's a given. But the man has secrets, girl, and you might be on the verge of a disaster." She tilted her head and considered Lily for a moment.

"I saw a drawing that caught my eye, Lily. It was on a poster, dockside. When I looked again to be certain of my suspicions, it was gone."

A feeling of dread blossomed within her as Lily stared in disbelief. "You saw it? You recognized me?"

May smiled. "It was a very good likeness, honey. But you really look more like a Lily than a woman named Yvonne."

"I thought I'd killed a man, May. Now I find that he's still alive and on my trail."

"I knew you had secrets of your own, first time I saw you," May said. She held up a warning hand. "Don't get it in your mind that I'm after a reward. My mouth is shut when it comes to Yvonne Devereaux, but everyone else on this boat might not feel the same way I do. Just don't let Morgan talk you into anything you won't be able to get out of."

The pause was short, but her heart pounded in her ears as Lily considered her words. And then they were spoken on an indrawn breath. "Like marriage?"

"Marriage? You're going to marry him?" May's demeanor underwent a sudden change as she sat down in a chair. "And how will that help you?" Her eyes narrowed as she seemed to consider the idea. "Or will it be for Morgan's benefit? Is he planning on using you for cover?"

"What do you know about him?" Lily asked softly.

"Not a whole lot, but enough to recognize a man at work." She glanced toward the piano, where Charlie played the song they were to practice. "I think it's safe to say that Gage Morgan is not what he appears to be, Lily. Just watch your step."

She rose and beckoned toward the sheet music Lily held. "Let's go over this again, Charlie. From the beginning. I think we've got it now." And with a short introduction, Charlie began the chords that supported their voices, allowing them to mingle in close harmony, May toning down her more powerful voice to suit Lily's softer tones.

Even as her voice rose, and her skills blended with May's accomplished presentation, Lily thought of the man she had left in the cabin. He was indeed a surprise package, and unless she was prepared to offer him her trust, their alliance could not work.

He'd been kind to her, even considering the bruises his hands had left on her arms and shoulders. His anger had marred her skin and she'd watched as he'd inspected the areas where his fingers had gripped her.

"I'm sorry," he'd said quietly, and then his mouth curved in a rueful smile. "I've had to apologize twice for hurting you. It won't happen again."

But if she allowed herself to care for him, the pain she might face in the future would be all the worse, once his work was finished and she became a hindrance to him. And who was she trying to fool, she wondered. As if she weren't already mightily attracted to the man. He was handsome and appealing, even given the harshness of his appearance and the cold deliberation that drove his actions.

She was between the devil and the deep blue sea, as the saying went, and the water was getting deeper by the hour.

"It's been a problem finding you all alone lately." The man who spoke remained in the shadows beneath the over-hang on the top deck, where he would likely be unnoticed by anyone. His words were low, but alive with a taunt Morgan could not ignore.

"I knew you'd find me once you had news for me. As to the other, I'm setting the stage for my next move."

"That's one way of putting it, I suppose," the messenger said. "I'd say your job has benefits."

"Not a word about Lily," Morgan warned. "You've never heard of the woman in case anyone asks you."

"Oh, they'll be asking all right. By the time we dock tomorrow there'll probably be lawmen waiting for the boat."

"I won't be on it," Morgan told him. "Nor will Lily."

"I figured that out already. I've got a skiff waiting to take you to shore after she finishes this show."

Morgan fished his pocket watch out and snapped open the lid. "Sure beats swimming, to my way of thinking. We'll be there in an hour. Make a commotion of some sort to cover us."

"I've been yearning for a barroom brawl for days," the man said. His low chuckle was warmer now and he spoke quietly and quickly. "Be careful, Morgan. Using the woman may be the best idea you've had. She'll be perfect cover, and easy to drop off somewhere down the line when the job is done."

"Right." Morgan lit a match and the light flared as he brought the flame to the tip of his slender cigar. "This *may* be the best idea I've had," he murmured, taking the words as his own. He leaned on the railing and the man slipped from the shadows to disappear down a nearby set of stairs that led to the saloon.

The cigar flared as Morgan inhaled the heavy, tangy smoke. He looked at it with distaste written on his features, and cast it over the side where the water swallowed it with but a moment's pause. The wave that sucked it up drew it under the surface and it was gone. And just that easily he might be disposed of, he thought, his expression grim.

Protecting Lily was his first concern for tonight, and that involved taking her from the boat in less than an hour. And then finding a stray parson to turn her into Lily Morgan.

The plan went smoothly, almost too much so, Morgan thought as he bundled Lily and her small valise into the skiff. From the saloon, shouts were raised and men were overturning tables and joining the fray. Strange how a few words could bring gamblers, and those who were making a business of drinking away the evening, to the point of battle, he mused. Taking up the oars, he cast off from the side of the steamboat and into the channel.

The suction drew him back toward the vessel, but his strength was equal to the task, and Morgan steered the small boat toward shore, eager to be beneath the over-hanging branches of the trees lining the river. It was to Lily's credit that she was silent. But given the choice of coming along quietly or being exposed to the sheriff at the next stopping place, she'd recognized the value of his plan. Holding her valise, she'd followed him from the cabin. She'd climbed down into the skiff, her skirt held high, taking her place on the far end, holding firmly to either side as Morgan joined her there.

The trees bent their curving, lissome branches almost to the water and in moments they were safe beneath the fo-liage. The boat was a hundred yards downriver from them, and the noise from the saloon faded, even as the flickering lanterns on the stern became two pinpoints in the darkness.

"Now what?" Lily asked in a soft undertone.

"Now we walk," Morgan returned firmly. "We passed a small town a couple of miles back. We'll head there and find a preacher to marry us in the morning."

He pulled at the overhanging branches to draw the skiff closer to shore and then dug the oar into the soft river bottom, until they were safely moored next to the bank. It was a stretch for him, but in moments he'd jumped to dry land and then tugged the boat from the water.

"Let me give you a hand," he said, offering his palm in her direction. She placed her own in it, and he was struck by the trust in that small gesture. By the firm grip of her fingers and the warmth of her palm. His Lily was brave—of that there was no doubt.

"Take my bag," she whispered, and waited while he tossed the tapestry valise upon the bank. Her grip was strong as she allowed him to guide her from the boat, and she followed him closely. In short order he found a place that was easy to traverse to the meadow that met the water's edge. Carefully they made their way through a sparsely wooded area to where a road headed in a northerly direction, and they set off walking.

"We'll need to stop somewhere to sleep for a few hours," he told her, his voice a low murmur in the darkness. And within fifteen minutes, he'd found a shadowed area beneath a grove of trees that offered a haven. The blanket he carried was spread on the ground and Lily lowered herself to its surface.

"Are you all right?" he asked, aware that walking in her new shoes was not a comfortable venture. They were made for beauty, not hard use, and he rued the fact that he'd not had the foresight to purchase a more practical pair.

"Fine," she said, reaching to undo the footwear, then sliding the bits of leather from her feet with a sigh. "But I think we need to look into a different—"

"—pair of shoes. I know," he said with a grin. "I've already decided that."

"Well, at least we're on the same track here," she whispered, her shoulder slumping as she bent her head and reached to pull the combs from her hair.

"Lie down, Lily," he told her, placing her fabric valise on the blanket. "I'll use this for a pillow."

"What about me?" she asked, slanting him a look upward, the moon giving her an unearthly look, silvering her dark hair and casting her skin with a pearly glow.

"You'll use me. My shoulder anyway." He stretched out beside her and beckoned her with an uplifted hand. "You're safe for now," he said.

"Am I?" She sounded a bit dubious, but did as she was

told, curling on her side to face away from him. "I feel like I've been here before, Morgan."

"Yeah, you should. We've slept this way for the past few nights." He tucked her neatly against himself and felt her soften beneath his touch as she whispered in the darkness.

"What will we be doing tomorrow night? Will you go on by foot, or can we afford transportation?"

"Tomorrow night?" he asked. "We'll worry about it when we get there." In the next twenty-four hours he was committed to finding a man of the cloth who would turn the two of them into husband and wife. Tomorrow night he'd have the satisfaction of knowing that Lily was his, every delectable inch of her.

For tonight, he could only dream.

Chapter Five

The church was small, the exterior a testimony to cleanliness that spoke well for the young minister and his wife. Even as the pastor swept the doorstep, his pretty helpmate moved to enter the building through the doorway behind him, a bouquet of flowers cradled in her arms. The young man did not resemble a minister, Lily thought, being clothed in overalls and a striped cotton shirt. She had become accustomed to a more formal representative of the church back home, a man who seldom busied himself with the upkeep of the building of which he was in charge.

"Good morning." His greeting was cheery, she thought as she smiled in response, leaving it to Morgan to set the stage for the proceedings.

"We heard we might find you cleaning house," Morgan answered. "I asked at the general store about a church where we might be married this morning, and they advised me to come in this direction. Said I'd probably find you here on a Saturday morning."

"Mary? Come on out here," the young man called, leaning through the church door to where the flowers had disappeared only moments ago. He turned back to Morgan. "What a surprise. We'll even have flowers on the altar table for the occasion," he said warmly. "Mary raids her garden every Saturday and strips it almost bare. Somehow by the next week she finds her supply replenished. It's made a believer out of her," he said with a smile that made Lily chuckle.

"What is it, Ray?" Behind him, his wife halted in the doorway and then hurried toward Lily, hand outstretched. "Good morning." The words almost bubbled from her, so warm was her welcome.

"These folks want to get married, honey." The young pastor set aside his broom and wiped his hands on his overalls. "I suppose I should go and change my clothes first."

"No need," Morgan told him quickly. "We don't have a lot of time to linger here. I think you'll do just fine the way you are. So long as we can record the marriage in your church records. We want everything legal and above-board, don't we, Lily?" His look in her direction was that of a man longing to own the title of *husband*.

Morgan acting as the expectant bridegroom was almost too much for Lily to swallow, and she could only nod affably and offer a smile at his words. The man was set on making an impression, it seemed, making sure they would be remembered in this town.

"I can do more than that for you," the minister said. "I have a stack of marriage certificates, just arrived from a printing house in Saint Louis the other day. They look kinda fancy. Makes it more of an occasion, I always think, if you've got something to hang on the wall and pass along to your children one day."

Lily swallowed her denial of that particular idea and nodded again. This was Morgan's show. She'd let him manage it as he pleased. And he no doubt would have anyway, she thought soberly. He was a man who was ob-viously used to taking charge and running things as he saw fit. She'd be hard put to have a say in much of anything once this day was over and he was truly her husband.

For a moment she froze in place, and then felt the weight of Morgan's arm against her shoulders as he claimed her attention. His eyes glittered like polished steel, the gray turning almost to silver as he shot her a warning glance. "Smile," he murmured, in a tone that carried no farther than her ear. "Act like this is the most wonderful day of your life, Lily."

And it might very well be, she thought darkly. Who knew what the future might bring? An accommodating twitch of her lips met his demand and his voice rose a notch. "Lily and I are hoping for a large family some day, parson. But we'll need to make this a real marriage first, I believe." He turned back to Lily. "Are you ready, sweetheart?"

"As ready as I'll ever be," she cooed, smiling sweetly for his benefit.

"Well, I'm glad I got here early," the minister said earnestly. "The inside of the church is ready for Sunday service and we're pretty much spick-and-span." He ushered them inside the small sanctuary and paused. "It's plain but it's a real church, sir," he told Morgan. "I always say every couple should marry in God's presence, don't you?"

"Yeah, I certainly hold to that belief," Morgan said earnestly. Lily stifled the urge to laugh aloud at his droll acceptance of the minister's view. And then she looked into Morgan's face and changed her mind. The man looked as sober as a judge, she decided. As if this were indeed an occasion to be celebrated properly. She'd thought the whole marriage idea was her own, but now it seemed that Morgan was not being dragged into it, kicking and fighting for his life to continue as a single man.

In moments they were standing front and center before the minister and his wife, the scent of flowers surrounding them and the luminous glow that shone through the window over the altar encircling them in a golden frame of sunshine. The moment was suddenly solemn and Lily shivered.

This is the real thing. I'm going to marry Gage Morgan, right here and now.

"I fear I haven't learned your names yet," the minister said quietly, his demeanor that of a man of the cloth, even though he resembled more closely a farmer just in from the field.

"Gage Morgan and Lily Devereaux," Morgan told him.

"Actually my name is Yvonne Lilianne Devereaux," Lily said quickly. "Although I'm called Lily."

"Well, we'll make sure it's legal and binding on your marriage certificate," she was told. "But for the ceremony itself, we'll go by the name you prefer."

She nodded and then stood silently next to the man who was about to take control of her future. As if he sensed her hesitation, he grasped her hand in his, his fingers long and tapered, his grip firm. His palm was calloused, and she felt her fingers curl inside it, as if she sought a haven there.

The words of the ceremony were brief and to the point. She made the proper responses when prompted by the minister, and in short order heard him speak the final words that turned her into a woman who would be called, henceforth, Lily Morgan.

"Would you like to kiss your bride?" The words spoken by the minister caused her to look upward into Morgan's face. His gaze glittered from between narrowed lids, his mouth was hard and unyielding as he pressed it against hers, and his arms bound her against him with a fierce possessiveness she knew she could not have escaped, had she tried.

It seemed Morgan took this business of marriage very seriously indeed. His lips softened after a moment and she was aware that his grip loosened, freeing her from the cage of long arms that encircled her. His eyes met hers and she thought his expression changed for just a moment, a touch of satisfaction edging the mouth that whispered her name.

"Lily? Do you feel married?" he asked, and then bent again to press another, more tender kiss against her lips.

What she felt was apprehension, she decided, even as she recognized the desire he made no effort to conceal from her. His nostrils flared a bit, as if he inhaled a scent that intrigued him, and a dark line of color ridged his cheekbones.

"Thank you, Parson," he said quietly as he turned Lily, holding her in front of him. "If you'll ready our certificate, we'll be on our way."

"Won't you stay for some coffee? I have a fresh pan of cinnamon rolls, just out of the oven," the young wife said. "It wouldn't be any trouble at all. We haven't had very many weddings here. We need to celebrate this one properly."

Lily could not resist the invitation. She'd likely never have another chance to commemorate her wedding. Back home it would have been different, with the church full of family friends from the surrounding community plus the people from the house known as River Bend, had she married there. Instead she'd settled for a youthful couple who exemplified a happy marriage so far as she could tell, and a pan of cinnamon buns instead of the fancy wedding cake her mother would have provided.

It wasn't a bad exchange, she decided as they followed the young couple from the church fifteen minutes later. The parsonage was warm and welcoming, and the coffee and cinnamon rolls filled the hollow spot in her stomach. Only the impatience Morgan was holding on to with a tight rein put a blot on the celebration.

He gripped her elbow after all the goodbyes had been

said, and Mary had pressed a single flower into Lily's hand with the instructions to place it in their family Bible as a keepsake.

"I will. I will," Lily promised, wondering where she was going to find such a thing. She doubted that Morgan's bag carried such a volume, and her own belongings were scant. She wore the second dress Morgan had bought for her, a flowered, full-skirted garment that suited her, but would certainly not hold up well on a long journey. Her other things were folded and squeezed into the valise, and unless Morgan decided to spend more money on her wardrobe, she'd fast be out of something to wear.

They left the parsonage and walked back to the center of town, Morgan carrying both bags, Lily touching his arm for balance as they trod the uneven, rutted road. "We'll go to the livery stable, I think," Morgan said. "See what we can find in a horse and buggy."

"I can ride if you want to get two saddle horses instead," Lily offered.

He looked down at her feminine garments. "Like that?" His brow lifted and she bristled.

"Buy me some trousers and I'll show you a woman who can outride you any day of the week," she muttered.

He laughed aloud. "I doubt that, sweetheart. Besides I want us to appear legitimate when we reach our destination. We're going into a ready-made existence, Lily, and everything will be provided for us for the next few weeks."

She chewed on that idea for a moment. Somehow this wasn't what she'd foreseen when Morgan had told her he would be using her for cover. "We're going where?" she asked. "What will we do when we get there?"

"You'll find out. Just trust me," he told her. And then dropped the bags to the ground beneath a tree at the town's main intersection, where a livery stable stood beneath trees that sheltered it from full sunlight.

A husky man held tongs in his left hand, their pincers gripping a horseshoe. He held it over the glowing coals in his brazier and then placed it on an iron block in front of him, lifting high the hammer he was using to form it. The horse tied at the stable door was waiting for his new footwear, and Lily was gripped by a remembrance of the barn in which she'd spent so many hours, that haven of horses and leather and vehicles that were used on the plantation.

Just so had the dark-skinned man, who served there as blacksmith, worked the iron horseshoes and sweat profusely over his task. Now the fellow they watched took note of them and nodded an abrupt greeting.

"Be with you folks in a minute," he said, holding up the iron shoe and examining the results of his hammering. With a deft movement, he held it in the coals for long seconds, and then the hammer went into action again. The sound rang in the air as they watched. Around them the town swept in all directions, the buildings low and clustered in long rows of storefronts.

"There. That oughta do it," the smithy said, laying aside his tools and allowing the horseshoe to cool on the iron block. He wiped his hands on the already soiled apron he wore, and then propped them on his hips.

"We're in need of a vehicle and a pair of horses to pull it," Morgan told him.

"You wanta rent it by the day or week?" the man asked.

"I don't want to rent it at all. I'd like to buy a team and a carriage or a wagon."

"How about a buggy and one horse?" the man countered. "I got a spare buggy and a mare that pulls it right well."

"Any room in it for our things?" Morgan asked, looking down at their bags.

"Yup. A nice covered place at the rear, oughta hold all that and more."

"Let's see it," Morgan said pleasantly, and then turned to Lily. "Why don't you go in the store across the way and see if there's anything you want to get before we leave, honey?" he asked nicely. And then bent forward, speaking in a lower tone. "Get something for us to eat for the next day, and see if they have a larger case for your things. You'll be needing a pair of sturdier shoes, too."

"All right," she answered. "Would you like to give me some money to pay for this?" she asked. "I'm almost flat broke, Morgan."

"I'll join you there in fifteen minutes," he said, and then turned her, pointing to the general store they'd visited briefly earlier. "Get going, Lily. We need to make tracks."

She did as he asked, buying a loaf of bread some neighboring farm wife had brought in fresh this very morning, according to the proprietor's wife. A chunk of cheese, sliced from an enormous wheel of the stuff, was wrapped along with beef jerky and a small bag of candy sticks.

She found a pair of shoes that looked to be sturdy, lacking in style, but making up for it by being formed from soft leather that would not leave blisters on her feet. Her eyes touched momentarily on a shawl, one of several that were folded on the counter.

"Ain't that a pretty one?" the woman behind the wooden barrier asked. Holding it up before her, she swirled it around and held it over her shoulders. "One of the ladies makes these to sell. Does a dandy business at it, too."

"We'll take one for my wife." From behind her, Morgan's smooth tones decreed she should have the small luxury and Lily turned to smile her thanks. "It doesn't take much to make her happy," he said.

"A good thing, I'd say," Lily murmured beneath her breath, holding her smile intact as Morgan paid for the small assortment she'd put together. She picked one up, a dark-blue specimen with a fringed border and draped it around herself. "Like it?" she asked sweetly, fluttering her eyelashes at him, and was gratified by Morgan's glare.

He bent to place his mouth next to her ear. "Watch it, lady. Don't push it too far." His hand slid into his pocket and he brought forth enough money to pay for their purchases and then watched Lily from beneath shuttered lids as the woman bundled their things in two packages.

Lily took up the one that held her shoes, leaving Morgan to deal with the food.

"You folks have a good trip," she chirped as they left.

"How'd she know we were going on a trip?" Morgan asked, gripping Lily's elbow as they descended the wooden steps to the street.

"I told her we'd just stopped here to be married, and we were off on our honeymoon," she said, hastening to keep up with his long stride. "And if you don't slow down and let me catch up with you, she'll think you're in a hurry to carry out the plan," she told him, breathless from the pace he'd set.

The buggy waited just outside the bank and he led her there, lifting her to the high seat with an ease that surprised her. The man held leashed power in those hands, she decided. He was broad-shouldered and tall, and his hands, though graceful when they shuffled and dealt poker cards, were strong and callused. "Give me your shoes. I'll put them in the back with the rest of our things," he said, looking up at her. "And where's the larger bag I told you to buy?"

"I decided we didn't need it. If I don't have any more clothes than what I've got with me already, it's foolish to buy something bigger to put them in."

He frowned. "I'll be in the market for a couple of things in the next day or so," he told her. "We'll need something to keep them in."

"Like what?" she asked as he rounded the front of the mare and climbed up onto the seat.

"Like some boots for me, suitable for farm life, a couple of dresses for you that don't make you look like a refugee from a saloon. And," he said finally, "a gun for you to use, and some shells."

She laughed. "You're going to trust me with a gun? And then expect me to use it? I'm the lady who uses a fireplace poker for defense," she said sharply. "I can shoot a long gun, but I don't think that's what you have in mind, is it?"

"No, you'll need something you can carry with you." He snapped the reins over the mare's back and the buggy set off, rolling quickly past the last of the storefronts and onto a wending road that traveled parallel to the river they'd followed.

"I didn't realize I was expected to shoot anyone," she said. "I thought you frowned on seeing my picture displayed on that wanted poster."

He cast her a patient glance. "I don't *expect* you to shoot anyone, Lily. I just want you to know how to use it if you need to."

She considered that idea a moment. "I have the feeling I'm getting in over my head, Morgan."

"Another thing. If we're married, you need to be calling me by my name."

"Gage?" she asked. "Morgan suits you better." *And speaking your name will make this whole thing too personal, make it a real marriage.*

"Gage sounds more like a husband," he said. "And I want to represent a typical married couple."

"Well," she began slowly, "maybe I just won't call you anything. That'll solve the problem. After all, any decent married man wouldn't really want to be associated with a woman who belongs in a saloon, would he?"

"Oh, yeah," he said softly. "I won't mind *associating*

with you, Lily. In fact, it will be my pleasure. And so far as the Gage bit is concerned, I suspect you'll be calling me lots of names before we get through this. In fact, I hope you'll still be talking to me. The best I can hope for is that the nicest thing you call me will probably be my proper name.''

And wasn't that a remark designed to make her stew, she thought, settling back in the seat, almost ignoring his comment about the association they would undertake. She'd deal with that when the time came, she decided, feeling like a veritable coward as she shoved the thought of Morgan's intentions to the back burner of her mind.

The town Morgan headed for was down the river, a small community in Arkansas, situated to the west of the Mississippi. Facing hard times, the farmers and ranchers there were being threatened by men who purported to represent the federal government, snatching up their property and reselling it for vast profits. The railroad right-of-way was valuable, as was the grazing land.

''Sand Creek has been a thriving town for years, and these folks own some pretty valuable property. The problem is that too many of them are being cheated out of it.''

''Sand Creek? This place we're heading for really has a name?'' she asked, sarcasm coating her words. ''You mean I really get to know something about this mess you're about to drag me into?''

He shot her a measuring look, his grin appearing. ''And you thought I was nothing but a two-bit gambler, didn't you, sweetheart?''

He wasn't too far off, he decided, from the look in her eyes that told him he'd come pretty close to reading her mind.

''Well, what are you exactly?'' she blurted and turned to look out over the gently rolling countryside as the buggy moved past open fields and wooded areas. As if she regretted her question, she refused to look back at him as he chose his words carefully.

"I work for the government," he told her. "This is how it is. When the men of Sand Creek went off to war the lack of money and shortage of manpower left in the community made farming an unprofitable proposition," Morgan said. "The farmers and ranchers left were too scattered across the landscape to unite against the thieves, and no one was ready to challenge them. At this point, one by one, they've become victims of the land scams. Most of them have lost their holdings already."

"And we're supposed to do what?" she asked. "Sit there and wait to be picked off when they decide it's time for us to turn over and go belly up?"

Morgan shook his head. "We're going to be working undercover as a married couple, taking the place of some folks named Blair. You'll be taking Sarah's place and I'm posing as her husband, Sam. Just to keep things simple, I'll be known as Gage.

"Having you along as my wife will give me credence," he said. And it would be up to him to keep her safe, with only the honed skills gained over the past years to protect the two of them on this assignment. He was playing a lone hand, with his life at risk.

"Won't the crooks we're after figure out that the folks who are moving over to make room for us have also taken on new names?"

"I doubt it. They only know that the Blairs' holdings are running alongside the land that's marked out as an ideal route for the train tracks that will head south from Saint Louis to Louisiana and then west to Texas. A secondary route, as a matter of fact, one scheduled to be started in a year or so.

"One thing in our favor is that there's a sheriff in Sand Creek who's prepared to help us."

She was silent for a moment and then apparently thought of another fly in the ointment. "Where will the Blairs be staying while we take over their lives?"

"They'll be living in town, out of danger."

"They'll be out of danger," she repeated. "And we'll be in the midst of it."

"Yeah, we will. In fact that's only one part of this whole thing I don't like, Lily. Not one little bit. And it's also the very reason I want you prepared to use a gun should the need arise."

"Morgan…" Her voice trailed off as she reconsidered the question she'd thought of tossing in his direction. Had he plotted in a cold-blooded manner from the beginning? Had he decided she was a likely prospect to fulfill his assignment? Had there been no real attraction for her in the scheme of things?

"What, Lily?" he asked quietly, as if he understood her dilemma and would not press for the query she'd suppressed. "What do you need to know?"

She launched out, cutting her ties with whatever security she'd gained over the last days. "Am I just a part of the plot, Morgan? Did you string me along and use me for your own needs?" For if he lacked any real caring for her, she'd just as well know right now. If she was bait for a trap, the least he could do was be up-front about it.

He refused to look at her, his jaw clenching, his grip on the reins tightening. And then he spoke, with reluctance, as if the words were drawn from him one by one, as if he must ponder the impact they would have on her.

"It began that way, Lily. I knew I needed to find a woman to provide cover for me. You seemed the ideal prospect, from the very beginning. The problem was that I couldn't sort out whether I was plotting to take you with me for my own benefit or the advantage it would give me to have you along."

He glanced at her, his eyes veiled, cool beneath half-lowered lids. "I knew when I said those vows back there that I was in this for longer than a few weeks. I don't make promises lightly. And once I claim you as my wife, I won't be turning you loose."

"You plan on dragging me along on all your little trips, Morgan?" She was amazed at the degree of calmness in her voice, when her insides were shaking, and she was feeling somehow as though the earth was trembling beneath her.

"No." The single word was emphatic. "I'll figure something out. I've got a few irons in the fire, Lily. This will be the last time I take an assignment." He hesitated and then pulled the horse to a halt by the side of the road. The silence surrounded them, the jingle of harness and the sound of hoof beats stilled, with only the song of a bird from a nearby tree filling the void.

He grasped her arms and turned her toward him. She refused to strain against his superior strength, knowing the struggle would be futile, and instead tilted her head back to look up into his eyes. Steely-gray this morning, they neither warmed now nor took refuge in evading her gaze.

"Yes, Lily, I'm using you as bait. I won't deny it. At the same time, I've promised you I'll protect you, and I will. You have my word on that." He waited, but she refused to give him the satisfaction of a reply, for indeed there was none to be offered. He'd only confirmed the facts.

"I married you because I wanted to, not because it was the only way to get your cooperation. I could have threatened you with exposure if you hadn't gone along with this."

"I thought that's what you did," she said quietly. "Back on the boat when you made that lovely remark about Colonel Weston *gnawing* on my bones."

"I was making a point," he said, and then he grinned. "It worked, didn't it?"

"The picture you planted was too vivid for me to ignore," she told him. "I know the colonel, remember?" The shiver that touched her spine could not be hidden, and as she watched, his nostrils flared and his eyes narrowed a bit.

"He won't hurt you again, Lily. When this is over with, I'll tend to the colonel."

And he would. Even not knowing the man beyond the past few days, she had no doubt that he would be her champion, that his words to her offered a promise she could not ignore.

"All this is irrelevant anyway," he said, releasing her and picking up the reins again. "We're married, we've got a job to do and we're in it together, like it or not. If you're not going to go through with your end of this thing, you'd best say so now, Lily. I need your cooperation for it to work. Will you abide by our bargain?"

The buggy rolled down the road and she was silent, knowing he awaited her decision, aware at the same time that she had little choice in the matter. She was a woman alone, in desperate straits without his protection. And that thought brought fear to her heart. For the first time in her life, Lily Devereaux was in danger from all sides.

Not only was she up to her neck in a deception that might well prove to be her undoing, but she was bound legally to a man who held all the cards. And who, she realized, held an attraction for her that Colonel Stanley Weston had never possessed.

She felt cornered, yet she refused to abjectly submit to Morgan. Her rearing as a Southern lady would not allow it. She'd been instilled with the pride of the Devereaux clan for over twenty years, and no mere man would make her bow her head in defeat.

With a feline smile that had been her defense more than once in her early years, she looked at Morgan, her head tilted to one side, her mouth pursed a bit as if she considered his demand and found it amusing.

"Yes, I'll abide by our bargain," she said softly. "It's to my benefit, after all. But once this is over, you'll take me home to my family and walk away, Morgan."

He hesitated, and she felt triumph rise within her. She'd surprised him, had caught him unaware. He'd expected capitulation and instead had gotten a counteroffer.

One brow tilted as he considered her for a moment in silence. And then he only nodded, choosing his words carefully. "If that's what you really want, Lily. If you still feel that way when this is over with, I'll take you home."

"And you'll walk away?"

"If that's what you want," he repeated, "I'll walk away."

Chapter Six

They spent the night in a small hotel, which had the distinction of being the only available spot within twenty miles that had beds available to weary travelers. On that count they definitely qualified, Lily decided, trudging across the small lobby to where the proprietor had designated they would find a place to eat. The sign in front of the wooden structure bore no name, only proclaiming the building as the Hotel.

Its dining room consisted of a fireplace and four mismatched tables, with chairs equally as nondescript, all in a half circle around the hearth, although in midsummer such amenities as a fire were not a necessity. Lamps lit each table and the young woman who carried in their evening meal wore a dingy apron, but the food she presented for their approval seemed substantial and smelled appetizing.

''Thank you,'' Morgan told the girl, then leaned across the table to murmur his thoughts aloud to Lily. ''I feared that when there was no choice of a menu to be had, we might be in trouble. I'm happy to report that my fears were in vain.'' He glanced at her plate and then back at his own. ''This roast beef looks to rival any I've ever tried.''

"You'd better hope it's not muskrat," Lily said softly, poking at the meat with her fork.

Morgan was silent and she ventured a look at him through her eyelashes. His eyes danced with laughter and his words echoed the emotion. "Trying to scare me off, Mrs. Morgan? It won't work, you know. I've eaten every creature known to mankind in my day. Muskrat wouldn't be my first choice, but it has left an unforgettable memory in my mind. And trust me, my dear, *this* is not that particular delicacy."

He cut the meat and forked a bite between his lips, then chewed and swallowed. "In fact," he offered, "I'll be glad to eat yours if it doesn't appeal to you."

Lily laughed aloud. The man had a sense of humor. A real, live funny bone. And she wouldn't have thought it, not for a moment. The meat was delicious, the vegetables a bit overcooked but edible, and the apple tart delicious, steaming and juicy beyond belief.

They ate, almost in silence, their appetites whetted by the food, and as if neither of them was willing to speak of the hours ahead, they chose, almost by mutual consent, it seemed, to spend their energy on devouring the food before them. The table did not boast a tablecloth, and there was not a napkin in sight, but Lily's handkerchief filled in nicely and she wiped her mouth with it.

Morgan's smile caught her attention and she felt a flush suffuse her cheeks. "What?" she asked abruptly. And then looked down at the front of her dress. "Did I spill something? Or leave crumbs on my face somewhere?"

He shook his head and pushed away from the table and then circled to her side, holding her chair as if they had just dined in an elegant restaurant in some expensive hotel, instead of in a dusty town with not a smidgen of elegance to its name. "You looked like a young woman who was thoroughly enjoying her meal,'' he said. "And the sight pleased me.''

"I did enjoy it,'' she said, rising as he took her elbow and assisted her. That his help was not necessary was a given, but the fact that he was treating her in a gentlemanly manner pleased her somehow.

"I haven't seen you look happy before,'' he told her, leading her from the small room to where the stairs climbed to the second floor. She gripped the banister, noting that it was rough-hewn, sanded a bit to protect its user's palm from splinters, but certainly lacking any beeswax or polish.

"I haven't been happy in a long time,'' she admitted, slowing her pace, as if she would prolong the time until they reached the room he'd taken for their use.

"A shame,'' he said. "For it seems that it takes little to please you, Lily.''

"Life has not been easy, Morgan,'' she told him. "I'm not looking for sympathy, only trying to explain the way things are. Or were, I should say. I have high hopes that my future will brighten immeasurably when this particular jaunt is over and I'm on my way back to Louisiana.''

"Louisiana?'' he asked, sliding the key from his pocket as they paused before the door of their room. "You hadn't told me before where you were from.''

And now the fat was in the fire, she supposed. She'd never learned the fine art of discretion. Mama had always told her that a lady is known by her ability to remain discreet and hold her mouth, giving away nothing but that which is required of her. She hadn't agreed at the time, of course, but perhaps Mama was right.

"Well, that's where I'm from,'' she said, sounding even to her own ears a bit disgruntled. Louisiana was a big place, and once he got her within a few miles of River

Bend, she'd elude him and never have to worry about seeing him again.

"It shows," he said, walking to the bedside table and lighting the candle there. "Your speech is soft, with just a bit of the lilt of New Orleans in it."

"But not proper English?" She sat on the chair and glared at him.

"I wasn't the one who said that," he reminded her, removing his jacket and hanging it on a hook. He unbuttoned his sleeves and shirtfront, then paused. "We'd better settle this here and now, Lily. I'm not sleeping on the floor, and neither are you. We shared my bunk on the riverboat, and we'll do the same here. Understood?"

She felt a distinct sense of relief. It seemed that tonight was not to be the beginning of their marriage, after all. He only wanted to share the bed with her, and there was room enough for two to lie there, side by side, without touching if they were careful of their movements.

"All right, that sounds agreeable to me," she said, leaning forward to slip her shoes from feet that felt suddenly tired, toes that cramped beneath her fingers. With a sigh, she leaned back and stretched her legs out before her, wiggling her feet and rotating her ankles in a distinctly unladylike manner. Somehow, it didn't seem to matter. This was only Morgan, after all. She needn't make a pretense of being dignified around him.

"Stand up and I'll undo your buttons," he said, offering his hand.

She eyed it for a moment before she took it, rising before him and then turning, offering him her back. Lifting her hair from her shoulders, she pulled it forward and began plaiting it as he dealt with the line of buttons that held her dress together. The cool air from an open window touched her exposed skin, and she shivered.

"Don't tell me you're cold," he said. "And I won't believe you're frightened of me, Lily."

"Neither," she said, seeking out a corner where the light was not so bright, where she might don her nightdress without his eyes taking in every movement. "The breeze caught me. It felt good, as a matter of fact. I don't know why we bundle ourselves up in so many items of apparel, when it would be more sensible to dress in fewer garments."

"You can dress in as little as you please around me, Lily," he said, amusement touching each word. "Especially at night. I've never been a fan of nightclothes."

"That's where I'll draw the line," she said sharply. Her bag was opened quickly and her nightgown drawn from its depths. She turned and looked at him, unwilling to plead for privacy, hoping he would give it freely.

"Am I supposed to shut my eyes or turn my head?" he asked, settling on the edge of the bed to remove his boots and stockings. "Not a chance, sweetheart. Just get yourself into that monstrous garment and get ready for bed."

Lily obeyed, not with grace, but with a semblance of dignity. She pulled the gown over her head and stripped from her garments beneath its folds.

"You've spoiled my evening," Morgan said. "I looked forward all day to watching you undress, you know."

"You did not," she said, gathering up her clothing, then shaking each item out and folding it neatly for tomorrow's use. He was a tease, she decided. She recognized that his smile was intended to assure her of her safety with him, and doggone if it wasn't working. He'd told her he'd take care of her, keep her safe, and then he'd promised to share the bed without coercion tonight.

"You have no idea what I've thought about all day, Lily," he murmured, standing and stripping from his trousers. His drawers were knit, clinging to every line of his lower body, allowing her a glimpse of his male attributes.

She turned away, feeling the heat of embarrassment creep up her cheeks again. The man had no shame, none whatsoever. Just because she'd married him—

His low laughter caught her ear and she knew again the threat of Morgan's appeal. For that was the bottom line. She'd married him, and as his wife, she could expect only what privacy he chose to give her, only the amount of restraint he exhibited. She stepped to the opposite side of the bed and pulled back the sheet and quilt, fluffing the pillow before she settled on the bottom sheet and drew the second one over her legs.

He stood beside the bed and she thought his attention was on the braid she'd formed. His words proved her theory correct. "Do you want me to brush your hair?" he asked, settling beside her. "You usually spend some time on it, and tonight you've stolen my pleasure at watching you. I'd be happy to serve as your lady's maid."

"That might be nice," she murmured agreeably, "but tonight I'm tired." She turned aside, hugging the edge of the thin mattress and heard his low chuckle behind her.

"Come here, Lily," he whispered.

Wonder of wonders, she did as he asked, twisting in the bed, her nightgown tangling around her legs, until she faced him. "What?" she asked, breathless from more than just the exertion of her movements.

"Now lift up and reach past me and blow out the candle," he told her.

She cast him a look of exasperation. "Why didn't you think of that before you plunked yourself down?"

He grinned. "I wanted to see you reaching over me." He waited until she sighed and then lifted herself on one elbow and stretched toward the candle. She blew with a mighty gust of breath and it flickered, then died, leaving them in the dark.

"Actually," he said softly, "what I wanted was to feel your breasts against me. Like this." He wrapped one arm around her and she felt the soft curve of her bosom press against his chest. His hand lifted and cupped her, as if he weighed and measured the firm fullness.

"Please, Morgan," she whispered, "don't do this to me."

"I'm not hurting you, Lily. I know better than that. I'm only touching you, admiring the lines of your figure and wondering how long I'll be able to keep my hands off you."

"Well, you're off to a bad start, I'd say," she hissed. "You aren't showing much restraint right now."

"Oh, sweetheart," he murmured, laughter coating each syllable. "You have no idea how hard this is for me."

She twisted from his grasp and sat up in the bed. "All right. I'm not going to worry and wonder every night when you're going to decide to make your move. You warned me that this would be a real marriage. So if you're going to do *that* to me, you'd might as well get it over with," she said harshly. "I'd *rather* have it over with, if you don't mind."

"Making love to you is not something that will ever be 'over with', Lily," he told her softly. "But here and now is neither the time nor place for it to happen. It will be in a more private, comfortable spot than this."

She lay back against the pillow and felt his arm encircle her waist. Then he rose over her and bent to touch his lips against her cheek. "I'm going to kiss you, though," he said. "No more than that, so don't be stiffening up on me."

She believed him. For some strange, unknown reason, she trusted the man, even in this. Her lips were pliant beneath his, her breathing calming as she relaxed beneath his caresses. The hand at her waist remained there and she felt just a small tinge of disappointment that he seemed content with his brief exploration of her breasts. She'd never enjoyed Stanley's attentions, had assumed that women were not meant to get pleasure from the acts that led to intimacy.

Now it seemed that Morgan might banish those ideas from her mind, and the thought of his possessing her body became less of a threat and more of a tantalizing promise of joy to come.

They journeyed another full day, and by the time sunset was upon them, Lily was yearning for a soft bed and warm meal to fill the void in her stomach. The cheese and bread were gone, and Morgan had devoured the candy sticks once he discovered them in the bundle. A patch of berries by the side of the road had yielded a treat during the afternoon, but had long since been digested.

"I'm hungry," Lily muttered, stretching her arms over her head in a distinctly unladylike manner.

"You have an appetite like no other woman I've ever met," Morgan observed. "I don't know where you put the food. It sure doesn't stick to your bones."

She smiled. "Is that a nice way of telling me I'm skinny? If so, it's not hurting my feelings. It's never been my aim in life to weigh a ton."

"You're not skinny, Lily. Not by a long shot. In fact, you've got the most nicely rounded—"

She sat upright with an abrupt movement and glared at him, cutting off his pronouncement before he could utter the final words. "Never mind my rounded whatever," she said. "I know what I look like, and as long as I'm decently covered, I can pass for an ordinary farmer's wife. I'd think that was the most important thing right now. I've never asked to be decked out in satin in my life."

"But it looks so good on you," he said smoothly. "Not that I want anyone else to see you dressed that way. But I rather enjoy admiring your charms."

"Well, admire them some other time. Right now we need a place to sleep for the night, and something to put in our stomachs."

"I thought about searching out a farmhouse and asking for the use of a barn," he said. "But there hasn't been a house to be seen in miles."

"Are we near a town?"

He shrugged. "I'm not sure. My map isn't up-to-date. From what I could tell, there's a place just west of here, a decent-size dot on the map. Maybe we should head in that direction."

"I can settle for sleeping on the ground if needs be," she said, "but I'm not sure how much longer I want to go without food."

"All right," he said agreeably. "We'll stop in a grove of trees and build a fire and I'll find something for you to cook over it."

"Something?" she asked. "Like what?"

"Rabbit, maybe. Or squirrels, if we're desperate enough."

"A squirrel is nothing but a rat with a furry tail," she told him. "No, thanks."

"Well," he drawled, pointing a finger ahead and just to the west of the wagon tracks they traveled, "if you look over there, you'll see smoke rising. I warrant we'll find a house if we cut across the meadow at an angle and take a look."

"Really?" She peered in the direction he pointed and her heart lifted as she caught a glimpse of a curling whisper of smoke that rose in the air from behind a stand of trees. "Maybe someone will be willing to sell us some food."

"We'll see," he said, turning the mare off the trail and

making a path through tall grass and wildflowers that were blooming in abundance across the landscape. They were beneath the shelter of tall trees in a few minutes' time, and then as the trees became more sparse, a house with several outbuildings appeared ahead.

"Looks promising," Morgan told her. The buggy bounced a bit, and Lily hung on to the seat, and then as they reached a lane that showed signs of wagon tracks, she relaxed beside him.

The door opened onto a porch, and by the time they rolled within fifty feet of it, a man stepped out to greet them. A long gun hung loosely at his side, but the threat was implicit. Morgan held up a hand in greeting and murmured a low message to Lily. "Smile nicely, sweetheart. We want the man to know we're friendly."

She obliged, aware that a family so isolated would be naturally wary of strangers.

"What can I do for you folks?" the man called out as Morgan brought the mare to a halt in front of the porch.

"We need a place to bed down for the night. We're more than willing to pay a fair price for the use of your barn," he said. "And if you'll throw in some supper, I'll make it worth your while."

The farmer looked them over thoroughly and then nodded, as though he found no danger in their presence. "You can sleep in the hayloft," he told Morgan. "And my wife, Anna, has enough food cooked to share. Come on in."

Four children sat tucked together on a long bench on one side of the trestle table, Morgan and Lily receiving the honor of using chairs. The farmer and his wife shared a shorter bench near the stove and though the meal was plain, the food was good and plentiful, as their host had said.

"My garden is doin' real good," the wife told them. "Fresh string beans and beets are comin' along. Picked the first batch of corn today.'' The golden ears had small kernels and were tender. The supply of butter was abundant, and Lily slathered it on her second ear of corn.

"This is wonderful," she said, biting into the tender kernels without delay, aware of the trickle of butter that trailed along the edge of her finger, and ignoring it with ease. "Do you make your own butter?" And then she blushed. "Well, of course you do," she amended. "And your own bread, too, don't you?"

A plate piled high with thick slices sat in the middle of the table and Morgan reached for a piece. "Do you know how to bake bread?" he asked Lily, and then grinned at their hostess. "We've only been married a short while. I have a lot to learn about my bride. I suspect I'll be in for a few surprises."

"Well, I don't mind telling you a few things," the woman said, directing her smile in Lily's direction. "We all have to learn sometime."

The hour after supper was spent with Lily obtaining all the knowledge she could gather, and the woman who shared it with her was obviously glad of someone to listen while she talked. "We don't get much company, here off the beaten path," she confided. "Had a couple of fellas stop by the other day, but they skedaddled when my Henry waved his shotgun at them."

"What did they want?" Lily asked, her ears perking up at the woman's words.

"Said they were with the United States government and they had permission to take our land for a right-of-way for the railroad. Henry told them to make tracks, and when he reached for the gun, they left in a dad-blasted hurry."

Lily frowned. "Did they threaten y'all?"

"No, but I sure didn't like the looks of them. They said they'd be back." She sniffed in indignation. "Henry'll show them the road should they ride up to the porch again.

The government's got no business tryin' to take our land. We got a deed that says it's ours.''

"Did they offer to pay you for it?" Lily asked, wishing that Morgan were listening to the conversation.

"Yeah, about enough to get us a couple of days in a hotel and a few hot meals while we looked for another place to settle. Henry let them know we weren't interested. Not one little bit.''

Lily held her peace until bedtime, and then earned a surprised grin from Morgan as she hustled him across the yard toward the barn. "I didn't know you were in such a hurry to spend the night with me, sweetheart,'' he teased. Arms filled with a sheet, a quilt and a pair of pillows, items Lily suspected had been pilfered from the children's beds, he followed in her wake as she opened the big door at the front of the barn and stepped inside the yawning interior.

"I need to talk to you," she whispered, looking back toward the house. She gripped his arm and tugged him inside the barn behind her, then shut the door, leaving them in a twilight cocoon. From the windows, sufficient light shone to illuminate the ladder to the loft and Lily clambered up quickly, holding her dress high. She reached down to grasp the pillows as he handed them, and then the bedclothes, up to her.

Morgan made short work of the ladder and stepped onto the floor of the hayloft. "Looks like Henry cut hay not too long ago,'' he surmised, eyeing the stacks of fragrant dried grasses that surrounded them. "It oughta make a decent bed.''

The window of the loft was open, and in the dim light, he tossed the quilt across a heavy pile of hay and aimed the pillows toward the center of their makeshift bed. "Listen to me, Morgan,'' Lily said in a low voice. "I think the men you're in search of were here a few days ago.''

Morgan's hands halted in midair as he was about to snap

the sheet and allow it to drift over their quilt. It hung before him and as she watched, his brows lowered and he bent closer to her. "Are you sure?"

"No, of course not, but Henry's wife, Anna, told me that two men came calling and offered them a pittance for their land. Said the government was claiming it for the right-of-way for a railroad. Henry shook his shotgun at them and they left, but they threatened to return."

Morgan nodded, and then seemed to withdraw. "Did you hear me?" Lily asked. "What do you think?"

"Let me consider this for a few minutes," he told her. "I hadn't heard that the scam was being worked this far north, but if what Henry's wife told you is fact, then we need to get out the word."

"To who?" Lily asked. "Who do you report to?"

He shook his head. "Not now, Lily. Let me think." He waved a hand toward the temporary bed. "Go on. Lie down and get to sleep." Walking across the loft, he stood by the open window and gazed out, as if he could somehow divine the circumstances she'd described.

"We didn't bring our bags up here," Lily said, thinking of her brush and the nightgown she'd planned to wear.

"Sleep in your shift," he told her. "We'll be in a small town tomorrow night and I'll get you a couple of dresses to wear. That one will do for another day, won't it?"

"All right," she agreed, making an effort to reach over her shoulders to work at the buttons. Morgan glanced back at her and made his way to where she stood.

"Let me help," he offered, and she turned her back to him, accepting his assistance with an ease she couldn't have imagined a week ago.

Her life had changed immeasurably, she decided, once Morgan came on the scene. The prospect of marriage, after Stanley had dashed her hopes of a happy-ever-after, had not been given a second thought. Indeed, she'd vowed to herself to totally avoid the institution at all cost. Once burned, her mother had said, a woman would do well to stay clear of the hot stove.

Now, she faced the foreseeable future with this man, a man who was her husband, yet was not. Though the owner of the warm hands touching her back with slow, methodical movements seemed to have more in mind than an offer to serve as a lady's maid. Lily bent her head a bit, holding her hair to one side as Morgan reached the top button and slid it from its mooring.

"There you go," he said softly, and as she allowed the dress to fall forward from her shoulders, he placed his lips on the vulnerable nape she presented. As though he touched her with a thousand butterfly wings, her skin responded, a quick shiver running the length of her spine.

And then he was gone, back to the window, while she slid completely from her dress and petticoat, then removed shoes and stockings before she lay on the quilt and drew the sheet up over herself. She watched him, noted the width of his shoulders, the narrow wedge of hips and thighs and the hand he placed on an upright piece of wood near his head. His hat was tilted low, a custom he observed frequently, she'd noted, as if he would screen the message his eyes might convey.

Even as she watched, he removed the wide-brimmed hat and held it against his side. Then with a spin, he sent it sailing to where she lay. It landed at the foot of her makeshift bed and she sat up in surprise. "Morgan?"

He turned his head and his face was shadowed in the gloom of night. "Yeah?"

It was a simple reply, and she found she had no response to offer. "Nothing," she said, after a moment.

"Go to sleep, Lily," he commanded her. The words were harsh, as if he harbored some grudge against her, and she watched him for a moment. But in vain, for he turned away, dismissing her, if not from his mind, then certainly from his sight.

An owl swooped past him from the depths of the loft and he showed no sign that it had almost brushed his head in its escape from the barn. As though made of stone, he remained where he stood, and Lily held his image in her mind as she slept.

Somehow, Morgan felt little surprise at the story Lily had told him, for this place was an ideal spot in which to gull a simple farmer. Isolated, with no close neighbors, Henry was at a disadvantage. Without a doubt, he'd been taken in by the visitor's claim of government backing. How long he would hold up to the threats the men might offer was a question Morgan had no answer for.

They might burn his house or barn. Intimidation of a man's family was a common ploy when such criminals attacked, and there were reports of men being shot and killed in front of wives and children. It was urgent that they be caught, and he decided to warn Henry in the morning just what he could expect. Keeping his gun handy was the best deterrent, but there were times when the man had fieldwork to do, leaving his family vulnerable.

The only solution was to bait the trap in Sand Creek and hope for a quick resolution to the situation.

The night air was warm, with no breeze to cool the loft, and he feared the night would hold little rest for either himself or Lily. But once she'd relaxed and fallen asleep, she seemed to find a degree of comfort on the resilient hay. He'd allowed his gaze to return to her, time and again, waiting until she should allow her weary body the rest it needed. If he went to her now, he feared the loss of the restraint he'd placed upon himself. A man who knew the meaning of abstinence, he nevertheless chafed at the thought of having a wife so close at hand, without seeking her out as was his legal right.

He'd told her that they would consummate this marriage in a decent bed, at the right time. Long years ago he'd learned not to allow his masculine urges to control his life. But, there were times when keeping his word was damn inconvenient, he decided.

Lily would no doubt allow him the use of her body, but that wasn't what he wanted. He ached for her as he'd rarely yearned for a woman before. But then, he'd never owned a wife, never spoken the vows of marriage before, having grown comfortable with years of bachelorhood. He was almost forty years old, thirty-seven to be exact, and for the first time in his life, he'd committed himself to marriage.

He could no longer fool himself into thinking that it was a matter of convenience, this marriage he'd undertaken, that Lily was expendable, that he could deliver her to Louisiana and wave farewell. He'd told her he'd do that very thing.

But he'd lied.

She curled beneath the sheet and then pushed it aside in her sleep, apparently too warm beneath the low, overhanging eaves. Her legs were exposed beneath the hem of her shift, and he examined them from his vantage point. Slender but well formed, with narrow ankles and slim feet, she was built along aristocratic lines. Her body was shapely, her arms and hands graceful, and he was struck with the dark beauty of his bride.

The owl was returning to the barn, a bit of prey in its claws, and Morgan stood aside, lest the bird's flight be on a collision course with the man who watched. It was time to lie down, if not to sleep, then certainly to rest. Tomorrow would come soon enough, he decided. Worrying about it tonight wasn't going to do a bit of good.

Wearing his drawers, he slid between the quilt and sheet

and rolled over to where Lily was curled. One leg was bent, the other straight beneath it and the need to fit himself to that perfect angle she offered was urgent. With a bit of persuasion on his part, he could take his pleasure and provide her with a measure of her own. He gritted his teeth against the temptation, inhaling the sweet scent of woman that rose from her warmth and lured him near.

He formed himself to her back, holding her loosely, lest she be frightened by his presence there. But it seemed he offered her no threat, for she sighed, then murmured his name, as if she dreamed of him, and the fantasy woven in her sleep was to her liking.

There would be no ease for him tonight. Only the pleasure he could snatch from her warmth, the soft weight of her breast in his palm and the knowledge that she slept unafraid.

Chapter Seven

Henry lifted a hand in farewell, his face set in stoic lines. Forewarned, he was apparently already making his own plans to foil the men who would take his land if they could. Behind him, his wife and four children watched the buggy leave the yard, the woman holding a hand over her lips, as though they quivered and she must hide the evidence of her distress.

"I don't feel good about leaving them this way," Lily said, turning back to face Morgan, once the farmhouse was behind them. Although more a cabin than a house, it nevertheless held a family that worked hard to make a life here. A family that deserved the protection of the law, and seemed unlikely to receive it, and instead would probably be forced to do battle to keep what was theirs.

"I don't, either," Morgan said, exasperation in his tone. "But we don't have a choice. I've told Henry about the scam this gang of crooks is running. It's up to him to keep an eye out and his gun handy."

Lily was left to fret in silence for the next hour, for it seemed that Morgan's mind was busy with thoughts he was not willing to share with her. The day was perfection itself, Lily thought, the sky blue with puffy clouds sailing toward the east, birds singing and butterflies drifting over the wild-flowers by the side of the wagon tracks they followed.

"Morgan?" At his distracted glance in her direction, she pressed her lips together. "I'm sorry," she said quietly. "I just was wishing this were a real adventure, a wedding trip, and there was no danger attached for us or the people who live here." She lifted her hand, moving it to indicate the area before them. "Everything looks so peaceful, and yet we're heading into danger. Why do you suppose evil seems to surround us? Life would be so much simpler if everyone followed the rules of society and did what was right and proper."

"I didn't know I'd married such a dreamer," Morgan said dryly. He tilted his hat back a bit and leaned his elbows on his thighs, the reins loose in his hands. "Life is real, Lily. Things are tough all over, and if you want a decent life you have to fight for it sometimes. Henry's battle to hold his land will take all his strength, but if he wins the fight, his victory will be all the sweeter. He'll have beaten the odds."

"I was raised to be a dreamer, I suppose," she said. "Life was wonderfully easy when I was a child. I was pampered and petted, and everyone I lived with seemed secure. And then war came and things changed overnight."

"And you with them," he agreed.

"Not because I wanted to," she told him. "I'd have stayed at home until I found a husband. I'd have moved on, probably not far from home, and raised a family, just as my folks planned for me."

"Then why did you leave with your colonel, Lily?" he asked.

"I don't think I want to talk about it right now," she answered. "It might be better done another time."

"All right," he agreed amiably. "We're coming up on

a town anyway, I think. See that dark line against the horizon? Looks like it might be buildings.''

Lily bent forward, shading her eyes with one hand. ''I think you're right,'' she said. ''In fact, there's a house over there to the left, closer to where the river runs.'' Excitement rose within her and she sat on the edge of the seat. ''Can we see if there's a hotel or somewhere to eat?''

''Didn't your biscuits and gravy stick to your ribs?'' he asked with a grin. ''You ate enough for both of us.''

''I did not,'' she said sharply, glaring in his direction. ''I was hungry, and Anna, bless her heart, kept passing the biscuits my way.''

''I'm teasing you, sweetheart,'' Morgan told her. ''And yes, we'll find some food. It may be at a general store, or in someone's kitchen, but we'll eat.''

The general store sat in a prominent position in the center of the small town, a place named Middleburg, according to a sign someone had placed on the edge of the community. It boasted a bank, three saloons and a barber shop, but the emporium was by far the largest establishment there.

This afternoon it held an assortment of townsfolk and a smattering of farmers. One lady came in with a basket of eggs, another with rounds of butter wrapped in waxed paper, both of them trading for staples. Again, Lily watched as the proprietor cut a chunk of cheese from a large wheel and wrapped it in brown paper. He covered the cheese with a netting of some sort when he'd finished and turned back to Lily.

''What else would you like, ma'am? I got pickled bologna here in a brine keg.'' He pointed to a large crock on the counter, a plate covering it. ''Want to taste it?''

She couldn't resist, and nodded her assent. The man fished in the brine and brought out a length of sausage, placing it on the plate and cutting a small portion. He held it on the end of his fork and offered it to her.

Tangy, meaty and worth a second bite, she decided promptly and told the man as much, then watched as he wrapped her purchase in waxed paper before he included it with the cheese. A basket of small bread loaves sat on the counter and Lily bought two of the brown, crusty specimens, her mouth watering as she faced the prospect of a meal.

"You find enough for a meal yet?" Morgan asked from behind her. "How about a can of peaches?" he asked the proprietor. "And maybe you can tell me how far we are from Sand Creek?"

"Hmm…" the man said, narrowing his eyes as he considered the query. "Probably about forty miles downriver, shouldn't take you longer than tomorrow, late, to get there, providing you stop for the night someplace."

"Anything available here in town?" Morgan asked.

"Not much," the man said. "A boardinghouse where you might get a decent meal, but the beds aren't much, and you'd probably be sharing a room with other folks. Mostly cowhands on the lookout for work or down on their luck stay there."

"I think we'll go on, then," Morgan said decisively. "I'm going to need a box or maybe a valise, too. I've found a pair of boots that fit pretty well, over there on the counter, and my wife could use a dress or two."

"You folks been on the road long?" the man asked, turning to where glass bins held assorted items of clothing. "Haven't seen you hereabouts before, have I?"

"No, we're on our way to Sand Creek to visit with my wife's relatives," Morgan said easily, the lie tumbling from his lips, sounding like the gospel truth to Lily's ears.

"Well, let's see what we've got that'll fit your lady,"

the storekeeper said, lifting a gingham dress from the bin he'd placed on the counter.

Morgan gave Lily a nod and she chose two dresses that would make her look like a farmer's wife without any trouble at all. The man behind the counter found a box in the back room for them to place their purchases in and Morgan tugged his new boots on before they left the store.

The box fit nicely in the boot of the buggy and he tied it firmly in place before he joined Lily on the seat. "Do you want to eat while we travel? Or should we stop somewhere?" he asked.

"Are we in a hurry?" She felt a longing for a brief time of peace, a few minutes of undiluted pleasure. An hour by the side of the road might provide that, she thought wistfully, sitting on the quilt and eating their simple meal with no thought of anything beyond the next minute.

Morgan looked fully in her face, his gaze touching her mouth and eyes, his demeanor softening as though he read her thoughts and contemplated granting her desire for the respite she craved. "Why don't we have a picnic?" he asked, lifting the reins and turning the mare toward the road out of town.

"Can we?" She sighed the words, feeling foolish at the rush of happiness his offer brought into being. Spending an hour with Morgan, with nothing more to do than share their meal and perhaps speak of something other than the realities surrounding them was a joy to contemplate.

"Of course we can," he said easily, and in moments the mare was trotting between the traces, her head bobbing in time to the gait she'd established. The road was smoother here, as though it was a familiar route to other wagons and buggies. "How about that bend up ahead? Looks like a neck of the river comes closer to the road."

She sat forward on the seat, eager to espy the spot he'd

designated. And there, before them, was a perfect place for the picnic he'd suggested.

Morgan pulled the buggy off the road, and it bounced through the glade until they reached the bank of the river. The horse cropped grass, Morgan easing the bit from her mouth, and he held his arms up to lift Lily from the seat. She slid down the front of him, aware of the hard body beneath his clothing, grateful for the strength in his hands and arms, and thankful that he did not cause her to linger there against him.

The man knew just how to please her, she decided, watching as he spread the quilt on the grass beneath a tree. The limbs spread wide above them, casting shadows on the river's edge. Lily went to the back of the buggy and began to untie the rope that bound the box in place. Behind her, Morgan's forearms reached on either side of her shoulders and solved the issue neatly, his long fingers releasing the knots he'd set in place. She looked over her shoulder at him and her mind went blank.

His eyes were dark, perhaps from the shade in which they stood, but that held no explanation for the taut line of his jaw or the ruddy streak that touched his high cheekbones. His nostrils flared as she watched, as though he'd searched for and found a scent that pleased him.

"What is it?" she asked. "What's wrong?"

He shook his head and stepped back, allowing her to delve into the box to retrieve their meal. Her fingers trembled as she brought forth the packages, and he deftly took them from her. The bread and canned peaches were last, and then she found a quart jar of lemonade tucked into the bottom of the container.

"I didn't see this in the store," she said. "Is it really lemonade?" Three or four seeds swam in the pale golden liquid, and sugar lay in a thin layer on the bottom of the jar.

"Looks like it to me," he told her. "I talked the proprietor's wife out of it. She had a big pitcher at the back of the store, and I bought the Mason jar to hold it. We'll have to share, though. I didn't get an extra cup."

"I don't mind," she said, delighted with the surprise. "My throat is dry. This will be wonderful." She followed him around the buggy to where he'd spread the ground cover and sat on one side of the faded quilt. The food was easily accessible and she opened the packages quickly, then lifted the loaf of bread.

"I think we'll have to tear off pieces," she told him. "We don't have a knife."

"I have one," he said, reaching in his pocket and drawing forth a jackknife, the blade of which was long enough to slice halfway through the loaf. "Probably not very sanitary, but it'll work," he said, taking a clean handkerchief from his pocket and wiping the blade as he spoke.

And it did work. The bread was sliced, the peaches were opened with the sturdy blade, and the contents fished out to lay on a piece of the waxed paper. Morgan sliced the cheese and cut the bologna in pieces, and soon they were looking down on a veritable feast. "This is wonderful," Lily told him. "You're a handy man to have around, Mr. Morgan."

"Thank you, ma'am," he returned, doffing his hat in a gesture of mock courtesy. He placed it on the edge of the quilt and took up a piece of bread. "I haven't had a picnic in years," he said, and Lily thought she detected a note of wistfulness in his words.

"I haven't, either," she admitted. "Not since my mama invited the neighbors over after the cotton was harvested one year and we ate in the yard at big, long tables that my father and the men put together. Rather," she amended, "the men sat at the tables and the women and children sat on blankets on the grass."

"I'd have chosen to sit on the grass with you," Morgan said idly, watching her as she bit into the sausage she held. "You eat with such gusto," he told her. "I get a kick out of watching you."

She wrinkled her nose at him. "You're teasing again, aren't you?" she accused him, to which he shook his head and frowned.

"Of course not. Would I tease my wife?"

She felt her heart slow its beat, knew a moment of insight, felt a rush of wonder as she heard his words. So simply, so easily he seduced her. She who had vowed to renounce any tie with a man, who had been badly bruised by male cruelty, was now halfway in love with a stranger she'd met only days since.

Yet it seemed he was not deliberately leading her into a seduction that would result only in the giving of her body into his keeping, but one in which she feared she would lose whatever fragile control she held over her heart. Morgan could steal her soul in this moment, for if he offered his hand, she would take it. If he bid her follow, she would rise and go where he led.

It was frightening. More than that, it was a harsh glimpse of what her future held when he completed the terms of their bargain and followed the rules she'd insisted on. *If that's what you want, I'll walk away.* She'd bid him repeat her terms, and he had. Without a murmur, with no pretense of begging her to change her mind, he'd agreed.

And now she knew in a heartbeat, in the instant when he smiled into her eyes, that life without Gage Morgan would be like a day without sunshine. So readily he'd crept into her heart, so easily he'd persuaded her to his will.

Now she lowered her eyes to the food she held on her lap, and her words were but a cover for the feelings running rampant within her breast. "Of course you'd tease me, if you thought you could get a rise out of me," she said glibly. "But this time it won't work, Gage Morgan. I'm too involved in my picnic meal to rise to the occasion." A smile that was hard to come by curved her mouth, and she bent to the task of finishing the food that now tasted miserably akin to the paper it had been wrapped in.

He laughed at her gibe and leaned back on one elbow, propped up on his side to face her. "This was a good idea, Lily. We've been pushing hard today, and it's gonna be a long ride to Sand Creek. Hard to say if we'll find a decent place to stay tonight."

Rolling to his back, he closed his eyes, his hands beneath his head. And then one eyelid lifted and he grinned at her. "Want to join me? Take a nap together?"

She shook her head. "No, one of us has to stay awake and keep a weather eye out."

"We're pretty safe for now, Lily," he said softly. "I wouldn't risk you by sleeping if I thought we were in danger here."

"Well, I'll just straighten things and walk down by the water while you nap," she said. The need to be apart from him, if only for these few minutes, was pressing. She could smell the faint tang of soap he'd washed with this morning, knew the scent of his clothing, with its aroma of hay from the loft they'd slept in. His hair lay against his head, the waves more in evidence today without his usual dousing of water to keep them tamed.

In minutes, she'd repackaged the food and cleared up their picnic. After a quick glance that told her he was either asleep or making a good pretense at it, she rose from the quilt. It was but a short stroll to where the bank dropped off to the shallow inlet, and she made her way there, careful not to stand too close to the edge.

A school of minnows swirled before her, their tails moving in unison, as if they followed some unknown leader. And there, at the river's edge, a frog leaped into the shallows and the minnows milled and circled, then swam as one for the safety to be found downstream. Across the small inlet, where the river's narrow branch had made inroads on the landscape, a small animal came to the edge of the water, bending its head to drink.

Behind it, at the edge of the sparsely wooded area, a doe stood, her head lifted as if to scent for danger. Beside her, a smaller deer watched and waited. And then, with graceful steps the pair approached the water's edge and drank. They ate with dainty relish the grass at their feet, the larger deer lifting her head, apparently to listen for danger.

Lily watched, intent on the small drama before her, hearing the chatter of a squirrel, the call of a hawk overhead. In the tree beneath which Lily stood, a smaller bird called out, and then, leaving the branch he'd perched on, flew low in a circle over her head, and with a flutter of wings landed on a branch directly above her.

"Do you have a nest up there?" she murmured, and smiled at her own foolishness. No doubt the creature was guarding his territory against invaders, and she must seem like a giant to the tiny, winged creature. She tilted her head back, looking upward through the branches, where shimmering sunlight dappled the leaves and filtered to the water before her.

"You look like the statue of a woman on the prow of a ship I saw one day on the East Coast." From behind her, Morgan's words caught her unaware and she spun in place, her eyes wide. "I didn't mean to frighten you," he said, reaching to grip her arms, lest she fall into the water. "I just watched you here, with the breeze blowing your dress against your body, your hair tangled and curling over your shoulders, and I had to touch you."

"Touch me?" She felt dazed, whether because of the

sunlight glittering on the water, or the desire blazing from the eyes of the man who held her.

"Only a bit," he said softly, persuasively. "Like this." His head bent and he kissed her, a sweet, seeking union of lips that made her breath catch in her throat. His hands held her firmly, and it was fortunate, she thought, for her knees threatened to buckle beneath her. Her body softened, and she leaned forward until she was supported by the firm strength of the man.

"You draw me like a magnet, Lily." He lifted his head and she felt the heat of his gaze, touching each increment of skin on her face, felt the beating of her heart in her throat and knew the wonder of being a woman. Of sensing her value through his eyes, of recognizing the power he gave her with his words.

"You've surely been with women more accomplished than I," she whispered. "Women who know how to be with a man, how to please."

"Have I?" he asked after a moment, as if he mused over the thought. "Maybe so. But right now I can't remember any of them. I only see you, Lily." He bent to her mouth again and this time he edged her lips open with his, nibbled on her and persuaded her to allow him full entry to the warm, dark place where his tongue sought out the secrets that tempted him.

She caught her breath, then reluctantly drew back and pressed her hands against his chest. "You flatter me, Morgan," she said, feeling her lips tremble. With a deliberately casual air, she pressed them together and tilted her head to peer up at him. "I think you're trying to get on my good side."

"Do you have one?" he asked, joining the game. His fingers loosened their grip on her and moved to clasp behind her waist, swaying with her for a moment where they stood. He examined her face, bending to look at one side, then the other. "You look pretty good to me from either angle," he told her, and she laughed aloud, pleased that he had so easily diffused the moment.

"You've managed to frighten the deer I was watching," she told him, pointing across the inlet to where the small cove held not a trace of animal life. "I think our picnic is over," she said, even as she regretted the end of this small respite, "and you didn't even get your nap."

"No, but I rested awhile." He released her, they walked back to their picnic spot, and gathered up their things. "Here. You carry this and I'll get the quilt," he told her.

It was with a sense of sadness that Lily looked back at the spot as the mare jerked the buggy into motion. They set off at a smart pace, Morgan looking jaunty, she decided, with his hat set at an angle, and one foot propped on the front of the buggy. She settled back to enjoy the ride, in the back of her mind aware that it might be the last peaceful interlude they would share for some time to come.

It was a toss-up, Morgan decided. They needed to stop for the sake of the mare, yet it was probably only a few more miles to Sand Creek. The sun was setting rapidly, and he needed to make a decision. "Lily, I think we'd better plan on sleeping outdoors tonight," he said, hoping she didn't have her heart set on a genuine bed upon which to get a good night's sleep.

"All right." Her reply was quick and he was caught by surprise. The woman had taken him aback again. He'd thought to coax her, bribe her with some treat for tomorrow, and instead had been the recipient of a smile and instant agreement.

"Keep an eye out for a sheltered spot," he said, slowing the mare to a walk. The trees surrounded them, the road they followed was narrow, and now he was on the lookout for an area that would hold some sort of solid protection behind them for the night. The land was a bit hilly, with rocky areas that might offer protection from the elements or the chance of strangers finding them vulnerable. It was with that in mind that he looked for a change in elevation through the trees.

And then Lily saw a spot first, touching his arm and pointing off to the left, where a miniature cliff rose from the ground, jutting out so as to offer a sheltered spot beneath its edge. "Look," she said, "see that place over there?"

He nodded and swung the buggy into an opening between the trees, then jumped down from the seat and led the mare through the narrow passage to where Lily had designated they go. The shale formed layers of rock that had been tamed by long years of water running past, forming a cave of sorts beneath the overhang, and he eyed it with approval.

"I think this will work just fine," he told her, coming back to lift her down. "I'll tie the horse and give her a handful of oats, and then we'll spread our quilt."

By the time he'd settled the horse, stripping her from the harness and leading her to a spot where the grass was heavy, Lily had unloaded the things they would need for the night. She'd done a quick job of cleaning up the hollowed-out area and placed the quilt there, then brought their bags to be used as pillows again.

"Do you want to wash in the river?" Morgan asked her as she sat to take off her shoes and stockings. "It's quiet and doesn't look very deep."

"I can't swim," she said, looking up to where the twilight had made inroads, leaving only a faint blush in the sky. "I think I'd be more comfortable in the daylight, when I can see better."

He grinned at her. "That'll work. I'll be able to see better, too."

"You have a mind that seems to be stuck in a rut," she told him, sniffing her disapproval. She rose and looked to where the river formed a pool, a small inlet edged by trees at the waterline. "Maybe I could just wash piecemeal," she suggested, "not get in all the way."

"Whatever you want is all right with me." He planned on submerging his weary body in the water, scrubbing off the dust of the road and allowing the breeze to dry his body, no matter how primitive it might seem to Lily. "I have a shirt you can dry off with," he offered. "It's old, but clean."

"You're tempting me." She bent her head and pulled her hair over her shoulder. "Will you undo me, please?"

It was to his credit that Morgan did not linger over the task, but did as she asked with a minimum of dithering. He watched as she shed the dress and the petticoat beneath it, and he handed her his extra shirt and a bar of soap, along with a bit of towel, just about large enough to wash with. "If you don't take off your shift, you won't have anything to sleep in," he warned her.

"I thought of that already," she said. "I'll dry on the shift and sleep in your shirt. I have a spare in my bag. It's old and almost threadbare, but it'll do for one more wearing." She walked gingerly through the grass to the edge of the water and then turned to look back at him. Her request was unspoken, her need for privacy understood, and he turned his back.

"If you need help, call me," he said, wishing for a moment that his gentlemanly instincts were not so finely honed.

He heard her muffled intake of breath as she splashed at the edge of the water, then the gasp as she settled to the bottom. "It's not very warm," she told him, and he grinned. The better to make her amenable to his arms around her tonight, he thought, his gaze sweeping the surrounding area lest a stray animal should approach the water and frighten her.

She lasted about three minutes, and Morgan was not surprised when he heard her feet splashing through the shallows as she emerged. "I'm almost done," she called to him. And then she appeared, his shirt wrapped around her, reaching her knees, the sleeves trailing past her fingertips. "Your turn," she said, handing him the soap and cloth he'd given her to use, then placed her shift across a bush to dry.

"I won't be long," he told her, stripping from his clothes, stashing them to one side, and then making tracks to the water. Before he stepped in he deposited the soap and rough cloth she'd used on the ground, then walked ten or twelve feet from shore. A sloping drop-off gave way under his feet, allowing him enough depth to swim. Without hesitation he dived in at a shallow angle and caught his breath at the chill.

Perhaps she watched, he thought, and yet he doubted it. Lily was not ready for a naked man yet. She'd already seen him very near that state one night, but tonight was not going to see him coaxing her into his arms for anything but providing a bit of comfort on her behalf. He sensed that each day brought her closer to the point of allowing his possession. He was willing to wait.

Sand Creek, Arkansas, was only a step above the last place they'd stopped, Morgan decided. A sheriff's office and jail drew his attention as the buggy rolled down the road. The man who stood in the doorway wore his gun as if he were accustomed to strapping it in place every day. His clothing was worn, but clean. Close-shaven, but for a mustache, he wore a hat that shaded his face from close scrutiny.

Morgan lifted a hand in a salute as the buggy rolled past the sturdy building and received an answering wave. "We'll go on down to the general store," he told Lily, "and you can look around and see what we need, find some basics. I'll stroll back and talk to the sheriff and see how the land lies."

She nodded, and he sensed that she was on edge. She wore one of the new dresses and her hair was pulled back into a neat braid, giving her the look of a female far removed from the saloon on a riverboat. Looking like a farmer's wife, she presented exactly the picture he needed, and it was with a sense of satisfaction he lifted her down and watched as she made her way into the building that probably held most anything a woman could ask for in order to run a home and cook meals for a family.

Tying the buggy to the hitching rail, he turned back toward the jailhouse, where the lawman stood, his gaze narrowed on the man who strode toward him. "Morning," Morgan said, tipping back his hat as he approached. "We just arrived in town, and I suspect you're the man I should be talking to."

"Well, you've got that right," the sheriff said. "Caine Harris." He held out his hand in greeting and Morgan felt his fingers caught in a firm grip. "Who might you be?" the lawman asked, even as he scrutinized the man before him.

"Gage Morgan," was the reply. "I was told you were expecting me."

"They told you right," Harris said. "Things are not to my liking these days. I'm about ready to pull Sam Blair and his wife off their place and tuck them away in the hotel for safekeeping. I think you've arrived just in time.

They've had threats for the past couple of weeks, and things are getting downright dicey."

"Can't the law do anything?" Morgan asked harshly.

"We're waiting for them to play out their hand," Harris said. "We need to catch them red-handed, and then we'll have them nailed. If these were the only men involved, it would be one thing, but they're not. There are three pair of them working up and down the river in small farming communities."

"I'd think the government would lend a hand," Morgan said bluntly.

Caine Harris nodded and grinned. "They have. They sent me you, didn't they?" He looked toward the general store where Lily had disappeared from view. "Who's the woman? I didn't know you were working with a partner. Not that I'm disputing the idea. It will look more natural if a couple are at the farm."

"She's my wife," Morgan said. "And before you ask, she knows what's going on, and understands that she's providing my cover."

"Kinda risky, isn't it?" the sheriff asked. "Is she trained?"

Morgan shook his head. "I'm going to work with her on handling a gun as soon as we're in place. In fact, I'd like you to lend me one for her to use. And I'm counting on you as backup when the time comes."

Harris nodded. "I've got men lined up, several of them who showed up here when they were rooked out of their property in the past month. They're not sworn deputies yet, but that's easily tended to when the time comes. And as to the gun, I'll find you one."

They entered the jail, and Harris sat down behind the battered desk. Pulling open the bottom drawer, he lifted two pistols from it. "Either of these will work. The fella that wore them last won't be needing them anymore," he said with a grim smile.

"I'll take them both," Morgan said. "It won't hurt to have a spare. I could use a holster, too. The gun I carry is handy, but I'd rather have one that represents a show of force, and will give me a longer range."

"The government planning on paying me for outfitting you?" the lawman asked, snagging a leather holster from a peg on the wall.

"I wouldn't be surprised," Morgan told him. He listened intently as Caine filled him in on the particulars of setting up his post in Sam Blair's farmhouse. "I'm heading for the general store," he told the lawman. "Lily is probably champing at the bit, waiting for me. I told her to buy whatever we'll need for the next little while."

Settling the holster belt below his waist, he shoved the gun into it. "Ammunition?" he asked, waiting as Harris dug into another drawer for a supply of bullets for both guns, then stashed them in a leather bag before he handed them to Morgan.

"You can fill your belt later, but you'd better load the guns now. I don't want you caught unaware." He paused as if he would issue a warning, and then shrugged. "I think you can handle most anything that comes up. I just hope your partner is ready for what she's gonna find out at the Blair place."

"What's that supposed to mean?" Morgan asked suspiciously. "Isn't there a farmhouse there? They told me I'd be in a secure place."

The sheriff grinned with a total lack of humor. "You'll find out. Now," he said, rising to his feet, "that oughta do you for bullets for a while. If you want more, the general store has a good supply. I'm going on out to the Blair place in about an hour. It's just about three miles from town, on the road west. A gray house, not very big, with a barn and outbuildings. There's a grove of trees out front, almost hides the place if you're not looking for it.''

"I'll find it," Morgan assured him. "We'll probably beat you out there. It shouldn't take long for me to finish up at the store."

Chapter Eight

"For the life of me, I don't know why anyone would want this place." Lily looked around her at the small house, then toward the barn, a sturdy, well-kept structure that made the living quarters look somewhat like a chicken coop. But even the place where the chickens lived was a disaster, providing scant shelter for a handful of hens. Beyond it, an outhouse leaned precariously, the door seeming to be permanently ajar, just past the kitchen garden.

Unless you were willing to live in the barn, the garden was the only bright spot, Lily decided. Neat rows of vegetables, well tended and thriving, gave evidence of Sarah Blair's diligence. Too bad it hadn't inspired Sam to give his wife a decent place to live and work.

Instead, Sam Blair had chosen to invest his finances in the herd of horses that fed in an enormous pasture. Centered with a large pond, which lent credence to the story of the Blair place holding water rights that made it a valuable property, the pond provided the herd with an unending supply of fresh water and the luxury of lush grasses on all sides. They grazed there, probably fifty or so animals of various sizes, looking like money in the bank to her untrained eye.

That gentleman who owned the sleek horses sat on the porch, shotgun across his knees and hat pulled low over his forehead as Morgan and Lily approached, the mare slowing her gait at Morgan's tug on the reins. "Whatta ya want?" the farmer asked, his jaw grim as he rose to confront the callers, lifting his gun to point in the direction of the buggy.

"Caine Harris sent us out to see you," Morgan said, carefully keeping his hands in sight, and away from the gun he wore.

"You the fella that's gonna squat here for a while?" Sam asked, squinting up at them.

Lily thought Morgan's voice was taut with anger as he answered. "Yeah, that's me. This is my wife, Lily." .

The gun lowered from its threatening position and Sam Blair shouted out a single word. "Sarah!" Without turning toward the door behind him, he uttered the summons, and in mere seconds the woman stood, framed in the doorway, wiping her hands on the front of her apron. "These folks are here to stay for a spell."

"Sheriff said we were to go into town," Sarah told Morgan, stepping out onto the porch. "But I surely hate to leave with my garden just coming in good."

The farmer laughed, the sound grating to Lily's ears. "She ain't much good for anything else that I can see. It's a good thing she's a right hand with growin' food for the dinner table."

The woman lived a drab existence, Lily decided. She might be better off if the crooks gave her enough money to hotfoot it out of town and leave Sam in the dust. He'd certainly demonstrated his lack of husbandly devotion in the past few minutes.

"You'd better pack up your things and be ready for Harris. He'll be here to escort you back to town," Morgan told the couple. And then he looked at Lily. "Are you sure you can handle this?'' The words were an undertone, his eyes showing the doubt he felt as he cast another long look at the ramshackle house he was about to move Lily into.

She only shrugged, and then added words that failed to surprise him. ''I've slept on the ground and sung in a saloon. Served drinks to the scum of the earth and run from a man who would have ruined me for all time.'' She lifted her chin defiantly. ''Staying here for a short while doesn't seem like any big chore to me. There might even be a decent bed in there and a stove to cook on.''

Morgan grinned down at her. ''Don't count on that, sweetheart.'' He stepped down from the buggy and raised his arms to her, lifting her to stand before him. ''Take a deep breath, Lily. You're about to become Sarah Blair, and I fear you're in for a few surprises.''

Caine Harris arrived as the Blairs went into the house to do as they were bid, and it took the lawman less than thirty minutes to bundle up his charges and set off for town. Lily watched as the farm wagon followed the sheriff, who mounted on his horse and led the way. Sarah cast one last look at her garden as they passed the small enclosure, and Lily was tempted to call out a reassurance that she would tend the garden plot well.

''That poor thing,'' she said instead, facing Morgan in an outburst of disgust. ''She'd probably be better off if Sam called it quits and left her behind.'' She looked up at Morgan, wondering at his silence, noting the grim set of his jaw. ''What are you thinking?'' she asked quietly.

''Just that I've probably dragged you into a mess,'' he told her. ''This isn't what I was expecting, Lily. And unless I miss my guess, old Sam is hoping we'll settle things for him and he can dicker later for a payoff. I doubt he's as averse to selling out as he lets on. It wouldn't surprise me if he's planning on holding out for a good price, considering the water rights on this property. The man knows horses—that's obvious—but he sure as hell hasn't provided well for his wife.

"My guess is that once he lays his hands on a bankroll, he'll hightail it out of here and find a soft spot to land with cash in his pocket to tide him over."

"Then why was he waiting for us with his shotgun handy?" she asked.

"Making a show of strength," Morgan surmised. "He knew help was on its way. Once we showed up, all he had to do was leave and expect us to fight his battle for him."

"Well," Lily said, shrugging her shoulders in a gesture of futility, "that's exactly what we're doing, isn't it?"

"This," Morgan told her bluntly, "is the part of my work that leaves a bad taste in my mouth. We're putting our lives on the line for a man who's willing to let his wife carry the load, a man who hasn't got enough ambition to keep his house in order."

"And if we get rid of the threat to him, what will happen?" More, she wondered what would happen to the hapless woman who'd worn herself to a frazzle in this place.

"He'll probably keep raising horses, providing them with good feed and an abundant water supply, and a barn full of hay for the cold months. I'll be willing to bet he has ranchers lined up to buy that herd. There's a lot of good horseflesh out there, and a total lack of pride on his part when it comes to the rest of his surroundings."

Morgan's voice revealed his anger, and Lily could only be thankful it was not directed at her. The man made a formidable enemy. He would do this job, and count it as a thankless task. But somehow, he'd be sure that Sam Blair paid penance for expecting the law to fight his battle.

"Let's go inside," Morgan said, taking Lily's arm as she climbed onto the porch. The single step was held in place by two nails, and it shifted beneath their feet. "This is the first thing I'd better tend to,'' he said, holding open the door for her as they walked into the kitchen.

Clean, but shabby, was Lily's impression. Sarah had evidently done what she could to keep house, but Sam had not provided her with the necessities for the job. The floor was clean, but the planks that formed its surface were uneven. The stove's oven door hung by one hinge, and Sarah had propped it shut with a length of two-by-four. A stack of wood lay on the floor, unevenly chopped, as if an amateur had used an ax, without the strength to cut the wood, managing only to mangle a log into scraps and pieces.

''I'll warrant that Sarah cut her own firewood,'' Morgan said, shaking his head at the sight.

''It's a wonder she didn't hurt herself.'' Lily could only imagine the weight of an ax head, lifting it over her head and then feeling the shock of iron striking a heavy log. ''I'd say anything that got done around here was because of Sarah,'' she said.

She glanced back at the doorway that led to the porch. ''The first thing you're going to do is mend that outhouse door, Gage Morgan.'' Her words were scornful as she took another look at the ramshackle necessity. In this she would brook no opposition from the man who met her gaze.

''Yes, ma'am,'' he said nicely. ''I already had that figured out.'' He looked around the room they stood in and grimaced. ''I'm not in any hurry to see the rest of this place, if this is anything to go by.''

''Well, it's clean, anyway,'' Lily told him. She lifted the stove lid and felt the heat of coals within rush upward. ''I'll add to the fire and put together something to eat.''

''Lily?'' Morgan spoke her name and she rose from bending over the stack of firewood, a shredded log in each hand. ''I got a gun from the sheriff for you and I want you to keep it close at hand.''

''And where would you like me to stow it?'' she asked,

thinking that handling a gun was not something her mother would approve of, should that lady ever be privy to these circumstances. The chances of that coming about were dim, but Lily was reminded how far she had come from her beginnings.

"See if there's another apron around. They usually have pockets, don't they?" Morgan asked, looking at a row of hooks by the back door. "I'll look in the bedroom. Maybe Sarah has an extra tucked away in there."

"I'll take care of it," Lily told him. "Get the gun and show me how to shoot it. I'm not going to worry about being accurate. If someone is threatening me and he's close enough for me to feel intimidated, I suspect I can wave a gun around and offer a threat of my own."

Morgan nodded, his lips curving in a smile as he headed for the buggy. The woman was unique, that was for sure. She was staunch in her support of their situation, ready to do whatever the circumstances dictated. He couldn't have asked for a better partner if the government had sent him their top woman candidate. And he wouldn't be having the pleasure of Lily's company had that happened. Women agents were few and far between, not usually available for the sort of assignments he handled.

He'd find out how good a farmer he'd make over the next few days, perhaps. Depending on how long it took the men to show up again, he'd be saddled with the chores, including milking a cow. It had been years since he'd done that particular job, but he suspected that once learned, it was a skill he could recall without too much trouble. Chickens were simple. Feed them and gather the eggs. They seemed to have the whole yard at their disposal, the gate to their area left open for them to roam.

Hopefully they would head for their roosts come evening. If not, he was probably going to be elected to chase them down. And at that thought he swallowed a grin.

Wouldn't his boss in Washington like to see him in search of a flock of laying hens? Somehow that wasn't the picture he'd painted for himself when he'd accepted this assignment. But then, he hadn't known he'd end up a married man, either.

The barn yielded an assortment of tools, and Morgan chose a hammer and found a box of nails. The hinges on the outhouse door cooperated with him, and the wood held firm. He found two pieces of two-by-four to shore up the far side of the structure and checked the inside, pleased to find that Sarah had extended her cleaning streak this far.

As he turned aside to head back toward the barn, a flash of color caught his eye. He watched Lily as she bent over the vegetables growing closest to the house. An apron tied around her waist reminded him of the weapon he'd meant to give her. Chastening himself silently, he retrieved it, tucked away beneath the buggy seat, and took it to where she worked. Her apron was held in front of her, the hem lifted to provide a fabric basket for the produce she'd harvested.

"Hi," she said, lifting a flushed face to him. Her hair curled over her brow and against her cheek, a faint line of perspiration on her upper lip. "Do I look like a farmer's wife?" she asked. "Look." Holding her apron from her body, she displayed an assortment of small carrots along with leaf lettuce and three tomatoes. "I haven't picked a garden since I was seventeen years old," she told him.

Her head lifted and her nostrils flared as if she caught a whiff of some pleasing aroma. "Just smell the earth, Morgan. There's nothing like it."

"You think not?" he asked, enjoying her pleasure. And then he doused her mood by drawing forth the gun he held. "I hate to be a killjoy, sweetheart, but here's the gun I want you to carry."

Her face fell and the glow of delight left her eyes. "All the time?"

"I'm afraid so. If anyone comes around and I'm out in the barn or beyond, where I can't see or hear you, you'll have to be prepared. Bear in mind that all you'll need to do is fire a shot in the air and I'll come running. No matter where I am, I'll hear it."

She took the weapon from his hand and held it gingerly. "Just point it and pull the trigger?"

He shook his head. "No, you'll have to cock it first." He reached from behind her and held the gun, her hands beneath his as he pulled back the hammer until it clicked. "That alone will no doubt make a man think again about facing you down, Lily. Just be sure you're standing behind some sort of protection. If he's armed, don't risk yourself. Fire the gun in the air and then aim for your assailant next."

"I don't know about this," she said dubiously. "I'm not sure I could shoot to kill."

"You'd better be ready to do that very thing," he said harshly. "Trust me, if it comes to you or the other fella, you'll do it."

"Let me take my vegetables in the house and then I'll practice with it," she said.

He followed her from the garden to the porch and then into the kitchen. She spilled out her bounty into a dishpan and added water from a bucket near the stove. "They don't have a pump in the kitchen," she said. "I used the one by the watering trough. I can't believe Sarah doesn't even have a sink or water in the house."

"I'll do water duty from now on," he told her. "Is there only one pail?"

"No, there's another, but I think they used it for milking."

"Carrying water in it won't hurt anything," Morgan

said. "In fact, I'll fill them both right now so you'll have enough to last through the evening until I go out to take care of the cow."

"Sarah had just made butter," Lily told him. "She washed out the churn and formed the round before she left."

"Is there any meat to cook?" Morgan asked.

"Just a side of bacon hanging in the pantry. I'll slice some off and make a skillet of eggs. Do you like lettuce and tomatoes mixed with bacon grease dressing?"

"Never had it, but I'll give it a shot," he said, pleased at her willingness to adapt.

"Well, that's another thing, Morgan. Have you ever killed a chicken?" she asked, slanting a questioning look at him. "I'm not real good at the bloody stuff, but I can clean it and get it ready to cook for dinner tomorrow, if you've got the nerve to chop its head off."

"Can Sarah spare a laying hen?" he asked.

"I saw a couple of young roosters out there, strutting around like they owned the place," Lily said. "One rooster is all any flock needs."

"You seem to know all about this stuff," Morgan said, settling in a chair at the table. "A regular farm girl at heart."

"I used to help in the kitchen. Probably got in the way more than I helped, now that I think about it, but Susanna put up with me. I learned how to do any number of things. I bake a dandy biscuit, Morgan."

"Seeing is believing," he teased, enjoying her sparkle as she flitted around the simple kitchen. It felt almost as if—

He shook his head. This was an interlude, fraught with danger. He'd be remiss if he forgot for a moment to keep up his guard. But the temptation to imagine, just for a few minutes, that Lily was cooking for him in their own kitchen, that the words they exchanged were as ordinary as any between husband and wife...

She'd set the boundaries, though. He would take her home. That far he'd go, and gladly, but the rest of it might not be to Lily's liking. Whatever faced her in Louisiana, he would be a part of it.

He looked up at her, catching a pensive expression as she came to a halt, standing silently beside the table. "What is it?" he asked. "Did I hurt your feelings, sweetheart, doubting your ability to bake decent biscuits?" Something had spoiled her mood, and in all probability it was something he'd said.

But she shook her head, and though it failed to touch her eyes, her smile was ready. "Of course not. I'm just thinking. Wondering how long we'll be here, how long the supplies we brought will last."

"Yeah, well they won't do us much good tied on the back of the buggy," he said, rising as he thought of the foodstuffs they'd purchased in town. He went out the door and automatically scanned the horizon. The barn was the place to watch from, he decided. Open at both ends, it held numerous places a man could lie in ambush. Stalls lined the main aisle and there was no doubt a tack room. The loft held hay, he'd warrant, and probably straw. Old Sam had done well for his herd of horses.

To the west, a line of trees caught his eye. When danger came, it might appear on that front, the trees providing good cover until an assailant was within a couple hundred yards of the house. Of course, he thought, untying the boxes of food, and lifting one into his arms, they might come right up to the porch, demanding that the occupants move out and leave the property to the government.

Caine Harris said that the Blairs had not been face-to-face with their foes, had only received written notice that the property was to be vacated by the middle of the month.

It was the twelfth today, if he remembered right. At most, they had two or three days leeway before they could expect visitors.

The kitchen door stood open and Morgan carried his load inside, settling it on the table, then returned to the buggy. If he was any judge of it, Lily had bought enough food to last them the better part of a week. Along with what the garden produced, they should be well fed. He brought the second box to where Lily was putting up canned goods and sacks of basic food items.

"I hope this stuff won't spoil," she said, frowning as she looked down at the piece of sausage she held. "Maybe I should make it for breakfast. I got a chunk of ham, and that'll hang in the pantry." She stepped back and considered her purchases. "I think we have enough, Morgan. I bought coffee and sugar, and Sarah had oatmeal and flour."

"Biscuits and gravy for breakfast?" he asked, aware of the plea in his words.

She shot him a glance. "I thought you were doubting my ability to produce biscuits."

"Not for a minute," he swore, holding his hand over his heart. And then he smiled, as her saucy smile appreciated his gesture. "You know what, Mrs. Morgan?"

"No, what?" she asked, returning to the stove where bacon sizzled in the skillet.

"I like you. I really like you, Lily."

She was silent, her head bent as if the sizzling bacon fascinated her. For a moment he had second thoughts about his declaration. Then she turned to him and he caught a glimpse of dampness on her cheek, one she brushed away with the back of her hand.

"Do you?" she asked, and he thought the query held more meaning than the words implied. "You don't mind getting tangled up with me and having me on your hands while you finish this assignment?''

"Hell, yes, I mind," he said sharply. "I'd like to have done this a different way. I wish I could have met you somewhere other than in a riverboat saloon, and that things were different in several ways. But all that aside, you're…'' He paused, unable to speak the words that hovered in his mind.

"I've enjoyed every hour I've spent with you, Lily," he said after a moment. "Even when I spent some long minutes wondering how far I could trust you, even when I found you'd not been honest with me." His voice lowered as he spoke his intentions. "Even then, I had no intention of giving you up."

"Giving me up? I don't think there's a choice, is there?" She tilted her chin and he saw the effort she made to remain indifferent to his words. "We've established the limits of our relationship already, if I remember rightly."

"We don't have a relationship yet," he reminded her softly, and knew that he would remedy that fact before very many hours had passed. Lily would not escape him so easily. He was a man jealous of what he claimed as his own.

And Lily was his.

The bed was decent, and that was the best that could be said for it, Lily decided. The sheets were fairly clean and she debated for a moment whether she would trust herself to lie where Sam Blair had placed his body the night before. Her natural inclination for cleanliness won out and the sheets were stripped from the mattress. The quilt was spread quickly over the striped ticking and she searched out another coverlet from a chest in one corner of the room.

Kneeling before the wooden box, she handled its contents with gentle hands. It was no doubt a part of Sarah's dowry, remnants of what she had brought to her marriage. A small flannel gown was folded in one corner, a hand-worked baby quilt beneath it. There'd been no sign of children about the place, and Lily could only imagine that Sarah's life was barren in more ways than one.

She felt nostalgia grip her, knew a rush of tears that she could not contain, and wiped them away with the edge of the apron she wore. The weight of the gun she carried was a reminder of their circumstances and she drew it from its hiding place and placed it beside her on the floor.

"It just isn't fair." She'd cried the words aloud to her mother one day, years ago when it seemed that chaos reigned and their existence as a family had come to a halt.

"No one ever said life was fair," the small, elegant woman had said. "We just all do the best we can, and face the future one day at a time."

"Mama." Lily uttered the single word beneath her breath as a flood of yearning almost overcame her. She'd sworn never to go back home, but now, with Morgan's aid, it seemed she would once more see her family. And if they chose to welcome her, she would sort out her life and seek a modicum of peace of mind there on the plantation where she'd been raised.

"Lily?" Morgan's voice called her name from the doorway. "What are you up to, sweetheart? I could have helped you with the bed if you'd called me."

"I'll wash those sheets tomorrow," she said, blinking back the tears that flooded her eyes. "I thought we'd sleep on top of the quilt for tonight."

He was silent, save for the sound of his footsteps across the bare floor. And then he was behind her, bending to place his hand on her shoulder. "Are you all right?"

"Of course," she asserted firmly. "Just looking for something to put on the bed. I think we'll settle for this," she said, lifting the coverlet from the depths of the trunk.

She rose, holding it before her, refusing to meet his gaze. "Do you know, Sarah doesn't even have a parlor. That miserable man scrimped by with as little output as he could manage, with only a bedroom and kitchen in this place."

Morgan laughed, a sound of derision. "I'm surprised he provided her with that much. From the outside, I figured it would be one room. His animals get treated better than his woman." He stepped to the bed and picked up the quilt, inspecting the mattress. "This isn't bad, Lily. I think we'll get a decent night's sleep, anyway."

He turned then, catching her unaware, and his eyes narrowed as he focused on hers. "You've been crying," he said softly. "You never cry, Lily. What's happened?"

"Oh, I've been known to shed a few tears on occasion," she told him. "This is one of them." She waved a hand at the trunk, and then reached to lower the lid over the sparse collection of treasures Sarah possessed. "I found all the things Sarah holds dear in that box," she told Morgan. "Including a baby's gown and blanket, both of them used and then stored away."

"She doesn't seem to have had an easy life, all the way around," Morgan said. "I hope she's enjoying her stay in the hotel, having someone else do the cooking for a few days." His hands reached then for Lily and his arms drew her to him, holding her in a comforting embrace.

She leaned against him, welcoming his warmth and the sheer strength of the man, finding the solace her aching heart sought. For a moment they stood in the center of the small room, the twilight gathering outside the window and the shadows creeping into the corners of the house. Lily straightened and leaned back to look up at him.

"I'm fine now, really," she said, "Just one of those *woman* things."

"I don't know much about women, I suppose," Morgan said ruefully. "At least not that part of womanhood."

Lily laughed softly. "I suspect you know your way around women quite well. You've certainly managed to make an impact on my life."

"Are you sorry?" he asked. "Would you do things differently if you could go back to that first day on the riverboat?"

She considered the matter, and then shook her head. "Probably not. You were the only one I could trust, besides May. She's a good person, you know. I'd like to meet up with her again some day."

"Not much chance of that," Morgan surmised. "But I don't think she'll last long riding up and down the river. She's got more value than that."

"Down on her luck, do you suppose?" Lily asked. And then murmured her suspicions aloud. "I think she was involved with Ham Scott."

"No doubt," Morgan agreed. "You know she stood up to Ham for you."

"So did you." And he had, she thought. He'd pulled her out of danger, perhaps not life-threatening, but certainly a perilous situation, one she was unable to cope with on her own. "I thought I'd chosen the lesser of two evils at first," she admitted. "And then I realized you were a gentleman at heart."

"I'm not a gentleman tonight, Lily," he warned her, and then set her away from himself, paying mind to the buttons that closed the bodice of her dress. "I've milked the cow and set the pail aside until morning. The chickens are penned up and the horses are settled out in the pasture. Even closed the barn doors," he told her. "Now it's time for us, for the two of us to think about the situation we're in."

"I've thought of little else lately," she admitted, lowering her head to watch as the last button was slipped from its mooring. Morgan's hands were warm against her skin as he lowered the dress over her shoulders, allowing it to fall to the floor. She wore a shift beneath it, a petticoat tied at her waist, and stockings held up by plain garters just below her knees.

It seemed she was about to lose every bit of her clothing, if Morgan had anything to say about it, for he showed no signs of stopping with the removal of her dress. His fingers worked at the ties of her petticoat, and then he watched as it joined the dress on the plank floor beneath their feet.

"Sit down on the bed and I'll take off your shoes and stockings," he offered, a lazy smile appearing to curve his lips. He had a nice mouth, Lily decided, the bottom lip fuller than the top, his teeth even and white when he smiled. In fact, there wasn't much about the man she could find fault with. He was dark and muscular, tall yet not overpowering with his size.

She complied with his request, knowing he would not take her refusal as an answer, and so decided to go the route of least resistance. His long fingers worked at her shoes, and then slid up her legs to where the garters held her stockings in place.

"These are too tight," he said, easing the elastic down to her ankles and then sliding the circles from her feet, the stockings with them. She curled her toes at his touch and he laughed softly, looking up into her face. "Are you afraid of me, Lily?" And at the quick shake of her head, his smile widened. "I thought not," he said, satisfaction alive in his words.

She was in her shift, only a pair of drawers beneath it to protect her modesty and he was apparently not going to stop until he had stripped her of everything she wore. But as if to give her a bit of respite, he stood and unbuttoned his shirt, then tossed it aside with an impatient gesture. His trousers were next, his fingers moving quickly to undo the front placket, shoving the denim fabric to the floor, his drawers joining them. His feet were bare.

In fact, she noted with embarrassment, he was as naked as the day he was born, and seemed to have no problem with her seeing him that way.

She lowered her gaze to her lap, finding that her fingers were clenched tightly, a detail Morgan seemed to pay special mind to. He squatted in front of her and she looked up, startled by the sight of his broad chest, muscled arms and the dark hair that formed a triangle, its color matching that which covered his head. He seemed pensive, she thought, his hand reaching out to enclose both of hers in his palm.

"I think we can get rid of the rest of your clothes, Lily," he said quietly. "It's almost dark out, sweetheart. I'd like to have a candle or lamp lit, the better to see you, but I'll defer to your modesty for tonight if you like."

She nodded, wiggling to loosen the shift from beneath her bottom, then pulling it over her head, leaving her bare, but for the drawers she wore.

"Stand up," he told her, rising before her and waiting until she should do as he asked. There didn't seem to be much choice, she found, for his hand drew her to her feet. And then she felt his palms on either side of her waist, long fingers causing her drawers to fall around her ankles.

"No other man will ever see you this way again in your life, Lily," he vowed, his voice dark and filled with promise. "You belong to me now. I promised to take care of you and keep you safe." His tone lightened a bit as he revised his words. "At least as safe as I can for the next little while. I'll do my best."

"I can't ask for more than that," she whispered, hearing the tremor in her words and knowing he sensed her apprehension. "Please, Morgan," she murmured, unwilling to look into his face, but needing to ask this one boon of him. "Please don't hurt me."

"Now?" he asked, the single word slashing the air between them. "You think I'd cause you pain, Lily? Here on this bed?"

She lifted her shoulders in a silent gesture of unconscious dread, aware that a man's needs caused harsh treatment sometimes, that a man's hands could leave bruises in their wake, and that her body might not give way readily to his possession.

"For tonight, I don't think I want to know what has happened to you, Lily, to make you fear this. And don't shake your head at me. I know what fright can do to a woman. You're smaller than I am, more fragile and vulnerable. You're trembling, sweetheart." He drew a deep breath and his fingers cupped her chin.

"Whatever happened in your past, no matter how many men have been in your bed, this is where it all begins, Lily. From now on, it's just you and me. I don't want you to forget that."

"About my past—" she began, halting abruptly as his fingers rose to cover her mouth.

"I don't want to hear it," he said, his voice sounding harsh for the first time. As if he could not abide the thought of another man's hands on her, another man possessing her body.

But there's only been one. Only one man to know me before. The words burned in her mind, but his hand denied their utterance and she closed her eyes in recognition of his demand.

I don't want to hear it.

He'd given his word to take care of her, and if he was too proud to allow her to speak in defense of herself—so be it. She would do as he asked.

Chapter Nine

Morgan bent to her, his lips taking the place of callused fingers against her mouth. The kiss was gentle, his hands careful as he lifted her from her feet. One arm swept beneath her knees and she was placed carefully on the bed, his mouth more demanding now, holding fast to the territory he'd claimed.

It took her breath, this warmth and kindness that flowed from him, saturating her to the marrow of her bones. And yet, beneath the patience, she knew a storm brewed, knew that the man who came down beside her held his passion in check, sensed that he was on a tight rein and might not be able to give her much more time to welcome him into her body.

Lily tunneled her fingers through his hair, reveling in his weight as he pressed her into the mattress. Safe and secure. The words had a new meaning, she found, as they applied to her position beneath Gage Morgan. There was no threat in his loving, only the promise of pleasure, and she sighed, offering her mouth for his taking once more.

He murmured beneath his breath and spoke her name. "Lily...you're sweet."

A sound of amusement was born in her throat and she

smiled up at him, laughter whispering in her words. "I'm not, you know. Sweet, I mean. My mama said I was too sassy for my own good."

He lifted his head and she thought she espied a dimple in one cheek as he touched her lips with his index finger. "Your mama looked at you a different way than I," he said. "She never tasted the fresh flavor of your kisses." He scanned her face with an all-encompassing look. "Trust me, Lily. What you're giving me is sweet, something I've never tasted before. It's as if you're brand-new, fresh and clean."

"Being here with you in the midst of all this…" She hesitated, pressing her lips together. "I can't explain it to you. Only say that I've never been *here* before. In fact, I don't know how good I'll be at what we're doing," she said quietly, feeling she must warn him in some way of the limited experience she'd gained over the past years.

"I'll take what I can get," he murmured, bending again to taste her mouth, this time granting his tongue permission to touch the inside of her lower lip.

She allowed it, opening her lips, offering what he sought from her, and he groaned, a sound that vibrated from his chest as he explored further. Meeting his tongue with her own, she found the experience she'd found distasteful in the past to hold a whole new measure of delight. Morgan's mouth welcomed her, his tongue fenced with hers and his pleasure was apparent.

Her cheeks and temple were visited by his lips then, as if he must explore each inch of skin visible to him. She turned her head to one side, then the other, knowing the thrill of a man's mouth seeking out the places that brought delight to her body, causing her to shiver and cling even tighter to him. He lifted a bit and she felt his gaze touch her breasts, knew that even in the dim twilight, he could make out the form of her curves, that his eyes could gauge the fullness displayed before him.

His hand moved to cup her, his fingertips tracing the smooth surface, then caressing with care the tender crest, which hardened and formed a tight knot beneath his touch. A soft chuckle escaped him as he spent long moments at the game, and she felt the spiraling pleasure he brought into being, knew the warmth he teased into life as he tantalized and petted her with tender care.

"Do you like that?" he asked, bending to suckle before she could form a reply, then watching her from beneath heavy eyelids.

She lifted from the bed, jolting as if a wire were connected from the place where he took his pleasure to that other part of her she knew he would soon allow his fingers to search out. A sound that embarrassed her was borne on a whisper as he fondled her, his touch becoming more firm, his fingers learning the shape and form of her body.

"Lily." He breathed her name, as if it were the only word he could speak, breathing it again and again as he spent long minutes in exploring her curves, his mouth opening against her skin. And then repeating it again as he rose to kneel between her thighs.

She stiffened, drawing away from his hands, knew a moment of panic as he touched her, there where she was most vulnerable, where she could so easily be bruised by a rough hand or a man's harsh use.

"I won't hurt you," he said, repeating his promise again, and she fought the rise of apprehension that threatened to engulf her. This was Morgan, she told herself. He was her husband. He had the right to use her as he pleased.

And even with all of that, she found herself tensing, knowing a measure of fear as he tested the place where he would penetrate her body. Where he would join them, the power of his manhood mating with the soft female part of her. Her breath caught audibly in her throat as his hand stroked her, and at that his movements slowed, seeking out the welcome her body provided him. His sound of satisfaction could not be mistaken, as moisture from within greeted his touch, as if her body had been made ready by his tender care. With a sigh of surrender, she lifted her hips to accommodate his entry.

But it seemed he had other ideas, for only that single finger made the journey within the heat of her body. As if he explored some unknown area, he visited each increment of flesh within her, pressing first here, then there, as if he waited for her to give some response to his touch. Unable to remain silent, she moaned aloud, and her hips rose in a movement that appeared to please him.

The dampness increased as he answered her unspoken demand, and she felt the slick entryway stretch to accommodate his exploration, allowing him to delve to the depths of her womanhood. An aching need possessed her, a yearning for completion, a hunger for something more than the teasing promise he offered.

"Morgan?" Surely that was not her voice, that whispering, breathless calling of his name. But it seemed it was, for he bent to her and kissed her, deeply and thoroughly, even as his hand brought new sensations to life, there where she opened to him without reservation.

As though she scaled the heights, she yearned toward the pinnacle he seemed to hold just beyond her reach and she strained, moving in the rhythm he set. Until, with a glorious surge of heat, a blinding flash of rapture, she found the crest, and began the downward slide.

He moved then, filling her, offering her his masculine need, surging into the place he'd readied for his taking, and she gripped him tightly, lest he leave her bereft. But it was not to happen, for even though he moved, easing from her possession, he returned, each thrust bringing more sensation to life, until she knew she could not contain any longer the joy he offered.

"Morgan!" It was a cry of fulfillment, and it triggered his own movement, as if she offered him leave to find his pleasure as he would. In moments he fell against her, his big body relaxing, his arms barely holding his weight from her. And still he sought her mouth, pressing kisses there, leaving the warmth of his breath on her skin, testing her earlobe, then her throat with the edges of his teeth.

But there was no pain, no residue of disapproval to convey to her that she had not pleased him. His touch was all that was tender, his kisses gentle now, his body still one with hers. He had given her that which she'd thought never to own, the knowledge that she was wanted, treasured and cherished by the man who claimed her.

The tears would not be contained and she wept.

Lily awoke in his arms, her breasts flattened against his chest, her legs tangled with his and her hand resting against his back. Broad daylight teased her eyes open, and she caught her breath, wondering for a moment if she could wiggle her way from his arms before he awoke and held her fast against himself.

"You cried, Lily," he murmured, his early-morning voice rasping in her ear. "Did I hurt you, then? I tried not to, sweetheart."

"No." She shook her head. "No, of course you didn't." Words of explanation were hard to come by, for she wasn't certain herself why the experience had brought her to tears. Only that the beauty of Morgan's loving had released the floodgates she'd put in place so long ago. When she'd decided that no man would be given freely that which the Yankee colonel had taken by force.

Now she looked up, facing the man she'd married, the man who owned her as surely as if he'd purchased her, body and soul, that night on the riverboat. She belonged to him. Of that there was no doubt, and she would not quibble over the fact. For now, she was Morgan's wife, to do with as he would. And she could not bring herself to feel sorrow at the thought.

It seemed there was more to do in the running of a kitchen than Lily had thought possible. Morgan carried in buckets of water, heating them on the stove in readiness for her chore of washing the sheets and the assortment of clothing they'd worn. She found soap on a shelf, bits and pieces swimming in a jar of water, the whole thing looking more like a gluey mess than anything else. But it formed suds nicely when she poured a measure of it into the wash-tub.

The yard seemed the best place for the chore, beneath a tree where Morgan set a bench in place for her use. He found a length of rope in the barn and she scrubbed at it in the warm water before handing it to him to stretch between two trees. And with every step, every movement she made, the weight of the gun she carried in her apron pocket reminded her that this peaceful moment might be shattered in an instant of time.

While the sheets soaked, she poured the cream from last night's milking into a pitcher and set it aside, handing Morgan the bucket for disposal in the pigsty. A sow rooted there, a clutch of piglets surrounding her, greeting the splash of milk in their trough with squeals and snorts.

Then, her sleeves rolled midway to her shoulders, Lily scrubbed at the sheets, liberally distributing the suds. Setting them aside, she concentrated on her soiled dresses, then the shirts and trousers Morgan offered her with a reluctant grin, bending to whisper in her ear that he'd never had so lovely a maid to tend to his needs.

She barely restrained the amusement his teasing brought

forth, unwilling to meet his gaze. It seemed that he took the events of the night before in his stride, but Lily found herself remembering each touch, each lingering caress as she worked at her task. And found that the memories had the power to make her blush.

The clothing scrubbed as well as she could manage, she called to Morgan and he carried clean water, dipped from the horse trough for her use. Wringing the clothes out made her hands and arms ache, and after a cursory attempt, she gave in to the temptation to allow the breeze to do the job for her. There were no clothespins it seemed, so the dripping shirts and dresses were hung to dry over the taut line, and the tub was carried back to the house.

"I'm going out to the barn." As though he was hesitant about leaving her alone in the house, Morgan stood at the back door. "I'll be in earshot if you need me," he said, and then his impatience was spoken aloud.

"Damn it, Lily. Will you look at me? I'm beginning to feel like I've done some terrible thing to you. You've ignored me all morning," he said, sounding a bit like an angry man to her ears. And then his words only served to prove her right.

"You said I didn't hurt you last night, and I know, sure as shootin', that you enjoyed what we did together. So how come I'm getting the silent treatment this morning?"

Lily chanced a look, fearing the anger, yet willing to face up to her own apprehension. His frown was daunting, and his stance that of a man ready to pounce on the object of his indignation. She could not bear it, could not hear him speak with such frustration filling his words, and then not respond.

With silent footsteps, she approached him, the small kitchen making it a short journey, and with an honest heart she replied to his accusations. "I've never before known the pleasure that you gave me, Morgan." The blush returned, and she recognized the heat that crept up her throat to touch her cheeks with color.

"I can only tell you again that there was no pain for me, only a time of feeling like a woman who is wanted by the man she married. It was what I'd hoped for, and yet I found that I wasn't ready for what you gave me. My body was used for a man's convenience more than once, and I had no way of knowing—"

"Hush, Lily," he whispered, his soft words interrupting her halting explanation. "I suspected you were cautious, and I was certain there was some fear mixed in."

"You suspected right," she admitted, finally able to look up with a measure of ease into his silvered gaze. She swallowed, then uttered the words that begged to be spoken aloud. "Thank you. I can't say it any other way, Gage Morgan. If nothing good ever comes my way again in this life, I'll have the memory of one beautiful night, when I felt a man's loving to the depths of my heart."

His arms opened and she stepped into his embrace, her face buried against his chest, there where his heart beat in a steady, sure rhythm. *Safe…secure.* The words were alive in her mind, as if she spoke them aloud.

"Don't ever be sorry you married me, Lily," he said, his words almost harsh, as if spoken in warning.

She stepped back and looked up at him. "That sounded like a threat." What had begun as a teasing response became the truth as she caught a glimpse of the man buried deeply in the facade that was Gage Morgan. At least the Morgan that most people saw and recognized as the man who earned his money as a gambler. A man whose contacts were scattered far and wide, who was never quite what he seemed to be.

"Sometimes," she began haltingly, "I don't think I know you. You seem to be one man, and then in a moment of time you become someone else."

"How so?" he asked, his eyes darkening as he challenged her.

She thought for a moment. "Back on the riverboat, when we met that first night, I thought you were a gambler, even a gentleman of sorts. And then…" Her pause was long as if she considered those few days and searched for answers.

"Then you became someone else, right before my eyes. You decided I could be useful to you, Morgan, and you used that Wanted poster to threaten me. In that moment I feared you and what you had the power to do to me."

"You didn't have to marry me, Lily," he reminded her gently. "That was your choice."

She nodded slowly. "I know it was, and at the time my reasons seemed to make sense to me. I thought I could use you in turn, make you agree to take me home if that was what I wanted when this assignment of yours came to an end."

Lifting a hand, as if to clear her mind of the clutter it seemed bound to sort through, she caught a glimpse of steel in his demeanor, of dark challenge in his eyes. "I saw another part of you when we arrived in Sand Creek. Your plotting and planning to catch these men is first and foremost in your mind. You really don't care what it takes to finish the job, and if I get in the way, you'd sacrifice me, if need be." And then as he shook his head in silent rebuttal, she simply closed her eyes and turned aside.

"I don't know you at all, do I?" she asked him in a whisper. "I've given myself to a man, and now I find he's not who I thought he was."

"I'm Gage Morgan, Lily. I'm the riverboat gambler you met and the hard-nosed man who forced you into this situation. They're one and the same man, they just wear two different hats." His hands touched her shoulders and he tugged her back a step until she felt his heat against her spine.

"I'm your husband," he said, more quietly now, almost as if this were the most vital part of his soliloquy. "I'm using you, I'll admit that much, but I thought you knew the whole plan before we got here. Remember, sweetheart," he said, and his voice was harsh as he spoke the endearment, "you asked for this. You came with me of your own free will. No one forced you into it."

"Do you feel anything for anybody?" she asked, knowing that the real question was much more personal. *Do you feel anything for me?* For if he didn't, if he'd used her last night, as he had all along, persuading her to his will, one way or another. If that were the case… Her thoughts spun as she waited for him to form a reply.

"I can't let myself feel," he said. "This is a job, an assignment I've taken on. If I let you, or any other distraction, mar my concentration, it could mean failure on my part."

His fingers were almost painful as he clutched at her shoulders. "I can't afford to give you any more than I already have," he said. "When this is over, when we've caught the men we're waiting for, and when I'm a free agent again, maybe then I'll be able to be what you want. For now, this is it, Lily."

She shivered, knowing that he was being honest with her. And after all, she thought, she didn't need him. She'd managed to get along by herself for quite some time, working here and there, saving her earnings and then setting off again. Moving, always moving south. Finally down to the silver combs she wore, down to the last of her valuables, she teetered on the brink of disaster, and only Morgan's strong arm had kept her afloat for the past week.

"All right," she said, facing the facts as she saw them. "I'll forget that we spent last night together, set it aside as an error in judgment on my part. Or maybe the price of the protection you offered me.'' She stepped away from him and felt his hands slide from their grip. Strangely bereft, she walked from the kitchen and on into the sparsely furnished bedroom, where the bare mattress reminded her of the hours of darkness spent there in Gage Morgan's arms.

He followed her and halted in the doorway. ''You made a bargain with me, Lily.''

She thought his voice held a new edge, a harshness heretofore missing in his demeanor. ''I won't renege on it,'' she told him. ''I told you once before that I pay my debts. I know what I owe you.''

''I told you from the beginning that this would be a real marriage, once we spoke the vows that made it legal. Don't try to back out of that part of it,'' he warned her.

''I don't want last night to be repeated,'' she insisted stubbornly, knowing the words for a lie.

He laughed. Not a chortle or a murmured sound of amusement, but a full-blown laugh, as if her words were too entertaining to ignore. ''To begin with, you have no choice in the matter,'' he told her. ''In the second place…'' He approached her and she wished fervently that there was an escape route handy.

''There is no second place,'' he said, as if he had decided not to elaborate on the problem. ''You're my wife now, Lily. If I want you to sleep in my bed, you will. If I want to make love to you, I will. And if you want to make an issue of it, we'll hash it out right there on that mattress.''

''My,'' she said wryly, ''doesn't that sound like a fair situation. How much do you weigh, Morgan? Two hundred pounds?''

''Give or take a few,'' he assented, and then his gaze measured her, and he made a guess that struck too close to reality for comfort. "I figure I outweigh you by about seventy pounds, Mrs. Morgan. Am I about right?"

"Give or take a few," she said, repeating his words.

"Do you think you stand a chance of fighting me?"

"I won't even try," she said, feeling as if a large tomcat had her in his clutches and she was being tormented like a creature backed against the wall. His smile was feral now as he reached to touch her face, one long finger tracing the line of her cheek and jaw.

More like a panther, she decided, or perhaps a mountain lion. An opponent so sleek and dark and wonderfully appealing, a woman stood little chance of besting him in any battle.

He pulled her against himself and she allowed it, yielding to his will. But it seemed it was not enough, for he held her before him and his gaze was impatient, edgy, as though he was of two minds as to his next move. Then he spoke.

"For now, Lily—just for now, do as I ask. Keep your gun handy, watch your back and be careful. You've held up thus far. Give it two more days, and things will have come to a head, and this will likely be over with." He lifted her chin, forcing her to face him fully. "Will you do that?"

She nodded. And it seemed to be enough for him. He released her and left her where she stood, striding through the small cabin and out the door.

The gun bumped against her thigh as she followed in his wake, and she found herself watching the tree line to the west as she stepped out onto the porch. The wind had blown one of her dresses from the makeshift clothesline and she walked to where it lay on the ground. Picking it up, she shook it and held it before her. It was already dry and she placed it over her arm, then continued on to where the rest of her washing hung.

Only Morgan's heavy trousers still held dampness in their fabric. The sheets were dry, as were the small clothes they'd worn. With a cautious look to where the barn door stood open, she gathered the remainder of the laundry and went back to the house. In less than ten minutes she'd put the sheets on the bed, fluffed the lumpy pillows as best she could and slipped them into the cases.

Wearing an unironed dress did not appeal to her and she sought out Sarah's irons, finding them tucked beneath the stove. A towel held the clothes she sprinkled down for ironing and she wrapped them tightly, stowing them in the bedroom until morning when she would sort out the task of ironing.

They finished the evening meal by dark, and Morgan carried in the milk pail shortly afterward. He'd gathered eggs earlier, then called the chickens into the pen by the simple means of shaking a shallow pan full of feed and waiting for them to join him for their evening meal. The horses were on their own, except for one that looked to be limping, Morgan said. He'd brought her into the barn and checked her out, deciding to keep her inside for the night.

"She's got a problem of some sort," Morgan told Lily. "I don't know a whole lot about it, but I'm going to keep her in the barn overnight and take a good look at her foot. She's favoring her right foreleg."

"Shall I come out and help?" Lily asked, looking beyond the porch where the barn and outbuildings stood in shadow. The sun was buried beneath the western horizon, only faint crimson streaks in the sky telling of its presence just out of sight.

"Are you afraid to be alone in the house?" he asked.

She shook her head. "No. A little wary for some reason, but I'll stay here and clean up the kitchen as long as you don't need me."

Morgan headed for the barn, and within moments Lily

saw the glow of a lantern within the structure. The mare was tied in the aisle and Morgan was crouched beside her, lifting her foot and examining it intently. A rifle lay on the floor beside him, and he wore the holster he'd borrowed from Caine Harris. She found the weight of her own weapon strangely comforting as she watched him. Easing out onto the porch she kept a sharp eye out, looking toward the west again, and then beyond the barn to where the pasture held the herd.

From around the side of the house, she heard a soft whicker, and then the snort of an approaching horse. Perhaps one of the herd had gotten through the fence, she thought, and without thinking, she stepped off the porch to investigate. A rider came into sight, hat pulled low over his forehead, sitting easily in the saddle, and before she could retrieve her gun from the depths of her apron pocket, he lifted a hand in greeting.

"Evening, ma'am," he said quickly. "It's Sheriff Harris, ma'am." Swinging down from his saddle, he led his mount to where she stood and doffed his hat, revealing a face she was familiar with.

"I was halfway to shooting my gun," she told him. "Problem was, I couldn't get it out of my apron pocket as quickly as I wanted to." Her smile trembled as she thought of what might have happened, had her visitor not been the sheriff.

He apparently had the same thoughts, for he glanced down at where the heavy weapon swung against her thigh. "My advice would be to swing that thing upward, still in your pocket, and fire it in the air," he told her. "You ought to practice cocking it with one hand, Mrs. Morgan. One shot in the air and I'll warrant that husband of yours would be here like greased lightning."

"I think he's on his way right now," she said, watching as Gage stepped from the barn and approached, rifle in hand. His stride was long, his stance purposeful as he neared the porch, and then, with a hard glance at the lawman, he halted and nodded a greeting.

"Evening, Sheriff," he said. "I wasn't expecting to see you here tonight. Do you have news for us?"

"I came at dark so I wouldn't be so obvious if there should be someone keeping an eye on the place," he told Morgan. "Thought you ought to know that a farmer north of here was shot and killed day before yesterday. His wife rode into Middleburg on their farm wagon last evening. One of their neighbors escorted her so she'd be safe. They'd wrapped the fella's body in a quilt and brought him along so she could bury him right and proper."

"What happened?" Morgan asked sharply.

"The story I heard was that they had visitors, two men who showed them identification and said they were authorized by Washington to take over the farm for railway right-of-way."

"Hell, how many acres does any railway need? If there was such a plan going on, a man would be compensated for three hundred feet or so along the edge of his property."

"Well, as it turns out, the woman said they were the same fellas who'd been there before. Old Henry aimed his gun, but the odds weren't in his favor."

"Henry?" Lily felt dizzy, the blood rushing from her head and a great roaring enveloping her as she sought the edge of the porch. She sat heavily, leaning against the post, as Morgan took three long strides to reach her. He touched the back of her head and bent it forward to touch her knees.

"Take it easy, sweetheart," he murmured. "You're about ready to pass out on me. Just lean over and let the blood back where it belongs."

"Henry?" she repeated. "Do you suppose..." She

looked up the sheriff, shaking her head in helpless sorrow. "We met a couple," she said softly. "His name…"

Caine Harris nodded as she spoke. "It was probably the same family. The woman said they'd been warned by a man and his wife a few days ago that they were in danger, but Henry thought he could handle it without help." The lawman shook his head. "He was wrong—dead wrong. Two against one are pretty poor odds to run up against. And that bunch of young'uns will never get over watchin' their pa get shot, right in front of them."

"We stayed overnight there," Morgan said quietly. "I warned him, sure enough, but I was afraid of something like this happening. I'm just surprised they let his wife go without a fuss."

"They gave her a bank draft for a hundred dollars, and packed her up on Henry's farm wagon, body and all. Said she had an hour to be off the property. She got away with just their clothes and a few essentials." Caine's face took on a harsh expression and he shoved one hand in his pocket.

"At least they let her bring Henry's body with her," he said. "They're makin' arrangements to have him buried in the churchyard in Middleburg tomorrow."

"How'd you hear so soon?" Morgan asked.

"They put out word right away, warning folks to keep an eye out. The thing is, Henry's wife signed over the deed to the men, and unless they can be caught red-handed, they'll probably get away with it. The deed is made out to a corporation of some sort. The men are just working for somebody else."

"Isn't the government able to do more than they're doing?" Morgan asked.

"We live on the edge of civilization," the sheriff said. "Washington has better things to do than to worry about a few farmers gettin' rooked by some scallywags. Besides, they sent you here, didn't they?'' He looked at Lily and then back at Morgan.

''If we can catch them here, we'll have them. They're too smart to try their scam close to town, where there's some protection and neighbors to help out. It's folks like Henry, simple farmers who can be fooled into thinking they have to sign over their land, who are being cheated.''

''The thing is,'' Morgan said, ''once the word is out, they'll cut their losses and head to another area, where they haven't been heard of. And then the deeds will have been left in the name of some big shot who'll take the railroad for a bundle when the time comes to lay the track.''

''When is the line coming through?'' Lily asked.

''Supposed to be next year, from what I hear,'' Harris said. ''They'll sign their papers in New York or Chicago or some other big city and head on down here with the rights all signed, sealed and delivered.''

''What do you think comes next?'' Morgan asked.

''They won't make the mistake of hitting too close to Middleburg. More likely come on down in this area. There's three farmers just south of Sand Creek and then the Blairs' place here that have been approached.''

''Well,'' Morgan said, ''I don't know about the others on the other side of town, but we'll be ready for them here. How much backup will you give us?''

''I'm sending two men out here in the morning to stay with you,'' Harris said. ''You'll have to keep them out of sight, and it's up to you what you do with them. Just get some food in their bellies and give them a place to lay their bedrolls at night. Between them, they should be able to keep a good lookout, taking turns sleeping.''

He turned to his horse and reached for the saddle horn, his reins held loosely. ''I've got my ear to the ground, Morgan. If I suspect anything, if anyone sees strangers hereabout, I'll hightail it out here, quick as I can.''

"Well, I suspect I can't ask for much more than that. At least Lily and I aren't going to be in this alone."

But for some reason, his words failed to give her any comfort as Lily watched the sheriff ride off into the night. Behind her, Morgan stood in the shadows, clothed in the darkness, a man with secrets, a man who drew her to him as a moth is drawn to flame.

Chapter Ten

"I don't think there's any reason for you to be looking out the window, Lily." From the bed, Morgan's voice was amused, and she could visualize the lazy grin he was sending her way. "Our bad guys won't be showing up in the middle of the night," he said. "They'll want to confront us, and they need a signature on the deed to have the transfer of possession legal."

"Well, seeing that we don't own the place to begin with, we couldn't sign it over to them anyway, could we?" His words of teasing assurance were not enough to lure her from her post, and she crossed her arms, standing at one side of the window frame, lest she expose herself fully should someone be out there, keeping watch over the house.

"No, but don't worry about that angle. We're not going to let this go that far," Morgan told her. "Once they demand our cooperation and offer a bank draft for the property, we can arrest them and haul them away. Caine has a cell waiting for them."

"Who's going to arrest them?" she asked, turning her head to look toward the bed. He lay propped on both pillows, his head turned toward her, and even in the dim light, she could see the glitter of his eyes and the naked beauty of the man who awaited her presence beside him.

"I can arrest them," he told her. "I'm carrying a note from government headquarters in Washington giving me that right."

Another facet of his varied past, she thought. *My husband, the government man.* She smiled then, to think that a woman on the run might carry around her very own protector, an agent from the nation's capitol.

"I'm not sure I like the bent of that amused look you're wearing," he said. "I'd say your mind is working a mile a minute, trying to find a hundred reasons to keep you out of this bed tonight."

"Tell me, Morgan," she said impulsively, "what happens if your boss finds out you've been harboring a criminal? Will you lose your job?"

"Well, if I were in this for the high salary, it might be a concern, but since the government is not known for making their employees into rich men it wouldn't be any great loss," he said. "And on top of that, you have to understand something, Lily. Men who are willing to do what I do for a living are few and far between. They manage to overlook a lot when it comes to their operatives."

"Even having a wife with a price on her head?"

"Are you worried?" he asked, shifting to lean on one elbow. He patted the mattress next to him. "Come on over here. Let's talk about it."

"I'm not easily persuaded," she told him. "I kinda like it right here by the window. In fact, I may pull that chair over here and just spend the night keeping an eye out for trouble."

"I don't think that'll work," he said, and as he spoke the words, he turned and swung his legs over the side of the bed, rising with not a stitch of modesty to cover him from her sight.

"Get back in bed," she said, turning back to the window. But nothing she saw outdoors could shake from her mind the sight of Morgan in all his masculine beauty. He approached her silently and she closed her eyes, visualizing the breadth of his shoulders, the muscles of his upper arms, the dark whorls of hair that decorated his chest, and the stubble on his jaw that needed the attention of his razor on a daily basis.

He was a male animal, a primitive specimen of manhood, a creature with all the natural inclinations of any man who was closed up in a bedroom with a woman, who was, by her own admission, in his power. A woman he knew he had every right to claim as his own. She sensed his approach, knew the instant his hands hovered over her shoulders, and she closed her eyes against the shock of his fingers pressing into the fine bones that formed her body.

One long index finger reached to measure her collarbone, tracing the length of it beneath her skin, then resting at the base of her throat. His hand shifted and his thumb sought out the place where her heartbeat could be felt in the hollow beneath her ear. Strength flowed from his hand to her flesh, tightening his grip, allowing him to turn her head a bit, revealing her face to his scrutiny.

She saw his uplifted eyebrow, the amused slant of his smile. "The bed's lonesome without you in it, Lily."

"You slept alone before I came into the picture," she told him. "You'll sleep alone after I'm gone from your life. What difference does tonight make in the general scheme of things?"

"I didn't have that problem to worry about before we met on the riverboat, and if the time comes that I lose you from my life, I'll probably never sleep as well without you beside me. But for tonight, you're here and I need you. Are you going to deny me?"

She was tempted to lean back against him, to entrust

herself to his hands, to relive the moments they'd shared only twenty-four hours ago. He seemed to take on a new cast in the darkness, shedding the hard shell he wore when his mind was filled with the strategies that bound their existence. As if the darkness gave him leave to relax, he was softer here, his mood more at ease.

Tomorrow might bring a renewal of their differences. In fact, she was dead certain that it would. Morgan was intent on the performance of his duty. She definitely took second place to the work he'd been sent to accomplish. But for right now, for these moments in this room, with the night surrounding them, he was once more the man who wanted her, who had married her because she would not follow him otherwise.

She'd asked for this. She'd demanded that he make her his wife, and in so doing had given him the right to ask for the use of her body, for the pleasure her womanly form could provide him.

"Lily?" He spoke her name, as if to remind her of the appeal he'd made to her sense of fairness. "Will you turn me away? Or were you just using your anger as a tool against me earlier today?"

"You said you could overpower me, Morgan. Two hundred pounds against my limited strength. Remember?"

"And you think I'll drag you to the bed and force you to lie beneath me?"

She shook her head, turning to look up into his face. It was set in remote lines, his eyes narrowed as if he would peer inside her to seek out her thoughts. "I don't think you'd pressure me," she said. "But if you did…" Her words faltered as he drew her against himself.

"If I did?" he asked, bending to whisk his lips across hers, tempting her with the faint pressure of a mouth that was sinfully made to entice a woman's hunger for its touch.

"If you did, it probably wouldn't be a battle of wills for very long," she said. "I'm not sure I could hold out against you, Morgan."

"Shall we find out?" he asked, bending to nestle his face against her shoulder, his mouth opening to allow him the flavor of her skin, his teeth touching the fragile, vulnerable bend between neck and shoulder.

"And tomorrow?" she asked, closing her eyes against the sight of his hair, against the sound of his husky murmurs as he spoke her name. And against the temptation he presented as she was caught up against the firm muscles of his chest and her legs were held imprisoned by the stance he'd assumed. He held her there, one hand sliding to mesh her body against the arousal he made no attempt to conceal.

For indeed he could not have hidden it had he tried. It was *there,* making itself known against the softness of her belly, reminding her of the moments when she'd offered herself into his keeping.

"Tomorrow will take care of itself." His words were firm, spoken in a husky undertone that allowed no quibbling on her part. It would be as he said. Tomorrow was another day, and tonight was all they might ever have. And she was not a woman to second-guess herself.

Lily lifted her arms, twining them around his neck, leaning into his strength and offering herself on the altar of desire. Passion was what they shared, she reminded herself. *Love* was a word she was not likely ever to hear from Gage Morgan. He might tell her he wanted her, and she could believe him, for that fact was evident. So for tonight she would settle for desire...for passion and pleasure.

"Take me to bed," she whispered. His breath was warm against her cheek as he lifted her; his arms were strong beneath her, and in three long strides, he'd reached the bed. She was placed carefully in the center of the mattress and then he was but a shadowed form, blotting out the moonlight as he lowered himself into her arms.

The two deputies were well-weathered, lean specimens who wore their years well. Spike and Levi were their names, and without any fuss they settled into the barn, chasing their horses out into the pasture, then carrying their bedrolls up to the loft. They made themselves useful as much as possible, though Sam's barn was obviously the target of his limited supply of energy.

The doors were closed to observing eyes as the men did what few chores needed their touch, and when Lily walked out just after noontime to offer dinner, they greeted her with enthusiasm. It was a simple meal, corn bread and soup beans, with a generous amount of ham swimming in the broth. The men fell to with a will and Lily watched, pleased that her cooking met with their approval.

"Have you seen Morgan?" she asked, walking to the far end of the aisle and peering through a cobwebbed window.

"He was in a while ago," Levi said, wiping his mouth on his shirtsleeve. Lily turned from the sight, wondering if she should have provided napkins. Her smile twitched as she freed the big door latch and slid it to one side.

"Ma'am, you shouldn't be doin' that," Spike said, his voice low as if he feared being overheard. And then, as if to emphasize his warning, a shot rang out and Lily looked toward the front of the barn.

"That was the other side of the house," she said quietly. "Do you suppose Morgan is there?"

"You don't know who might be out there, and you'd make a dandy target should those fellas we're watching for be heading this way," Spike cautioned as he motioned to the open doorway behind her. "One thing's for sure. That wasn't Morgan shootin' out front. It sounded like a shotgun, and he's carryin' a rifle." He waved an imperative hand at Lily. "Get away from that door, ma'am."

She stepped away, aware that his warning was valid. "I didn't think," she murmured, lifting a hand to slide the door back in place. A bullet twanged against the barn siding, the angle sufficient to send it askew, and Lily lost her balance and fell back, her breath forced from her lungs by the force of her body hitting the floor.

"Ma'am?" Levi bent over her, his hands touching her head, then dropping to rest on her shoulders. "I don't see any blood," he muttered. "But you never know."

"I'm not shot," she said, rolling to her side as she fought for breath. "It scared me, that's all." She sat upright, her hands against her chest as she finally managed to draw air into her aching lungs. "See if Morgan is out there," she said sharply. "Look out the window and pay special mind to the line of trees beyond the pasture."

But it seemed that Morgan had sought cover of his own. The two deputies flanked the barn, one at either end, and try as they might, Morgan could not be seen from the positions they assumed. Lily struggled to her feet, brushing straw from her dress and hair, and went back to the window.

"Why do you suppose they shot at me?" she asked Levi. "I wouldn't think I presented much of a problem to them."

"They killed a fella north of here a couple days ago," Levi offered, though his frown was dubious. "Other than that, I can't figure it, either. A woman ain't much of a threat, seems to me."

"Do you think they know you're here?" she asked, seeking any movement to be seen in the wooded area where she was certain the second shot had originated.

"Wouldn't be surprised," Levi admitted. "We didn't run into anybody on our way out here, but them fellas keep a pretty close eye on things, I suspect. They'll be wanting to clear us out of here, maybe take you prisoner to force Morgan's hand." He looked at her with a grin. "If you was my woman, I'd sure enough sign a deed over to keep you from getting hurt."

She felt a moment's warmth at the man's words of admiration. "You may be right, you know. If they wanted to kill me, they could probably have done it. Perhaps they were firing a warning shot."

"I sure enough feel well warned," Levi told her. "I don't mind a fair fight, but anybody who'd fire at a woman is pretty low in my book. You see anything up there, Spike?" he called out to where the other deputy stood peering from a narrow crack toward the house.

"There's somebody on the other side of the porch," Spike answered. "I think it might be Morgan. Can't tell for certain. He's kinda hid in the shade there, but I've a notion he's gonna make a run for it and skedaddle to the barn."

Lily turned and hurried toward Spike, and as she did, the man chuckled. "Yep, that's just what I figured he'd do," he said, sliding the door to one side, opening it just wide enough for a man's body to slide past the gap. "Sure enough, here he comes," he said. A spate of gunfire sounded outside and Lily closed her eyes, fearful of their target being the man who crossed the yard.

And then Morgan was there, looming in the opening, stepping into the dimness that enclosed Lily in its depths. "Lily?" His voice spoke her name, the sound relaying his concern. "Are you all right?"

"I'm fine," she answered, hurrying to his side. "I came out to give the men their dinner, and then we heard two shots, the second one coming from out back."

"Did you see anyone? Where did it come from? Out in the pasture?" he asked, gripping Lily's arms and bending over her, searching her face. "Are you sure you aren't hurt?"

She shook her head emphatically. "No, of course not. I think the gunman is farther out, maybe beyond the pasture, where the woods are pretty thick."

"I wouldn't be surprised," Morgan told her. "There's probably one there and another west of the house. He tried to get a shot off at me when I came in from the road to town." He angled a look at the two men who watched every move he made, and dropped his hands, allowing Lily freedom from his grasp.

"What were you doing there?" she asked, peeved that he should expose himself to danger without sufficient means of defense.

"Trying to force their hand. I wanted them to make a move," he told her.

"Are you happy now?" she asked. "They've certainly done just that. In fact, I'd say they have us pretty well stuck here between them."

"Well," Morgan said, a bit too cheerfully for her frame of mind, "at least I can have a bite to eat while they decide what they'll do next." He stepped to where the pan of corn bread sat, and bent to the kettle of soup beans. "This smells good," he told her, inhaling the succulent aroma.

He picked up the spoon and stirred the thick broth. "Suppose I've got time to have a taste?" he asked, and Lily's anger was fueled by his nonchalant pose.

"We're being *shot* at and you're worried about eating your *dinner?*" Her eyes flashed a warning.

If he'd thought to calm her down, he'd gone about it the wrong way. The lady was fuming. The rush of adrenaline had carried him across the yard and into the comparative safety of the barn, and for all of those fleeting seconds, his mind had been centered on Lily—whether she was still in the house and he was making a grave error in heading for the barn. His guess had been right, and perhaps the sight of her in one piece had been the reason he'd been filled with a sense of euphoria, his relief so great it seemed his heart swelled within his chest.

In fact, it was all he could do not to carry her to the pile of hay beneath the eaves and assure himself that she was safe and secure. "It's all right, Lily," he murmured, rising to face her, all his instincts telling him to hold her close.

"No, it isn't," she said, her voice soft but filled with an anger he welcomed. Lily in the depths of fury was easier for him to cope with than a whining woman would have been. He should have known that her responses would not be those of any ordinary female. His Lily was unique.

She stood before him now with her hand on the pistol she carried. Taken from her apron pocket, the gun was carried at her side and Morgan had no doubt she would use it if the occasion warranted it.

"You could have been shot," she said quietly. "I thought you'd be more careful than that."

"How about you?" he asked. "How did you manage to get from the house to the barn, carting your kettle and the pan of corn bread? I'll bet your gun was dangling in your pocket, wasn't it?"

She nodded. "I don't like this. Not one bit," she said in a low voice. "I didn't think it would be so dangerous, Morgan. I thought they'd come up to the house and very nicely ask us to sign the deed over to them and then we could turn them over to the sheriff and ride away, the job finished."

He stifled a laugh. "You really thought that?"

She lifted one shoulder in a negligent shrug. "I've never done this sort of thing before," she admitted. "When that bullet hit the barn siding, it put the fear of God in me, I swear it did."

"I should hope so," he told her, and then swallowed

the terror that threatened to choke him as he thought of Lily sprawled across the floor with a slug in her slender body.

"Hey there, Sam Blair!" From beyond the barn door a raucous voice shouted out a greeting. "You need to come on out here and tend to business."

"Whadda ya want?" Morgan's voice assumed a harsh, threatening tone as he called back a reply, one that imitated Blair's rasping voice.

"You know what we want. You were warned. Your letter said you'd better be ready to move your stuff out of the place by this morning. And you're still here. If you value your skin, you'll get that woman of yours and hit the road. You've got ten minutes to be on your way. All you gotta do is sign the dotted line, and you can leave with no trouble from us."

"Now, why," Morgan muttered beneath his breath, "don't I believe you?"

And then he stepped closer to the door and called out a response. "Where's the deed? And how do I know you'll let us go without firing on us?"

"You don't. But it's either that or burn up inside that barn. If you're not outta there in two minutes it's gonna be hotter than Hades inside."

Levi laughed, a low sound of enjoyment. "They don't know we're here," he said.

"What are you planning?" Spike asked him. "If we go out either door, we'll be cut down."

"How about the loft?" Morgan asked. "There's a window at the back and a door at the front. Maybe you can get off a shot from there."

"I can go up," Lily offered.

"No," Morgan said quickly. "I want you down here in case they set a fire. I'll need to get you out in a hurry."

Levi and Spike were already on their way up the ladder

as he spoke, and their footsteps gave indication of the direction they took, hay filtering through the cracks in the flooring and falling on the aisleway below. A double thump on the ceiling overhead told Morgan that one of the men overhead had caught sight of their quarry.

He heard the squeak of the window at the back of the loft as it opened, and then a shot resonated against the wall overhead. A loud retort answered and then was seconded by another gunshot from the front of the loft.

Morgan pushed Lily toward an empty stall. "Stay under cover," he told her, turning his back to make his way to the barn door. She watched him for less than a second and then turned toward the sliding door at the back. Moving it gingerly, she peered through the crack and then rested the barrel of her pistol there.

From the back of the pasture a man was making his way through the herd of horses, using the animals as cover, bent low and running from place to place. She watched him, noted the upward glance he shot toward the barn, and then as he neared the corral fence, he lifted his gun and took aim.

Without hesitation, she leveled her pistol in his direction, praying silently that she would not wound a horse, yet aware that should that happen, it would be the lesser of two evils. The man overhead in the loft might be at greater risk, she decided, tightening her index finger on the trigger.

The gun seemed to explode in her hand, the sound vibrating in her ears, the smoke rising before her. And at the back of the corral, the man lay in the dirt.

She swallowed, aware of the bile that gathered in her throat, hearing the shouts of men from the direction of the house and the sound of her own name being called out in rage.

"Lily!" Morgan was behind her and she turned to him.

"I told you to stay in that stall," he said, gripping her shoulders as if he would shake the stuffings out of her.

Behind them, Spike hit the barn floor. "You better be glad she didn't," he said, breathless and red-faced. "She nailed that fella. One shot, Morgan. Sure pulled my chestnuts out of the fire."

"You'd have gotten him," Morgan said darkly.

"I did," Spike said. "But I think her slug got there first. He shot at me, but when he got hit, it jerked him around and the bullet went wild."

"I'm going to be sick," Lily said weakly, her legs trembling, her heart pounding at a rapid pace. She opened the barn door and stepped outside, then caught sight again of the man lying in the dirt just thirty feet or so from where she stood. The ground came up to meet her and only Morgan's arm around her waist held her upright. The bile erupted from her mouth and she shuddered, aware of his handkerchief pressed into her hand and his strength keeping her on her feet.

"I'm all right," she managed to whisper. And then she looked up again as the man groaned and rolled over against the corral fence. "He's not dead, is he?"

"No, more's the pity," Morgan said with disgust. "Now they'll have to buy a new rope to hang him with."

"They're going to hang him?" she asked.

"Probably. It's against the law to cheat folks out of their property, Lily. He won't get away with it."

"Y'all in one piece in there?" The call from the front of the barn was loud, the voice familiar, and Morgan lifted Lily, easing her back inside the building. He led her to the front door and slid it open. Caine stood outside, his gun at his side, two other men flanking him. And there, next to the house, a body lay, unmoving.

"We got one of them here," Caine said. "Where's his partner?"

"Out back," Morgan told him. "Lily winged him."

From behind Caine, one of the deputies turned the dead man to his back and bent to reach inside his coat pocket. "Here's a bunch of paperwork," he called out. "Looks like a property deed to me."

"Hang on to it," Caine said. "We'll need it when we bring his friend to the judge."

"There are more of them working this scam," Morgan said. "But I've only had instructions to deal with these two."

"There's more of them," Caine agreed. "But they'll be scared off, knowing we found them out, and handled it here. Sand Creek won't be welcoming any more crooks, no matter how impressive their credentials look."

"They don't look like I thought they would," Lily admitted. "I was looking for ragged-looking criminals. These men are dressed like bankers."

"Meant to impress folks with their big-city fashions, I suspect," Morgan said. "But underneath, they're just criminals, like you'll find in any jail." He turned to Caine. "I've got the paperwork from Washington that'll put the one out back behind bars for a lot of years. Unless the judge decides to hang him."

"This is still the frontier," Caine said flatly. "He'll probably swing. If it warns off even one of this bunch, it'll be worth it. And the good Lord knows there's always men out there takin' advantage of folks."

Morgan looked down at Lily and then took the gun from her limp fingers. "Come on, sweetheart," he said. "Into the house with you."

It was to her credit that Lily did as he told her. Indeed, she could not have done otherwise. Morgan's arm supported her, assisting her up the step to the porch, his body providing a shield that blocked her view of the dead man whose blood pooled beneath him. The door opened readily and she was ushered into the kitchen, and from there to a chair, where she found her legs would not hold her upright a moment longer.

"I don't care what you say, Morgan. I'm glad he's not dead. I don't know if I could have borne it had I killed a man." She lowered her head to rest on the table and felt his hand brush her hair, knew the warmth of his lips as they touched her nape in a tender caress.

His whisper was breathed against her ear and she felt a surge of thanksgiving as he comforted her. "It's all right, Lily. You're not built for this sort of thing. I was wrong to take advantage of you and get you mixed up in it." His hand slid to her shoulder and he squeezed it once before he moved away from her.

She lifted her head and sought him out. He stood at the window, as if some great event took his attention, his hands widespread on his hips, his stance that of a man ready to do battle. "I came with you of my own accord," she said. Somehow, the man seemed to have retreated from her in the past few moments, and she felt a chasm opening between them.

"I had no right, Lily," he repeated. "You could have been killed out there."

"But I wasn't," she said, finding herself in the role of comforter instead of the one receiving solace at his hands. She rose, her legs steady now, as if she must prove her words to be true. "I'm fine, Morgan. I wasn't hurt." Silent footsteps took her across the room to where he stood. His shirt wore a line of dampness down the back, where he'd perspired and she caught the scent of male flesh and a musky aroma that drew her closer.

His voice sank lower, assuming a guttural sound. "I put a gun in your hand, Lily, and expected you to use it," he told her. "I didn't know I'd sunk so far."

"If I'd been an agent for the government, it would have

been my job." It seemed clear enough to her that by agreeing to this thing, she'd put on the same cloak he wore.

He turned to face her, and his eyes narrowed, as if he were taken aback by her proximity. "But you *weren't* an agent for the government," he said quietly. "You were a vulnerable woman. And I took advantage of you."

"You're stuck with me," she said, forcing a smile to her lips. "You married me, Morgan. Or have you forgotten?"

He shook his head. "No, I haven't forgotten," he told her. "But you'd be better off if you had stayed on that damn boat and kept going south."

She felt the pain of betrayal stab deeply in her chest. "Do you really believe that?"

He nodded. "You could have survived a few more days, Lily. Ham Scott would have kept a watch on you. He was happy to have you singing in the saloon, and by now you'd have been well on your way home."

She felt the blood leave her face, knew a moment's dizziness. And then she forced her spine to hold her upright and her chin tilted upward, her gaze meeting his head-on. "I certainly won't be in your way any longer than it takes to pack my bag, Morgan. I still know which direction to head to get to Louisiana."

With tears blinding her, she turned from him and crossed the kitchen. The bedroom door was only six feet away…now three…and finally she reached the threshold, crossing it and closing the heavy door behind herself.

From the other side she heard his voice, recognized the curses he spoke aloud, and then felt the floor beneath her shudder as his footsteps crossed the room in her wake.

A fist pounded on the door behind her and she leaned back against it as if her weight would keep him on the other side. "Go away," she said, recognizing the tears that clogged her words. "I don't want—"

"Stand aside, Lily." His voice was firm, interrupting her protest without hesitation. "I'm coming in, and I don't want to hurt you."

"You couldn't do a much better job of it than you already have," she said bitterly. "Just leave me alone."

Chapter Eleven

"Do you think you stand a chance of fighting me?"

The words rang in her mind as she considered the man on the other side of the door. And her own reply decided what she would do. *"I wouldn't even try."* She'd made the statement with the full knowledge that against his greater strength she had no chance of winning a physical battle.

A battle such as she was engaging in right now. Her eyes closed as she recognized the moment of her defeat. Her weight could not keep him at bay, and so she moved aside, feeling a twinge of regret as he stepped over the threshold. The man looked as though the hounds of hell were on his heels. His face seemed drawn, his eyes haunted, and they sought her out with a look of appeal.

"I'm sorry, Lily. I was wrong. I shouldn't have married you, and then I sure as hell shouldn't have used you that way I did."

"You used me? And how was that?" she asked, remembering the long nights of loving, and dying a bit inside as she recognized his regret that they had taken place.

"I made you sleep with me," he said harshly. "I threatened you if you wouldn't lie down on that bed and—"

His hand slashed the air as if he could not bring himself to utter the words aloud that would condemn him.

"You wouldn't have forced me," she said quietly. "I knew that. I came to you willingly. Not once, but twice." Her face flamed as she admitted the truth that begged to be spoken. "I wanted you, too, you know. I wanted to know what it was to feel a man's caring arms around me, to know tenderness in a man's touch. If either of us used the other, I must bear equal blame."

"You'd never have done what I demanded of you on that boat," he said, denying her claim. "You told me right off that you weren't what Ham Scott wanted you to be."

"And you didn't really believe me, did you?" she asked softly. "You never really believed that I wasn't a whore. It made it easier for you to take me to bed, if you thought I was well used already."

"No, it wasn't that way." The words shot from lips as if they could not be contained, and he stepped closer to her. "I never thought that of you, Lily. Not once I'd spent that first night with you, when we talked about Lily Devereaux. I knew then that you were a woman who'd been hurt, that no matter how you denied it, you're a lady at heart."

She smiled, a sad twisting of her mouth, and denied his words. "I can't believe that. I've known all along how…what you thought of me. You've never let me tell you…" She shook her head. "And now I no longer want to. It doesn't matter any more."

"Tell me what?" he asked. "About the men?" His jaw was taut, his eyes becoming dark with an anger he did not try to conceal. "What good would that have done, Lily? That part of your life is behind you. You needn't dwell on it."

She turned aside, her heart aching as though it would be torn asunder in her chest. The valise she'd carried into this house was against the wall, and she lifted it to the bed, sorting through its contents and then adding the nightgown that lay across the quilt. Her shawl, the gift Morgan had given her only days before was on the back of the chair and she lifted it, folding it carefully before she added it to the contents.

"I should leave this with you, I suppose," she said. "But I might need its warmth before I get home." She closed the bag and then looked toward the window. "I think the sheriff and his men have finished up out there," she told him. "You ought to go out and see if we need to do anything else before I leave."

Morgan strode to the window and bent to look outside. "I'll be right back," he said shortly. "Don't move your little fanny from this room, do you hear me, Lily?"

She was silent, unwilling to lie to him, and only watched as he walked into the kitchen and then out onto the porch. She heard his voice, that strong, deep tone that was identifiable even though she could not see him. No doubt, she'd hear those husky inflections in her dreams for all the nights to come, she thought. And then she bent her head, allowing the tears to fall unhindered.

He was sorry he'd married her. She was nothing but a burden, a woman he'd taken on and now needed to be shed of. Not that he'd said as much, but she was aware of his aversion to her past, knew deep in her heart that he would never be able to get beyond the memories of what she had been. She could not ask that of him, she decided.

Better that she leave him now, before the bonds between them bound her any tighter to him. Already she had fallen captive to the man, felt the first, tentative bloom of love in her breast. He was all she'd ever wanted, and yet could never own. The window on the far side of the room beckoned and she went to it, opening it wide and crawling through it to the ground below. Her bag was lifted readily and she set off at a fast clip, heading for the trees that offered shelter just a hundred yards or so to the west.

If she hurried, she would be able to reach them before Morgan found her missing.

"You'll have to come into town, sign some papers and file a report," Caine told Morgan. They watched as the two men were loaded on to a pair of Sam's horses, two who seemed willing to take the burden across their backs. The wounded man groaned and muttered harsh curses at the men who handled him, and for his efforts was given no solace. Only the presence of a rough bandage on his shoulder protected him from the jolting of the horse that carried him.

"That's about it," Caine said. He nodded toward the house. "Is your woman all right?"

Morgan nodded. "She will be. She didn't take well to using that gun I borrowed for her. I'll return it when we get to town. Probably not till later today. I think she's going to want to rest a bit." And perhaps he could make his position clear, he thought. Persuade her that their marriage could be dissolved with honor, could leave her unharmed, once he escorted her home to the safety of her family.

A man with his background had no business being involved in a marriage. Even though he thought to end his association with the government and find another way to earn his living, he still carried with him memories that would stain him forever. Lily was deserving of more than he could offer her.

He watched as the men rode off, Caine trotting his horse ahead to lead the line of riders. And then Morgan sat on the edge of the porch, feeling his way through the words Lily had spoken to him. Was she right? Had he condemned her for her past? Was he using his own sins to make a case against the marriage they'd entered into?

He stood and stepped up onto the porch, entering the door quietly. They needed to hash this thing out. *He* needed to know the facts after all, needed to hear her story, whether or not it was palatable. There certainly wasn't any cloud of righteousness hanging over his own head. He'd been involved too long in the business of death and deception to claim clean hands.

"Lily?" He stood in the middle of the small kitchen and called her name. The silence was ominous, but then he hadn't really expected her to reply. She was no doubt huddled on the bed or, perhaps, knowing her as he did, she might be ready to face him with all guns blazing. He grinned at that thought. At least she wasn't armed. He'd taken her weapon and placed it on the kitchen table earlier.

The bedroom door was ajar and he pushed it open. A tattered curtain blew in the breeze from the window on the far side of the room. A room that was empty.

"Lily!" He leaned from the window and looked at the field, the grasses growing in abundance, the trees that formed its western border. And he knew. Without the shadow of a doubt, he knew that she'd run. He looked behind him and scanned the room. Her bag was gone, a conclusion he'd already reached.

Now to find her.

He rode a mare he found in the pasture. Green-broken to saddle, she allowed him on her back, only tossing her head at the bit before she obeyed the nudging of his heels and the reins against her neck. She was tall, her legs muscular, her forehead broad. Darkening with sweat as she carried him across the field, she settled down as they neared the stand of trees.

Morgan pulled the mare to a halt, and called again. "Lily? Come on back." It was futile, as he'd known it would be and he entered the tall trees with care, looking down for a trace of the woman he sought. The branches were broken there, to his right, and he followed the faint marks of her passage, the bent grasses where her feet had trod, the scraping in the soil where her bag had no doubt been dragged past a fallen tree.

He circled the obstacle, continuing in silence, hearing the song of birds overhead and the chatter of squirrels, disturbed by his presence. She couldn't have more than a fifteen-minute lead, he decided, and if he kept on her trail, he'd find her within the hour. It was over thirty minutes later when he came out on the far side of the woods, and saw to his dismay that the road curved closely to the trees. Small footprints were clear in the dirt by the double tracks and then vanished.

She'd gotten a ride. Someone had reined in their horses here and picked her up. Not that it was unheard of for a man to stop his wagon and take on a passenger. But in this case, Morgan could only hope that it was a local farmer who had offered passage. The thought of Lily in the hands of a man who might harm her made Morgan's flesh crawl. He thought of the gun he carried, of the gun on the kitchen table he'd taken from her grasp, and wished fervently that he'd left it with her.

He set off in pursuit, the horse's sides becoming covered with foam as she fought the rider who bested her in the struggle they were engaged in. Morgan was a man used to recalcitrant animals, and though the mare tested him at every turn, he kept a steady pace as he followed the tracks toward town.

''Thank you,'' Lily said nicely as she climbed from the farm wagon. She lifted her valise from the back and waved at the man who'd offered a ride. If she went all the way to Sand Creek, Morgan would be after her in no time flat.

So she'd chosen to leave the Good Samaritan she'd flagged down, here where the woods provided cover for her flight, and she might find a friendly farmer's wife to offer her shelter.

The sun was no longer high in the sky, the afternoon coming on rapidly as she approached a farmhouse at the end of a narrow lane. A dog barked shrilly at her approach and she halted, holding her valise before her, in case he should attack. Instead, he circled her, his tail wagging as if he would herd her toward the house. She walked onward and the dog finally took up his place beside her, looking up with his tongue hanging from the side of his mouth.

A woman stepped from the doorway, her hand lifted to shield her eyes and watched as Lily approached. "What are you doin' all alone out here?" she asked, a frown well in place. "A woman alone's got no business wanderin' around the country."

"I know that," Lily admitted, pausing to allow the woman time to look her over. "I need a place to stay for a day or so. Can I sleep in your barn?"

"Ain't much out there to sleep on," the woman said. She turned and opened the screened door behind her. "You'd do better to come on inside." An impatient look back toward Lily provided the impetus to nudge her forward. The kitchen was warm, the scent coming from the stove was succulent, and Lily heard her stomach growl loudly.

"Sounds to me like you could use a bite to eat," her hostess said bluntly. "When was the last time you put food in your mouth?"

"Early this morning." Not that she'd eaten much, only a piece of toasted bread and coffee to wash it down with. The soup beans and corn bread had been left in the barn, and she almost smiled as she thought of the look on Sam

Blair's face when he discovered them there on his return home.

"Well, come on over here and sit," the woman said. "I'm Agnes Morley. My man's out in the field, and he'll be back before long for his supper. No reason why you can't have yours now, if you want."

"All right." Sitting at the table, she watched as the woman filled a plate from a kettle on the stove.

"It's just stew," Agnes said, "but I make a right tasty meal when I put my mind to it." She went to a dresser against the wall and gathered up a loaf of bread and a dish with butter beneath a glass dome. The bread was sliced quickly and she placed a generous portion on Lily's plate. "I baked this noontime. That's still a little warm."

The butter proved her right, melting into the coarsely grained bread, and Lily bit into it, the flavor making her smile with appreciation. "It's wonderful," she said. "I've always wanted to be able to bake bread like this. I'm good at biscuits, but I thought bread might be beyond my skills."

"Nothing to it," Agnes said stoutly. "Anybody who can take a decent pan of biscuits out of the oven can tackle bread dough." She sat down across from Lily and leaned her elbows on the table. "Now, you want to tell me who you're runnin' from?"

Lily bowed her head, concentrating on the stew before her. She lifted a bit of potato and a bite of meat to her mouth and chewed for a moment. "What makes you think I'm on the run?" she asked after a moment, then lifted her gaze to meet the knowing look Agnes offered.

"Any woman looks like you, all alone and walkin', is trottin' off from some man, somewhere," Agnes surmised.

"Maybe," Lily admitted. "But I won't be here long. Maybe just sleep in the barn till tomorrow."

"I already told you that barn ain't fit to sleep in. Especially not a woman like you." Agnes rose and poured two cups of coffee from the pot on the stove. "You look like the kind who likes cream in her coffee," she said.

"I can take it either way," Lily said. "If there's cream, I'll have some."

Agnes placed a pitcher on the table. "I kept some out when I churned this morning. My man likes it on his apple tart."

"You baked apple tarts?" Lily asked, then blushed as she recognized the tone of longing that tinged her words.

"Yeah, I did," Agnes said smugly. "Best you ever ate, I'll warrant. I've got a mess of dried apples left from last year, down in the fruit cellar. I manage to keep the mice away by hangin' them up in bags from the ceiling."

And wasn't that a lovely thought. Lily forced a smile to her lips. "I'll wait and have mine later, too," she said. "As it is, I feel guilty eating the food you cooked for your husband."

"Fat chance of that," Agnes said. "I always make plenty. Sometimes we have folks drop by." She leaned back in her chair and assumed a casual posture. "Don't suppose anyone will be lookin' to find you here, will they?"

"I doubt it," Lily said. "How far are you from town?"

"Sand Creek? Not far. Once in a while the sheriff comes by to let us know what's goin' on hereabout. Haven't seen him for a week or so though. Last I heard, he was hot on the trail of some fellas tryin' to rook folks out of their property. We been watchin' out pretty close, but from what Caine said, they're only buyin' up land closer to the river, where the road runs."

"I heard that some rich men up north are planning to put a railroad through here," Lily said.

"Well, whoever's been causin' trouble, I think Caine will keep it under control. He's a good man."

Lily agreed silently with the woman's assessment, and in a few moments had eaten the last of the stew on her plate. "Thanks," she said, the single word sincere in its meaning. "I was hungrier than I thought."

"I got an extra bed," Agnes said. "Take your bag on into the second room back there and take a nap, why don't you?"

The thought was tempting, and Lily managed to fight the allure of the woman's offer for less than a minute. "All right," she said. "I believe I will."

The bed was a bit lumpy, but the pillow was soft and cushioned her head, tempting her to close her eyes. It wasn't until the sun was low in the west that she awoke, her ears attuned to the sound of men's voices in the kitchen just beyond where she lay.

"...a pretty woman, dark hair and traveling on foot."

Lily sat upright, her heart pounding, her throat almost closing in terror. If the voice she heard wasn't that of the lawman from Sand Creek, it would be a small wonder. And if he wasn't describing her, she'd be ready to admit to another miracle. Not that she'd ever considered herself pretty, but there were enough looks from men cast in her direction to give her the knowledge that she was not hard to look at.

"Haven't seen anybody like that," Agnes said loudly. "What you want her for, Sheriff? Is she in trouble of some sort?"

"No, not really. Just that her husband is looking for her. He's pretty well frantic, worrying about her. She's been gone since right after noontime."

"Hmm..." Agnes mused. "Was he harsh with her? Why would a woman leave a man who was treatin' her right?"

"Any man as worried as Morgan is right now thinks pretty highly of his woman, to my way of thinking," Caine said firmly. "He's out scouring the countryside. He's afraid she's been hurt or someone might be holding her."

"I doubt it. There's not many folks hereabouts who'd take advantage of a woman alone," Agnes said.

Lily heard the scrape of a chair against the floor, and then Caine's voice sounded from farther away. "Well, if you see her, tell her her husband's wanting to know that she's all right." There was a long pause, and then Caine spoke again, his voice lower as if he hesitated to admit his doubts.

"You sure you haven't seen her, Mrs. Morley?" And then silence met her ears as Lily strained to hear the reply. "All right," Caine said quietly. "Just remember, give her a message if you see her."

"I'll do that," Agnes said. The sound of another man's voice meshed with Caine's as if the two men walked outdoors together, and Lily stood back from the door, hesitant to face the woman in the kitchen. She didn't have long to wait. The bedroom door opened fully and Agnes stood before her.

"I kinda thought you heard that," she said. "I wasn't too far off, was I, *Lily?*"

"He told you my name?" she asked.

"Yeah. Said a man named Gage Morgan was out lookin' for his wife, Lily. And I figured right off she was hidin' out in my spare bedroom."

"Why didn't you tell him I was here?"

"If you'd wanted him to know, I suspect you could have come on out and told him yourself," Agnes said bluntly. "When you didn't, I figured you didn't want to be found."

"Thank you." She turned away and found her valise. "I won't stay any longer, Agnes. I won't put you in the position of lying to protect me."

"Well, if you go trottin' out there right now, my husband is gonna see you and he'll probably take off after

Caine and let him know you're here. I'd say you better stick around till morning." She paused and eyed Lily closely. "Unless you're havin' second thoughts about runnin' off."

"Second and third," Lily admitted. "But I think it's for the best."

And that was how she came to tell Agnes her story. Alone in the kitchen, they shared more coffee, and Lily found the words rolling from her lips, offering details to another person that she'd thought never to share with anyone in her lifetime. Certainly more than she'd ever told Morgan. "I couldn't stay with him, not when I realized he was trying very carefully to back off from our agreement," she said, wiping her tears on the third square of cotton fabric Agnes had offered.

"Why don't you give *him* the choice? Not that I'm one to be giving advice, you understand," the woman said quickly. "But he cares about you, Lily. Did he ever hurt you? Take advantage of you? Other than takin' you to bed, I mean. And that's what men are prone to do, you know. Even a good man, like Gage Morgan seems to be." She hesitated a moment and then rephrased her words. "Especially a man like him."

Her head tilted to one side and she grinned knowingly. "He sounds like a real humdinger to me."

Lily could not conceal the smile that greeted Agnes's summation of him. "He is," she admitted.

"Then why don't you go find him and let him make things right between you?"

"I told you," Lily said. "He thinks I've been with more men than you can shake a stick at. And he doesn't want to hear the truth." She paused and looked out the window where darkness was falling across the horizon. "He doesn't *want* to care for me."

"I think he already does," Agnes surmised. "And I think you oughta give him the chance to prove it."

"I don't want you in trouble with your husband," Lily said, dubious over the plan they'd hatched, right after breakfast. Unaware of her presence in his house, Agnes's husband had headed to the barn, leaving the women to put the plot in motion.

"I told you, Jeremiah doesn't tie any strings on me, girl. When I told him I was takin' the buggy to town, he just gave me a wave and told me to leave him some food on the back of the stove."

"But you're probably not going to be back tonight," Lily protested. "And he'll be expecting you by dark, I'm sure. If you're taking me south farther than Sand Creek, you'll do well to get back by tomorrow."

"And when I tell him what I did, he'll come close to having a hissy," Agnes agreed. "But it'll be too late then to do much about it, won't it? Besides, if we get rolling, I may be back here right soon after dark. This standin' around talkin' about it ain't doing any good so far as I can see."

Lily nodded in reluctant agreement and tossed her valise into the buggy. She climbed to the seat and shoved the bag beneath it, stowing it out of the way. In moments, Agnes was picking up the reins, and the horse was setting off at a fast trot toward town.

A trail headed south before they reached Sand Creek, a seldom used branch of the main road, and Agnes turned the buggy there. "This cuts off a few miles, and we won't be going through town this way," she explained. "I know a woman who lives almost at the edge of Brightmoor, down the river a ways. I bet she'll put you up for the night and then see to it you get into town tomorrow."

"She won't mind?" Lily asked, her stomach churning

as she recognized the finality of the choices she'd made. The chances of Morgan finding her now were pretty slim, unless he dragged out that old Wanted poster and showed it around.

"I don't think so," Agnes said cheerfully, snapping the reins over the mare's back and urging the animal into a faster pace.

Her prediction was accurate, and Lily found herself ensconced in another unfamiliar bed when night fell. Agnes was well on her way home, shushing Lily's fears that she would not arrive there before dark.

"I've been taking care of myself for a lot of years," Agnes had said, hugging Lily to her bosom. She held her off and looked her over with a gimlet eye. "You think about what I told you, understand? That man ain't all bad. I'll guarantee it."

Sleep came quickly, Lily worn out from the past days' experiences. When morning arrived, her hostess provided her with breakfast and pointed her toward town, waving her a last farewell as Lily trod the lane that led from the farmhouse.

Brightmoor was a fanciful name for a town, she decided, as she passed a freshly painted sign that announced the town limits. Larger than Sand Creek, it was the county seat, according to the sign, and held a wide arrangement of stores and establishments. Though her pocket held little ready cash, Lily felt certain she could always sell her silver combs, should the need arise. And with that in mind, she strolled past the general store, casting a quick look inside its doors, and then to the hotel.

"How much for a room?" she asked the desk clerk.

He looked down at the single tapestry bag she carried, and she thought his brow lifted in a haughty fashion. "You're traveling alone?" he asked, and at her nod of agreement, he looked long and hard at the registry in front of him.

"I don't think I have any single rooms left," he said after a moment and with another disapproving survey of her dusty apparel and her lack of hat and gloves.

"Well, I'll just bet you *do*." The voice came from behind Lily, the syllables spoken in well-remembered tones, and she turned in surprise. May Kettering stood there, her smile wide, her arms held open in welcome.

"Miss Kettering? Is this a friend of yours?" the desk clerk said, his tone having taken a decidedly respectful touch. "I'm certain we can make arrangements for her to stay with us, if you'll just give me a minute." Clearly flustered, he fussed with the keys hanging on the wall and as he turned back, one in hand, May waved a hand at him in dismissal as she gathered Lily to her bosom.

"Miss Devereaux will be staying with me," she said firmly, her chin held at an arrogant angle, her arm around Lily's waist.

Either unwilling or unable to dispute her assertion, the young man only nodded his head as May gripped her guest firmly by her elbow, towing her toward the side staircase that centered the lobby.

"Don't drag your feet, girl," she said glibly, smiling with a flash of white teeth that could have charmed a whole roomful of men, and as Lily well remembered, often had. They reached the top of the stairs and May continued down the hallway before them, leaving Lily barely a moment to catch her breath.

"What are you doing here?" May asked quietly, fitting her key into the door that proclaimed it as Room 201. The door opened readily and she shoved Lily over the threshold before her, following her inside with a glance down the hall.

"What are you doing running around by yourself?" she

asked, her all-encompassing look taking in Lily's general air of dishevelment. "Where's Morgan?"

"Probably out looking for me," she answered. "I left him a couple of days ago. The job I'd agreed to do was finished, and I decided it was best if I went the rest of the way on my own."

"You can't be flitting from one place to the next that way," May told her firmly. "I saw a poster with your name on it down at the jailhouse yesterday."

"What were you doing there?" Lily asked. "Checking up on me?" And then she lifted a hand in apology. "Forget I said that, May. I didn't mean it." She looked toward the empty bed and her shoulders slumped. "I'm just so tired, I don't know what to do next."

"Well, I can figure that out for you easy enough," May said quickly. "You put your body down there and take a nap while I figure out what we're gonna do with you. I'm thinking the best place for you is right out in plain sight, Lily. Let me work on this while you rest a bit, and then we'll make plans."

Without a word of argument, Lily stumbled to the bed. It wasn't so much that she was physically tired, she thought wearily, but the fact that she'd about run out of steam. The impetus that had spurred her on that first day on her own was fast wearing thin, and she thought of Morgan's strength with a sense of longing.

The pillow was soft and she curled on her side, falling asleep before May left the room. Outside the window, twilight fell and the noise from the saloon across the street became too loud to ignore. Lily rose from the bed and stood at the window. Horses lined up at the hitching rail in front of the saloon, and men slapped the swinging doors with regularity. Most of them entered, adding to the level of racket that spoke of customers enjoying their leisure.

"You awake?" May came in the door, closing it behind

her and leaning against the solid surface. "I'm heading out to the saloon," she said. "Thought I'd check on you first, make sure you were all right."

"I'm fine," Lily assured her. She waved a hand at the window. "The saloon across the street?" she asked. "Is that where you're singing now?"

"Busiest place in town," May said with a smile of satisfaction. "Boss there pays good money, and it sure beats riding on that damn boat, up and down the river. Thought I'd never get on dry land again there for a while."

"I'm surprised Ham Scott let you go so easily," Lily said, and then rued her words as May's mouth tightened.

"He was pushing for more than I was willing to offer," May said. "The man was talkin' marriage. Can you believe that?"

"There's no insult in that," Lily told her quietly.

"I'll not tie myself to any man, not ever again," May said stoutly. "I walked off that boat and never looked back. Just a few days ago, in fact. Heard about this place from one of the gamblers, said they were lookin' for a singer." Her grin was pleased. "They like me, even if they don't understand half of what I sing to them. The boss man says I give his place *class*. How about that?"

"I agree with the boss man," Lily told her. "You're too good for a place like this, May. I'll bet you sang on stage sometime or another, didn't you?"

Her eyes darkened as May considered the query, and then she nodded. "I did, until I got lost in the bottom of a bottle. I let a man too close and he walked away. Left me hanging high and dry, and, fool that I was, I thought I could forget him. I did, too—every time I got drunk, that booze washed him right out of my mind."

"So you quit the stage?" Lily prompted.

"Or the stage quit me," May said, her smile weary.

"Ham Scott gave me a job and it worked out all right for a time. Then I decided I was better off moving on."

She shook herself and glanced out the window. "I'd better be shakin' a leg, Lily. It's past time for me to appear over there. I want you to stay inside tonight. Don't show your face downstairs. I'll send up a boy with some supper for you, but you stay out of sight. I've got an idea that might hold water. We'll talk later."

And with that she was gone.

Chapter Twelve

"Is that a wig?" Lily asked, stunned as May brought a carefully wrapped package from her trunk. The golden hair was wavy, flowing across May's arm as she held it aloft.

"Most expensive piece of hair I've ever owned," she said, touching it with reverence. "I wouldn't offer it to just anybody, Lily. But I think you'd do well to give it a try, see how it looks on you."

"Whatever for?" Lily asked, perplexed, even as the idea of placing the hairpiece atop her head intrigued her. Everyone in her family had dark hair, and she'd known a bit of envy as other girls in the community flaunted their golden locks in her face. Mama had always said that *her* daughter had the looks of a French woman, daring and attractive to menfolk.

Lily had certainly proved that right, the day the Yankee colonel had taken one look and decided she would be his for the taking. Back then, when he'd made his offer, and she'd traded her body for the plantation home's safety, she'd wished futilely that she was homely, that her slender form and curving bosom had not drawn his eye.

She shunned the memory, knowing it brought only pain.

"You want me to put it on?" she asked May. "Do you think no one will recognize me with blond hair?"

"That's the idea," May returned. "I talked to the boss at the saloon, told him a friend of mine was here and I offered to share the stage with you. He's willing to pay if the fellas like you, Lily. And he doesn't expect any more from you than that. Just sing a little and let the men listen to you."

"May, I can't begin to compete with your talent," Lily said quietly. "I'd feel out of place."

"Well," May began, settling in the chair. "I thought maybe we could do a couple of the duets we worked on while you were singing for Ham Scott. If you'd like to try, it would earn you some money, maybe set you up a little better, so you're not scraping the bottom of the barrel when you hit the road again."

"You'd do that for me?" Lily asked, feeling hot tears spring to her eyes.

"Sure I would, honey. You've got a strong voice and you make me sound good. Can't beat that combination with a big stick. Want to give it a try?"

The wig changed her appearance. There was no doubt that her golden complexion belonged to a dark-haired woman, but paired with the hair that May wound into an intricate fashion, Lily's features became exotic, and she viewed herself in the mirror with pleasure. Her dark eyes sparkled and her cheeks were flushed.

"I really look different, don't I?" she asked, leaning forward to twitch at a curl that drooped over her forehead.

"Don't mess with that," May said sharply, swatting at Lily's hand. "I just got it to where it looks like a man has touched you and tousled you a bit. Makes you appear more approachable."

"All right," Lily said agreeably. "If approachable is what you want, then I'm willing to give it a shot."

"Come on," May told her. "We'll walk over and see the piano player. He oughta be out of bed by now. We'll see if he can play for us."

The man was only too willing to provide the accompaniment May asked for, and with a few stops and starts as they refreshed their memories, the two women put together a credible performance. The owner of the saloon sat at a table in the corner and watched, a cigar held in his hand, the smoke rising to hover over his head.

"That's fine, May," he said finally as their impromptu concert came to an end. "What does this young lady plan on wearing? The dress she has on…" His voice trailed off as he scanned Lily's cotton frock. "Well, it just won't make it alongside of what you wear."

"I know that," May said soothingly. "I've got something she can get into. She's got a lot less meat on her bones, but I've got a needle and thread. We'll put it together by tonight." She waited expectantly as the man's cigar flared, and then took his nod as approval of her scheme.

"Come on, Lily. We've got work to do," she said in an undertone, leading the way from the saloon, across the street to the hotel. "Let's have a bite to eat first before we decide on which dress you're gonna wear."

The restaurant in the hotel was plain but the food served was more than adequate. Lily was reminded of the meal Morgan had purchased for them on another evening, and recalled the night they'd spent in that small hotel. She'd felt warm and safe with him.

Now she knew a moment of uncertainty, thinking of the hours ahead, when she would once more be on display to a roomful of men. May would look after her, of that there was no doubt, and for a few days she might be able to sing enough to earn hard cash. Cash enough to pay for the rest of her journey, so that sleeping in a barn would not be an issue.

"Eat up," May said, watching as Lily pushed the meat and vegetables around on her plate. "My stuff will never fit you if you don't get some meat on your bones, girl."

Lily smiled at the gibe and set to with a show of enthusiasm, cleaning her plate with an effort, but in truth enjoying the meal. "All right, now let's see what I can do with a needle and thread," she told May, lifting her coffee cup to her lips as the waitress cleared away their plates.

The choice lay among three gowns, and Lily had no hesitation in choosing one of brilliant blue, a satin creation that clung to her form. She put it on inside out and turned in a slow circle as May pinned the areas that would need to be adjusted for fit. Then she stood still as May's head tilted to one side and she offered Lily a complete once-over.

"That thing looks better on you than it ever did on me," May said, brushing the skirt so that it fell more smoothly. "Come on and get out of it, so we can get busy with the hem, and then work on the darts."

Lily had done her share of sewing as a young girl, her mother firmly believing that a lady should always know how to keep her family well dressed. Although they had servants in the house to do the mending and ironing, Lily had followed her mother's example and learned how to do fine stitching. Today that knowledge came in handy, and May's lifted eyebrow silently expressed her admiration for Lily's talent.

The dress was finished before suppertime, and placed across the bed, so that it would not wrinkle. Lily donned the wig again before they went down to the dining room for a quick meal, and then it was time to dress for work.

She stood before the oval mirror in the corner of May's room and viewed her image. If she hadn't known the details of her features, been so familiar with her eyes and mouth and the lines of her figure, she'd not have recognized the female who looked back at her from the looking glass.

"Is that really me?" The soft murmur of disbelief made May laugh aloud as she stood behind Lily. Her smile was triumphant as she tweaked a few curls in place and then ordered Lily to turn to face her while she applied a touch of rouge to the ridge of her high cheekbones.

"You'll do, I'd say," May said, pronouncing her work a triumph. "No one would ever recognize you as the woman on a Wanted poster, Lily." She held out a lacy shawl she'd dug from her stash of fancy apparel and placed it over the blue dress. "Let's go before you get cold feet."

The evening hours went by in a rush, Lily singing three times with May, hearing the men clap and cheer and stamp their feet in approval as the two women left the stage and retired to a table in a corner. That they were the object of stares and obvious speculation from the men in the audience was apparent, but May ignored the sidelong glances and Lily took her cue from the more experienced woman.

"They won't bother you, once they figure out that you're not looking for a man," May told her. "Just smile real nice, kinda like you like them all and can't pick out one to concentrate on."

And so Lily did just that, allowing her smile to touch faces that responded to the gentle curl of her lips, to the songs she sang, her voice harmonizing with May's higher tones. She sang as she'd never sung before, as if the disguise she wore gave her permission to leave her fears behind, allowing the full range of emotion she felt to be expressed in the music she sang.

It was well after midnight when they crossed the street to the hotel again, and Lily was weary as she took off the blue gown and spread it over a chair so that it would not be wrinkled. Carefully, she removed her golden hair, and watched as May placed it on tissue paper. Then without another word she slid her nightgown over her head and stretched out on the bed.

"You did well," May said, lifting the sheet to lie beside her. "This is going to work out just fine, Lily."

"Do you think it's safe to use my right name?" Lily asked.

"I only said you were Lily," May told her. "Even the boss doesn't know your last name. I told him you go by *Lily,* and that's it."

"I think they liked me." It was a contented murmur as Lily closed her eyes, and the last thing she heard was May's chuckle as sleep overtook her.

"Nope, I haven't seen that woman," the lawman said, looking down at the torn bit of paper. "Where'd you get the picture anyway?" He looked up suspiciously at Morgan. "It's not from a poster, is it?"

"Just a drawing of my wife," Morgan said, skirting the query neatly.

"Well, if she's in Brightmoor, I sure haven't seen her," the sheriff said firmly. "I don't know of anyone new in town, and I'd certainly recognize that face if I'd seen it. She's a real beauty, ain't she?"

"Yeah," Morgan agreed. "Unforgettable, you could say."

He'd hoped for some sign of recognition in the man's face. Surely this must be the route Lily would travel, the most direct way to where she'd said her home was located. He didn't have any specifics as to the name of the plantation where she'd been raised, but it made sense that she'd stick to the well-traveled roads to get there. A woman alone was more vulnerable away from civilization.

And if he'd had his head on straight, she wouldn't be in

this fix right now, he reminded himself. He shouldn't have trusted her to stay put, should have realized that she was primed to run from him. He'd pushed her almost to the limit of her endurance. Lily had offered herself to him and he'd taken the gift, and then trampled her feelings with his angry words. Words he'd give much to recall.

I shouldn't have married you. He'd made the statement so glibly, and even though he regretted the words spoken, it was the truth. Using Lily for his own pleasure was unforgivable. She was too soft, too fine…too vulnerable for a man like Gage Morgan to run roughshod over.

"I'll stay at the hotel for tonight," he told the lawman. "If you should remember anything, get in touch with me there."

"Yes, sir," the man told him. It wasn't often he had a government man come through town, Morgan realized. His willingness to oblige was obvious.

The hotel had vacant rooms and Morgan paid for one for the night, then went into the dining room and settled at a table. The waitress eyed him with an inviting smile, but he was oblivious to her, only ordering the special, then sitting back to wait for its arrival before him. It was fried chicken, and immediately he thought of the chicken he'd eaten with Lily, remembered her distaste at the thought of killing the creature.

He ate slowly, his mind recalling the hours and days spent with the woman he'd married. And now he was on her trail—and for what? To ship her off home to her family and walk away again? He'd told her that after this mess was over, he'd take care of the colonel in New York City. And that promise had totally slipped his mind.

He smiled. He'd use that as a lure, once he found her. Surely Lily would want to stick around long enough to gain some small revenge on the man who'd brought such sadness to her life. He was totally selfish when it came to

Lily, he decided, plotting ways to entangle her once again in his web.

Leaving a folded bill on the table, he made his way to the staircase and then up to his room. The brass numbers on the door designated it as Room 203, and he slid the key into the lock with ease. From the next room to his, from behind the closed door, a woman laughed, a joyous sound that made him flinch. Probably with a man, he thought. And then entered his own room, closing the door behind himself.

A low murmur of voices touched his ear and he recognized the tones as feminine, and then listened as the women left the room, closing the door with an audible sound and walking down the uncarpeted hallway, their shoes tapping softly as they moved along toward the staircase.

He lowered himself to the bed, looked to where the obliging desk clerk had left his bag in the corner, and in moments had closed his eyes. The sound of music roused him, but he pulled the second pillow over his head and went back to sleep. He could have used a drink, he supposed, though he rarely indulged. But it would be a long day tomorrow and sitting in a saloon went against his grain.

The sound of soft voices roused him again and he surmised it was the women from the next room, returning from a night of revelry. He smiled, remembering the last time he'd heard women performing in a saloon, and the thought of Lily's slender throat and the firm lines of her breasts beneath the dress she wore on that long-ago night. The memory brought him fully awake and he rolled to his back and looked up at the ceiling.

The voices stilled and he heard the creak of the bed in the next room. Apparently there wasn't a man there, just two women, perhaps ladies of the night, though neither of them seemed to be plying their trade tonight. Maybe he'd stay one more day, ask around a bit more before he headed south again. His eyelids drooped and he fell asleep, still wearing his clothes, uncaring of his comfort.

He rose early and ate, then spent the day visiting nearby farmers and stopping to ask the shopkeepers if they'd seen Lily. Receiving only a denial of any knowledge of the woman, he grew discouraged with his quest, though most of the folks he spoke with appeared to genuinely want to help. With no reason to dispute their memories, he conceded defeat and returned to the hotel.

A bath and a session with the razor made him feel measurably better, and he donned clean clothing before he set out for a meal.

"You goin' to hear the new singers at the saloon?" the waitress asked him as she poured his second cup of coffee.

"Hadn't planned on it," he said easily, leaning back to give her room. And then his ear perked up. "*New* singers?" he asked.

"Well, one of them has been there for a few days, the other one just started last night. I heard from several of my customers that they're a real treat to the eyes, if you know what I mean," she said with a grin. "And they can sing right well, too."

"Might be a good idea to drop by," Morgan said easily, drawn to the idea, even as a glimmer of hope came to life within him.

He finished his coffee and strolled across the street, entering the saloon and seeking out a spot where he might nurse a drink and watch the comings and goings at his leisure. A scantily dressed woman brought him a drink, and then at his smile and the subtle shake of his head, she deserted his table for richer pickings.

Morgan sipped reflectively at the whiskey, noting it was well watered, and appreciating the fact. He didn't want to stand a chance of drinking in a strange town and putting himself at the mercy of any stray man who might be looking for an easy touch. It was fully dark outside when the piano player changed the rhythm of his music and began a song that rang a bell in Morgan's mind.

Not the usual fare for a saloon, he thought, and then sat upright as he recognized the woman who stepped from the wings of the tiny stage to saunter toward the paying customers.

May Kettering. I'll be damned. He leaned back in his chair and listened as her voice rose in the melody that he'd recognized. Around him, the men quieted as she began, and by the time she'd gotten to the end, her audience was hushed, watching her avidly, as if they had been charmed by the music.

"Not the usual thing for a saloon, is it?" The owner of the bar stood behind Morgan's table and issued his query in an undertone. "I didn't think it would go over, but damn if the customers don't like her high-falutin' stuff."

"I've heard her before," Morgan ventured, his gaze fixed on May as she dropped her head in recognition of the applause. "She's got a good voice."

"Wait till you hear her singin' with the other one."

"Other one?" Morgan fought the urge to turn around, controlled the slight tremble of his fingers as he raised the whiskey to lips that had suddenly gone dry. "You've got two singers?"

"Yeah, some friend of May's. Came into town a couple of days ago. Kinda shy, doesn't say much, but she can charm the birds out of the trees with that smile. They make a good pair, both of them with yellow hair and voices that make you think good thoughts." He laughed, as if embarrassed by his own words, and walked away, leaving Morgan with his glass halfway to his lips.

Both of them with yellow hair. That let Lily out of the

picture, he decided, settling his glass back on the table. He watched as May sang again, and then heard her speak, bringing instantaneous stillness to the men assembled before her.

"Y'all liked my friend last night, and she's agreed to sing with me again. She won't be in town long, so you'd better listen to her while you've got the chance." She turned to the wing offstage, and with an expansive gesture of one hand, announced the woman who stepped upon the boards and allowed a smile to touch her lips.

"Here's Lily, gentlemen." Her voice became sultry as she lowered its volume and whispered a suggestion they seemed to embrace. "Enjoy."

The music from the piano changed tempo and the chords rolled from beneath the player's fingers in an introduction that the two women greeted with a smile, May tossing a kiss from her fingertips to the piano player, as if he pleased her enormously. And then they sang.

If Morgan hadn't heard them before, hadn't known the effect they would have on the men sitting before them, he'd have been enthralled. As it was he simply fumed. His Lily was all dolled up in a blond wig, her lovely dark hair covered by a piece of froufrou that was no doubt from May's collection.

And yet, even the golden hair, curled and arranged with seduction in mind, could not detract from the shimmering beauty that radiated from Lily's face as she sang. She met May's gaze and smiled, looked out at the audience and offered a wave of her hand as she opened her arms to include them in her music. She sang with innocence, with an appreciation for the words and music that made Morgan's heart ache, even as his anger built to enormous proportions.

The women left the stage, and the sound level rose as the men went back to their card-playing and general carousing. Morgan settled back in his dark corner and nursed another drink along as the night spun past. In less than an hour the two women reappeared and sang again to uproarious applause. And still Morgan waited, his patience endless, it seemed.

Just before midnight they stepped onto the stage again, and he noted faint circles under Lily's eyes, as if she had been too long away from a decent bed. Damn, he was ready to wring her neck. Fool woman. It was a wonder she'd made it this far without coming to harm. The music interrupted his thoughts and he listened throughout their final session. May blew kisses to the crowd, promising to see them the next evening, and then they were gone.

Morgan knew exactly where they were heading.

"You go on up," May told Lily. "I'm going to talk to the hotel manager if I can locate him. I need to find out if my room is available for the next week or so. If he gives me a decent price, I'll just stay on here. Otherwise I'll find another place to hang my hat."

"All right." Lily gripped the banister firmly and trod the steps, her feet weary from long hours in the high-heeled shoes she wore. Even though she'd worn such extravagant bits of leather on the riverboat, she was still unaccustomed to having her toes pinched in such narrow footwear.

The hallway on the second floor was lit by flickering kerosene lamps set on the wall at intervals, and she bent to slide the room key into the lock, turning the handle and stepping into the darkness. She closed the door and leaned against it for a moment. With a sigh, she pushed away from the firm support and made her way to the bedside table where a candle was provided for light. A box of matches lay beside it, and she fumbled as she struck one and held it to the candle wick. The flare of light made her blink and she turned from the flickering candle, only to see a dark form rise from the chair in the corner of the room.

"Hello, Lily."

It was to her credit that she didn't faint or scream and stumble toward the door. The truth was, she decided wearily, nothing Morgan ever did had the power to surprise her. Even appearing in this room at midnight, when she'd been dead certain he had no notion of her whereabouts.

She refused to cringe, ignored the escape offered by the nearby door, and only lifted her chin as if she would face head-on whatever the man had in mind. "What are you doing here?" she asked quietly, barely able to speak over the staccato beat of her heart. Her voice trembled a bit, yet that was to be expected after the long evening she'd spent, sitting in a closet-size room, as far from the smoke-filled saloon as she could get in between shows.

Tired didn't begin to describe her condition, but she fought the yearning to lie down on the bed and seek solace in sleep. With Morgan so close, she didn't stand a chance of peaceful slumber, at least not until he'd gotten his pound of flesh and walked away.

He was angry. She focused on his face, on the taut line of his mouth, the flaring of his nostrils and the dark, silvered glow of gray eyes gone pale and dangerous. His hands were fisted against his hips, and a holstered gun hung low against his right thigh. No, she decided with a small shake of her head, he wasn't about to shoot her. But Morgan could inflict hurt just by opening his mouth and speaking harsh words that would flay her heart wide open.

He was silent, refusing to answer her, as if it were beneath his dignity to reply to so foolish a query. Instead he attacked, turning her words against her. "I think that's a question you'd better answer," he told her.

She lifted her narrow shoulders in a shrug, trying for nonchalance, knowing she failed miserably. Not at her best in a quarrel, Lily was even more at a disadvantage when up against a formidable foe such as Gage Morgan. "What does it matter?" she whispered, slumping finally to the edge of the bed, too bone weary to remain upright. "Just go away, Morgan," she said. "You made yourself clear a couple of days ago, and I saved you the trouble of toting me home."

"I told you to stay put," he reminded her harshly. "You skinned out that window and took off like a scared rabbit. What's the matter, Lily? Couldn't you play the game to the end?"

She looked down at her hands, noting the trembling of fingers and aware of the chill that had penetrated her whole body. The lure of her pillow seemed almost too great to ignore and she turned her head, lifting her hand to halt his words. "Stop it," she said softly. "You needn't feel any responsibility for me. Just go away and let me be."

The door opened with a squeak of its hinges and May stepped inside. It was to her credit that she halted there just beyond the threshold, and even more telling that she didn't appear surprised by the appearance of the man who'd invaded the privacy of her room.

"Well, as I live and breathe," she said in lilting tones. "If it isn't Gage Morgan, come to collect his bride." She cocked her head and looked him over in an assessing manner. "She is your bride, isn't she, Morgan? You married her, didn't you?"

"You know I did, May." As if his patience did not extend to include her, he glared in May's direction and waved his hand at the door behind her. "Now, get yourself into the room next door." He drew the key from his pocket and tossed it to her.

With a knowing look in his direction and a quick movement of her hand she caught it midair and tossed it on her palm. "We're neighbors?" she asked. "How long you been there?"

"It doesn't matter," he said dismissively. "Long enough to find my wife." He turned the shimmering glare on her in full force. "Leave us alone, May."

"If you hurt her…" The pause was long as May's eyes flared with promise. "She's not ready for your anger, Morgan. She's—" her voice softened and she spoke a single word that he accepted with a nod of agreement "—fragile."

It was an apt description, Lily decided. For she felt that she might shatter like a crystal glass if Morgan touched her now, that she might break into a million pieces if her heart didn't stop the irregular cadence it had assumed in her breast.

She closed her eyes tightly, shutting out the sight of May abandoning her, hearing the click of the latch as the door closed and then the sound of Morgan's feet as he crossed to the door and set the lock. Behind her eyelids, red and silver lightning bolts flashed, and tears threatened to escape.

She would not cry, would not give him the satisfaction of seeing her fear and sorrow, for they were indeed both parts of her at this moment. Fear of what tomorrow might bring, and sorrow at the mess she'd made of her life and his, making that foolish demand of him. *The next time I run off with a man, he'll have to marry me first….*

"Stand up, Lily," he said, lifting her hands from her lap and pulling her to her feet. He frowned. "Your fingers are like ice. What's wrong?" He held her hands in one of his, and she felt the heat radiate from his flesh to hers and was tempted to curl her whole body against his even as her fingers sought the refuge he offered within the depths of his palm.

"I can't cope with you tonight, Morgan," she said wearily. "I just can't."

He turned her from him, and she felt the familiar touch of his hands as he undid the buttons that ran down her spine. "You don't have to cope with me, Lily. You only have to lie down on that bed and let me remind you that you're my wife." Her dress fell to the floor and he reached in front of her waist to undo the ties of her petticoat. It followed the dress, circling her feet and she was left in the scant covering of her shift and the stockings that were held up above her knees by blue satin garters.

"Pretty spiffy," he said, angling a look at the slender length of her legs. "May's?"

She nodded, aware of the chill that pebbled her flesh, bringing her breasts to a state of readiness for his touch. And how she could yearn for this man's hands on her skin was something she found foreign to her nature. She'd spent months shrinking from masculine admiration, knowing it was bent on her with an intent that had nothing to do with love, only that of a man's need to subdue and conquer her body.

Now the warmth of *this* man's gaze, even cloaked in anger as it was, had the power to make her tremble. She looked up at him, saw herself reflected in his eyes, and hated what she had become.

Morgan's woman. A woman he'd bought with a five-dollar gold piece from Ham Scott, and then legally made his wife with another handed to the young preacher who'd had them repeat their vows.

"Take that wig off," he said. "Why you thought you should cover up your hair with that monstrosity is beyond me." His look scorned the golden curls and waves and she felt a flare of anger. Nothing to match his, but a shred of rebellion that fought his decree.

"I like it," she said. "I hid behind it, and forgot how much standing up in front of an audience scares me."

"You don't need to hide behind anything, Lily." He reached for the hairpiece as she shrank from his touch.

"No, I'll do it," she said hastily. "May paid a pretty penny for this thing. I won't let you ruin it."

"All right," he agreed, impatient as she carefully removed the golden cap and placed it on the table.

"I need to unpin my hair. It needs to be brushed," she said in an attempt to gain time, to turn his anger aside. But he would not have it.

His hands touched her shoulders, his fingers tightened and he shook her, just once, but with the strength of a man fueled by a fury he barely held in check. "Damn you, Lily." He lifted her from the circle of clothing and placed her roughly on the bed, then bent to pick up the blue satin and tossed it across the room.

"Don't, Morgan. It'll be wrinkled," she whispered, watching as the fabric sailed through the air and then settled into a crumpled mass near the door.

"You won't be wearing it again," he muttered, his hands busy at his belt, undoing it and then dropping the holstered gun he wore to the floor. His shirt was stripped from him, and then he sat on the edge of the bed to remove his boots and stockings. When he rose, she saw the opened front of his trousers and the unmistakable bulge that spoke of a desire he obviously had no intention of denying.

"Don't do this to me," she said, turning her head away, as if she could make his jutting manhood disappear by denying its existence.

She heard the rustle of trousers as they fell from his body, felt the giving of the mattress as he sank onto the edge of the bed, and then knew the weight of his arm as it circled her waist and turned her to face him. "I've chased you over hell's half acre, Lily. Do you think I'll let you get away from me tonight?''

''We decided—''

He hushed her by the simple expedient of placing his palm over her mouth. ''*You* decided,'' he said harshly. ''You took it on yourself to run off instead of staying and sorting things out between us. You're a coward, Lily Morgan. I know I said I shouldn't have married you, and I still feel the same way. But the truth is, we *did* get married, and I won't walk away from it until I've done everything I promised.''

She was silent, her mind desperately searching, seeking out the promises he spoke of. ''I don't know what you're talking about,'' she said, and then she recalled. *If that's what you want, Lily. If you still feel the same way when this is over, I'll take you home.*

She spoke the words of his parole aloud. ''If you're talking about taking me home, I don't need you for that. I can get there under my own steam.''

''For now, it doesn't matter,'' he told her, dismissing the issue as he bent to her lips and claimed them in a rough kiss that took her breath. His lips were firm against hers, and then they opened a bit and she felt the damp touch of his tongue against her mouth.

''Don't.'' Lily squirmed against him and turned her face away. ''I don't want you to do this,'' she said, knowing the words for a lie. And yet, if she gave in to his seduction, she would not have gained anything by her flight. She'd be back in the same mess, with a man who represented the greatest danger of her life.

''Right this minute, I don't care what you want, Lily,'' he told her, his voice a low growl that made her shiver. His lips took hers again and he allowed no escape, one hand holding her head, his fingers entwined in her curls, his palm firm against her nape.

Chapter Thirteen

It wasn't true. He *did* care, but not for one moment could Morgan remove himself and walk away from her. Not now while his blood ran hot in his veins and his need for the woman he held within his grasp was so urgent. If she fought him—that was a different thing altogether, he decided. He would not force any woman. Certainly Lily deserved more than that from him.

But persuasion might influence her, and on that thought, he pinned his hopes. His mouth plundered where it would, first her lips, those lush, tender morsels of flesh that lured him, and then to the pure, clean line of her throat, where her heart pounded in an erratic drumming that pleased him.

She was soft, sweet, her skin resilient beneath his mouth, and he tasted her, knowing she was willing for this moment to be submissive to his touch. Her shift provided little cover for her breasts and he slid it over one shoulder, exposing the feminine lines he craved to explore. Lily's gaze was fixed on his face, her mouth swollen from his kiss as a whisper from her lips spoke his name.

In the grip of a need he refused to deny, he ripped the garment from her body, lifting himself as he tore it asunder and watched as the fabric shredded at his touch.

"Gage?" That whisper was bewildered now, and she pressed her hands against his chest for a moment, then brought her arms up to cover the breasts he had revealed to his sight. "Gage? What are you doing?" Her dark eyes held a mixture of surprise and fear, and he felt primal satisfaction flood him.

Good. She should be in awe of him, of the anger he held in check. Yet he yearned to see passion light her gaze, knew a moment of regret that he had frightened her.

"I like to hear you speak my name," he murmured, his gaze touching her hands and arms, shaking his head, and rejecting those pitiful attempts she'd made to hide the curves of her breasts from his sight. He grasped her wrists, holding them both in one palm and lifting them from her bosom, only to carry them over her head, where he pinned them to her pillow.

"Say it again, Lily," he told her, aware that his voice rasped the words, making them a command.

"Gage. Please," she whispered again. And still she did not resist, only blushed as he looked down at the lush curves he'd revealed.

"Yes, *please*," he said, repeating her plea, allowing a smile to touch his lips. "I'm going to please us both tonight, Lily. You won't call out or let May know, will you? You're too much a lady to upset the whole hotel, aren't you?" He focused on her throat, on the curls that drooped from loosened pins, and she shot him a look from eyes that defied his words—and then relented as she acknowledged the truth he spoke.

"You know I won't," she said quietly after a moment, and twisted her head away again.

"Because you want me, Lily?" His fingers sought out the rest of the metal fastenings and tugged them from the knot she'd formed atop her head. Her hair spilled from its restraints and he spread it across her pillow with his free hand.

"You turn me into someone I don't even know," she said, meeting his gaze with a stubborn glare.

His hand spread wide as curls wrapped around his fingers and clung to his skin. "That's better," he murmured, intent on the clean fragrance that rose to his nostrils. Part of it was Lily herself, for he recognized her aroma, would have known it if she stood amid a roomful of other women and he was wearing a blindfold.

He'd caught the scent of her that first night, when she'd been beside him at the ship's rail and his arm had slid possessively around her waist. Invading his senses, it had succeeded over the next days in turning him from a cool, calculating agent into a man who had lied and bullied her into this alliance. And now he must live with what he had become at her hands.

"You are what you are, Lily. I only bring forth in you the passion you've held captive for so long." He felt her fists clenching in his grasp and knew a moment of shame that he bound her so. "If I let your hands free, will you behave yourself?" he asked, bending to nuzzle against her shoulder.

"Behave myself?" Her words were incredulous. "I'm lying beneath a man who seems intent on forcing me to his will, and you think I need to *behave* myself?"

"Yeah, just long enough for me to talk you into this," he said, recognizing the slaking of his anger as she softened beneath him.

"I asked you not to do this, Gage," she said, repeating her plea. "I want you to go away and leave me be, while I can still walk away from you. I can make enough money to get home with from here. I don't need you."

And perhaps she didn't, he thought, lifting his head to look into her dark gaze. "But I need *you*," he said. "I need you to stay with me long enough to redeem myself, sweetheart. I told you I'd settle up the account with your Yankee colonel, and I said I'd see to it that you got home. You're gonna stay with me long enough to see both those things accomplished.''

"And in the meantime…what? You'll sleep with me?'' As he watched, the color rose again in her cheeks and she sighed. "Let my hands go. I won't fight you.''

"That's not good enough,'' he told her. "I want you more than just willing, Lily. I want you to meet me halfway.''

"I don't know how to do that,'' she whispered, shaking her head. And even as she denied his need, he released her hands. She caught a deep breath, then left them curled into fists, there where they lay. "I wanted you, Gage. From the beginning, even though I knew what you thought of me. I thought that you might be able to make me feel clean again, rid me of the memories.''

"And did I?'' he asked, pleased that she would admit to it. "Did you enjoy what we shared, Lily?''

She nodded and closed her eyes, as if her confession would not allow her to meet his gaze. "You know I did.''

He bent to her and his lips were soft, begging entrance to the sweetness of her mouth and she acquiesced, opening to him. If he'd thought to be a gentleman, that idea vanished with the first touch of her tongue against his. If he'd considered a slow seduction of her senses, it became impossible as she tilted her head, the better to receive his caress.

And when her knees rose to flank his thighs and he felt the heat of her softness against his throbbing flesh, he knew a moment of triumph that seemed almost primitive—his heart leaping within his chest as if it would not be contained.

There would be no cringing from his touch, no crying

in protest of his loving. Lily was too honest a woman to deny him that which her body cried out for; and for that inborn integrity that ruled her very life, he was thankful.

His movements were slow, Morgan forcing himself to a pace that would bring Lily the greatest pleasure. Her arousal was all-important to him, he realized, craving the knowledge that she would not regret this time of loving. And in that he succeeded. She clung to him, whispered his name in a trembling voice and moved at his bidding.

Fingers, lips, and the whole of his body accomplished what he'd set out to do, and when he finally took his ease within her, she wrapped her arms around him and once more he heard his voice murmured on a sigh.

Her face burrowed against his shoulder and she trembled—long, slow shimmers of delight she made no effort to deny. "Gage…" His name came more easily now, it seemed, and she spoke it again, a hushed syllable that resonated in his breast.

He turned with her in his arms, adjusting her for her comfort and clasped her to himself. His hands moved slowly, touching the soft skin, fingers threading through her curls and waves to hold her head still for his kisses. And yet it was not enough.

"I've missed you, Lily," he said quietly, admitting the truth aloud as he faced it for the first time. "You're under my skin. I've never known a woman like you, and God willing, I'll never have to look any further than this to find some degree of peace in my life."

She was silent in his arms and he felt his patience ebb, admitting to himself that he needed a reassurance of sorts that her own feelings were involved in this marriage. She'd let him know that he was important to her; and yet, perhaps that was only for her own reasons. After all, he'd promised to take her home.

Maybe…just maybe, if he was able to free her from the

stigma of her past, if he could seek out and avenge her innocence—the ways and means of which evaded him—perhaps she would find herself willing to accept their marriage.

"Are you awake?" he asked quietly, pressing his lips against her forehead, gathering for himself a measure of that elusive peace he'd found in her arms. "Are you all right, Lily?" Concern laced his words as he nudged her head back, the better to see her face.

Behind him, the candle burned low, but he blessed its presence as Lily's eyes opened to reveal a warmth he welcomed. No hint of anger marred the dark depths, no trace of apprehension remained to taint him with the brush of savagery. Even though he'd sensed a primitive force within himself that had brought him to the brink of force, he'd subdued it with the knowledge that to damage Lily in that way would be unforgivable—both for himself and her.

"I'm all right," she whispered. "Just feeling as though I've been swept away in a whirlwind, I think." She lifted her hand to his face and touched his mouth with her index finger, brushing it across his lips. "I think I wish you weren't nearly so accomplished at this, Gage. You make me feel like a rank amateur."

But we both know that you're not. Unbidden, the words sprang to his mind, and he forced them from his thoughts, aware that those things he did not know should not matter. He had secrets of his own, and Lily had not asked for them to be revealed. On the other hand, she'd made the offer to tell him of her past, and he'd denied her the catharsis such revelations might provide for her peace of mind.

"You obviously haven't had a whole lot of pleasure at the hands of any other man," he said, smiling into her eyes. "And that's just fine with me." She seemed almost untried, unused to accepting the joys inherent in a man's touch, and he wondered that she had not found passion before this.

"What will you do, Morgan?" she asked softly. "I've told May I'd be here for a few days. I can't break my word."

"Let's talk about that tomorrow," he told her, a glimmer of a plan forming in his mind. "I'm going to visit the sheriff to see if an idea of mine will bear fruit." He slid his hand to rest against her waist, pulling her close, luxuriating in the cushion of breasts against his chest as she snuggled in his arms.

"Go to sleep, Lily. I need some rest. It wore me out watching you up on that stage, ready to shoot the first man who reached for you. I don't think I want to spend my evenings doing guard duty." And his words were not an untruth, he found, for he'd been poised to leap to his feet, had he thought for a second that she was in peril. Watching her perform during the days to come might prove to be beyond his endurance, but there was no possibility of his missing a moment of the time she spent on that stage.

The sheriff shook his head at Morgan's story, sorting through his own stash of posters until he found one with Lily's picture on it. It was folded and pushed to the back of a drawer, and he looked a bit sheepish, Morgan decided, as he displayed it. "I didn't put it up," he said. "Couldn't imagine a woman who looks like that tryin' to kill a man."

"You knew when I showed you her picture, didn't you?" Morgan asked. "You'd already seen it then."

The sheriff shrugged. "Yup, I saw it all right." He folded it again and Morgan reached to take it from his hand.

"I want you to notify the authorities in New York that this woman is here, in your town."

"She's here? In Brightmoor?" Surprise lit the lawman's

face as he heard Morgan's request. "I sure haven't seen a dark-haired beauty like this anywhere around here."

"She's been wearing a blond wig," Morgan said, leaning back in his chair. "Stop by the Red Dog Saloon tonight and you'll be able to hear her sing."

"That gal's name is May," the sheriff said. "I was in there three or four days ago and took a gander. She don't look anything like this woman."

"You haven't heard that May has a friend working with her now?"

"And the friend is Yvonne Devereaux?" The sheriff mangled the name, reading it from the poster as if he were unfamiliar with the French pronunciation.

"The very one," Morgan said. "And to make it even more of a problem situation, the lady is my wife." He ignored the grin on the lawman's face as he laid out the plan he'd formed.

"I'll send a wire, today—this morning, in fact. It goes to this here fella?" he asked, pointing to the name in small print on the poster. "Here where it says she tried to kill Colonel Stanley Weston? What is he, some kind of war hero?"

"He's the worst sort of man," Morgan said angrily, his nonchalance gone as if a wall had appeared at the mention of the colonel's name. "I can't tell you much for right now. Just notify the authorities, and I'm sure they'll get in touch with the good colonel."

"Whatever you say, Mr. Morgan. I try to get along with any government men who pass this way. Don't see very many, but I'll warrant you're the one they're talkin' about upriver a ways. What do you know about the land scam some shysters were pulling on farmers up there?"

"That was my last job for Washington," Morgan said. "For right now, I'm on a break. I thought I'd spend a few days here, until we hear back from New York, anyway. Let's just see what kind of a fuss we can stir up.''

The lawman's eyes lit with good humor. ''We've been downright dull around here lately, Mr. Morgan. It sounds to me like things are gonna perk up.'' He stood up behind his desk and extended a hand in Morgan's direction. ''I'll get working on this right now.''

It took Lily over an hour to get the wrinkles out of the blue dress and even longer to tame May's mood to something approaching acceptance of Morgan's behavior.

''He tossed this thing across the room, did he?'' May sputtered. ''He didn't have to work long hours to earn money for a wardrobe, I can see that.'' Her fingers were deft as she plopped on a chair and worked at the wig, watching as Lily ironed the dress on a makeshift board.

''And I suppose he sweet-talked you into bed, didn't he?'' she asked, shooting a look of censure in Lily's direction. ''That man has a silver tongue, that's for certain. But, you know, he never gave any of the girls on the boat a tumble, just sat there and counted stacks of money every time he played poker. He's a gambler, sure enough.''

''He hasn't run out of hard cash,'' Lily said. ''He doesn't spend a lot, but he seems to have enough to go around.'' She halted in her task, the iron in midair. ''I'd give a lot to know more about him, but he doesn't say much. I don't even know where his family is from.''

''Somewhere in the South,'' May surmised. ''You can catch a little touch of a drawl in some of his words.''

''Could be Texas,'' Lily said. And then she looked at the iron she held. ''This thing is cooled off too much to do any good.'' Another iron sat on a metal stand, wrapped in a thick towel, and Lily picked it up, fastening the handle atop its weight, and touched the dress gingerly with it.

''I'll take the other one back downstairs to heat,'' May

offered, placing the wig on the dresser and taking the cooled iron with her as she headed for the door. It opened beneath her hand, and Morgan looked at her from the other side of the threshold.

"You going somewhere?" he asked, and Lily looked up at the sound of his voice. She felt a shiver run the length of her spine as he shot her a glance. His eyes gleamed with an appraisal she could not mistake, and his mouth curved in a smile that suggested his thoughts were of the night before.

He held the door for May's departure and she sailed past him, calling back to Lily over her shoulder. "I'll be a while, waiting for this to heat. Might even pick up something to eat while I'm at it."

Morgan closed the door behind himself and leaned against it. His fingers touched the key that rested in the lock and he was tempted to turn it, assuring privacy. Then, with another look in Lily's direction, he changed his mind. She was ironing that dress as if her life depended on getting every wrinkle out of the skirt. And was probably calling him a whole slew of names as she worked at it.

"I'm sorry I wrinkled the dress," he said politely, walking across the room toward her, assuming a hat-in-hand approach.

She looked up and her eyebrow lifted, a cynical gesture if ever he'd seen one. "Are you?" Bending back to the task, she spoke her mind, and he was left in the position of being obliging. "I'm going to sing at the Red Dog tonight, Morgan."

"We're back to *Morgan,* are we?" he asked. "I kinda liked it when you called me by my name."

"I noticed," she said sharply. "And if you'd like that sort of thing to continue, you'd do well to loosen the reins where I'm concerned." She looked up at him, her jaw set in a determined way, and he smothered a smile.

The woman didn't realize she was playing right into his hand, with her announcement of spending her evenings at the Red Dog Saloon. There wasn't a chance of taking the wig away from her, but he could unmask her when the time came. For now, he'd just sit and watch, and wait.

"I mean it, Morgan," she said. "I've made a promise, and I always do as I've said. I hope we aren't going to have trouble over this."

He shook his head. "Nope. Not as far as I'm concerned. I can use a few days off, anyway. I'll just take it easy and wait for you to wear yourself out singing. I figure a week oughta do it, don't you?"

"You're not going to interfere?" she asked dubiously.

"Not unless you call it interfering for me to watch you from a table in the back. I won't let you go over there without me being in the background, Lily. That's where I draw the line."

She looked at him for a moment, then bent to her work, stretching the blue satin over the board with a pressing cloth against the fabric. "I won't argue about that," she said after a moment. "But I have a notion that you've got something up your sleeve. You've given in too easily."

"Just trying to be a gentleman, sweetheart." He moved to stand behind her and bent to kiss the nape of her neck. Her hair was already pinned in a knot, with only a few tendrils falling from the arrangement as she worked. Her skin was damp, just a bit salty tasting to his tongue, and he felt the urge to tug her away from the ironing board and talk her into spending a half hour on the bed with him.

Only the thought of May finding the door locked in the middle of the afternoon and surmising what was going on behind it halted his yearning. It wouldn't bother him, but he'd lay odds that Lily would be embarrassed. He nudged her ear with his nose and whispered a promise there, words that made her turn her head abruptly in his direction.

"Behave yourself," she said sharply. "We will do no such thing, Gage Morgan."

"There," he said with a grin. "You *said* it, sweetheart. Now just call me Gage one more time and I'll leave you alone for a while."

"Well, be sure you come back in time for a late supper, *Gage*," she said. "I'll need some food to fortify me for the evening."

And with that he had to be satisfied, knowing that he'd assured himself of at least a week in which to work out the plan that was still forming in his mind.

The next days passed slowly, with Morgan doing as he'd said, unobtrusively watching from the back of the saloon while May and Lily performed for the ever increasing number of men who gathered nightly to hear the rare treat. If he felt a twinge of jealousy touch him on occasion, he brushed it aside, recognizing that Lily's beauty would always draw the eye of a discerning male, no matter where she was.

On top of that, she spent her nights in his bed, and as soon as the third show of the evening came to an end, he hustled her across the street to the hotel and placed her there. May laughed at his impatience, fluttering her hand at him as he attempted to escort her to her room, telling him that a woman alone could always use a friendly drink once the night was over. Because the saloon owner kept a watchful eye on her, Morgan just nodded agreeably and then took Lily in hand.

She seemed amused, he thought, by his protective streak, became haughty when she decided his possessiveness was out of control, his long fingers tugging the front of her dress a bit higher, lest she show more curves than he deemed appropriate. But when he rubbed her sore feet, she only crooned, sighing and wiggling contentedly on the bed.

"I think you're spoiled," he told her the fifth night of their stay in Brightmoor. "I wonder if any other man would sit around all evening watching his woman display herself on a stage and then spend an hour making her comfortable."

She yawned and stretched, her body showing to advantage beneath the new shift he'd bought her at the general store. As though his attentions had made her more secure, more certain of her place in his life, she'd blossomed beneath his care.

He watched as her toes curled, then stretched wide, noted the high arch of her foot and the slim line of her ankle. "You've got pretty feet," he said, lifting the subject under discussion high enough for it to catch the candle-glow. His movement also exposed a bit more of her legs than she realized, and he grinned as he enjoyed eyeing the slender curves displayed below the hem of the muslin shift.

"On top of that, you smell good," he said softly. He bent to brush her foot with his nose and she laughed. The look he shot her made her laugh even louder. "You're supposed to be taking this seriously," he said, one long finger reaching to tickle the sole of her foot. She twitched it from his grasp and sat upright in the bed.

"You may think you're getting away with something, but you're not," she told him, her eyes half-closed, her mouth twitching a bit as if she held some secret to herself, and was relishing his seductive techniques.

"I beg your pardon," he said with just the right degree of arrogance to aggravate her, and she was quick to respond.

"I've got your number, Gage Morgan. You think giving me a foot rub is going to earn you—"

He bent closer and snatched a kiss. "Well, I'm aware it won't earn me a place in heaven, but I was thinking more about an hour of paradise right here and now."

Her eyes filled with quick tears and he reached for her, pulling her into his lap. "What did I say? Whatever it was, I'm sorry, Lily."

She shook her head, and wiped furiously at her eyes. "Don't, Morgan. I'm just being foolish and I'd appreciate it if you'd ignore me."

He held her firmly, tilting her face to his. "Not a chance, lady."

"All right," she said capitulating after a few moments. "I was just thinking that this seems like we've stolen a few days, and I'm afraid when we leave here, our time together will…" She sobbed once and Morgan felt a rush of emotion fill his chest.

"This doesn't have to be the end of it, Lily. That's up to you. You know what I told you, and I refuse to tie any strings to our agreement. You'll be the one to make the final decision when we leave here."

"I don't want to talk about it now," she said, straightening on his lap and searching beneath her pillow for the handkerchief she'd left there. "Are you still sorry we got married?" she asked, wiping the tears from her cheeks.

"I'm sorry I forced you into this mess," he said quietly. "I told you last week that we shouldn't have made such an agreement. But—" he ran his finger down her cheek and she stilled, as she were frozen in place "—but, the fact remains that we did, Lily. And I think we're going to have to live with it."

"What are you planning?" she asked. "I've seen you talking with the sheriff twice now, and I know there's something afoot."

He was hesitant, unwilling to frighten her with the threat of Stanley Weston. Yet, he couldn't let her be shocked and floundering if the man showed up in town. And if he had the good colonel figured out, he was even now on his way to Brightmoor. A man with the capabilities to frighten Lily, as the good colonel had, must have committed foul acts against the woman.

No wonder she'd gone after him with a poker. Morgan would warrant that the man would be seeking his revenge on a personal level. And Morgan was ready for him.

"I've got a couple of things in place," he said.

"Now that told me a whole lot," she retorted with a narrowed look that amused him. Lily was at her best when she was riled.

"You'll find out as soon as it works out, sweetheart," he told her. "You just do what you've been doing, and I'll handle the rest of the plan."

Her sigh was weary as she nodded and curled against his chest. "All right, Morgan. There's no arguing with you. You're the most stubborn man I've ever known."

"Is that bad?" he asked, brushing her hair from her forehead before he bent to kiss her there. He leaned her head back over his arm and she lay quiescent in his embrace. "You know I don't take my promises lightly, Lily. I always keep my word. When I said I'd take care of you, I meant it. No one will hurt you."

"You can't fight the law, Gage," she whispered. "If Weston holds a warrant for my arrest, your hands will be tied."

"Don't you believe it," he said, his gaze turning cold. He knew he looked formidable when angered, and her words filled him with a wrath he could not contain. "I'll do whatever it takes to protect you. The good colonel is dealing with an underhanded man here. I've learned all the tricks, Lily, and I'm willing to use them to my advantage."

"Well, I'm awfully glad you're not out after my hide," she said, sliding from his lap and crawling between the sheets.

"Ah, but I am," he said lightly. "In every possible way.

I'll take you on the bed, in a chair or against the wall, Lily. Any way I can get you."

"The wall?" She glanced at the far side of the room as if trying to imagine such a thing, and then she smiled. "You're teasing me, aren't you? Trying to embarrass me."

"Shall I show you how it can be done?" he asked, leaning over her to rub his nose against hers, whispering the words as a seduction. And almost succeeded in his quest. But she shook her head after a moment, just when he'd thought he stood a chance of success.

"I suppose I believe you," she admitted, "but the wall and a chair are not my first choices."

"Well, one of these days, I'll demonstrate, Lily," he promised. "And remember, I always keep my word."

She looked askance at the chair that sat so innocently on the other side of the room, and then turned her gaze on him again. "Maybe the chair," she whispered. "I think I can figure out how you might arrange for that to work." And then she shook her head. "But not the wall."

She was an innocent, he decided. A woman who'd been used, but not courted. A female whose body had been exploited by men who were uncaring of her—who had used her for their own pleasure.

And in that moment, he swore silently he would not join that line of male creatures who had combined to hurt his Lily. She would know no harm at his hands.

Chapter Fourteen

"Morgan!" The sheriff's voice called to him as Gage left the hotel, and he looked up to see the lawman hustling across the road, a scrap of paper clutched in his hand.

"Just got a wire from New York. Our fella is on his way. Left four days ago. In fact, I can't figure out why he's not here already, as fast as those trains travel." He looked down at his paper. "It says he'll take a riverboat from Saint Louis and arrive here posthaste. Whatever that means."

Morgan smiled, a wolfish grin of satisfaction twisting his mouth. "It means he's in a big hurry to catch up with my wife."

"If he's carrying a warrant with him, we may be in trouble," the sheriff warned him. "I can't disobey the law. You know that."

"Does a warrant from New York hold water in your jurisdiction?"

"Hmm…I may have to ask a judge about that. I could always find a reason to check up on it for a couple of days, couldn't I?"

"I'll do it for you," Morgan told him. "I know some of the ins and outs of these things. There's always a way to block an opponent.'' He felt a surge of anger at what the good Yankee colonel had done to Lily. ''I'd give a whole lot to get my hands on him.'' And then he shot the sheriff a look that silently promised his cooperation. ''I know what you're thinking,'' he said. ''But I'll stay within the law, no matter what.''

''I want you to keep a sharp eye out today,'' the lawman said. ''I'll check the dock and find out when the next riverboat will be going past. If the fella is headed here, he'll no doubt come ashore in a skiff, if the captain isn't planning on stopping here.''

The sound of music from the Red Dog carried in the air as Morgan left the jailhouse and cut across the street. He took a hasty detour and pushed the doors open, halting on the threshold to allow his eyes time to adjust to the dim interior of the saloon.

''Come on in,'' May's voice called from near the piano. ''Lily's not here right now, but she'd ought to be on her way over. We've got a couple of new songs to put together for tonight's shows.'' She eyed him as he approached. ''Everything all right?''

Morgan forced a smile and nodded, tipping his hat back a bit. ''Right as rain,'' he said. ''Just biding my time while Lily fulfills her bargain with you.''

May cut him a narrowed look. ''Somehow I don't think that's quite the whole story, Morgan. I'd say you've got something on the back burner and it's convenient for you to play this game a little longer.''

He feigned surprise. ''Why, May. Surely you're not doubting my word?''

She shook her head at his antics. ''You're a smooth talker from way back, Gage Morgan. You may have Lily bamboozled, but you don't fool me.''

''Lily's not *bamboozled*,'' a voice said from behind him,

and Morgan turned his head to cast an admiring look on his wife.

"I didn't think you were." He held out a hand and she stepped closer to his side, her eyes holding questions.

"Anything I need to know?" she asked, and at the shake of his head, she spoke again, her words a quiet warning. "Don't set me up, Morgan."

If there was any one thing that merited his full concern, it was Lily's well-being. His arm slid to encircle her waist and he turned her aside, leading her to where the bar stretched the length of the saloon, empty now except for the bar keep arranging bottles twenty feet distant.

"You're part of my plan, Lily. You have to be for this to work right. But you surely know I'll protect you. With my life—if it comes to that."

"But still, you aren't going to let me know ahead of time, are you?" she asked. "I'm to be kept in the dark?"

"Lily." He turned her to face him, uncaring of the audience who watched. If May and her piano-playing friend wanted to be voyeurs, so be it. "Can you find it in yourself to trust me?" He bent to touch her lips with his, a soft kiss of persuasion, asking nothing more than her confidence in the bridge of faith he'd been attempting to form between them. He watched as her eyes opened, their dark depths still wary.

"I trust you," she said quietly. "Insofar as you're able, you'll protect me, Morgan. I know that. I just don't know how far your arm reaches."

"I don't, either," he retorted, honesty alive in his words. "But, we'll soon find out, if my hunch is right." He released her from his embrace and turned her toward May. "Go on and practice your music, Lily. I'll be around."

"There's a riverboat passing this way in the morning," the sheriff said, his voice an undertone as he stood behind

Morgan's chair. The saloon was filled with men who'd come to town on a Saturday night to celebrate the end of their workweek, giving them a chance to spend their earnings. Yet no one was near enough to overhear the sheriff's words.

"Will you be out there watching for it?" Morgan asked him. "Should I take an early walk to the dock?"

"If you like. If our friend is on this boat, he won't know you. He'll be intent on finding me."

"I suspect he'll head for the jailhouse."

"Yeah. I may beat him to the punch, if I'm on the lookout for him." He was silent then, but Morgan felt his presence there. And then the chair next to him was pulled out from the table and occupied. "She's quite a woman, ain't she?"

"I think so." And wasn't that an understatement, Morgan thought with a smile. If he'd ever wondered about the eventual end to his bachelorhood, it had never included a woman such as Lily playing a prominent part.

He'd thought of returning one day to Texas, to the family holdings there, to the prosperous ranch his father and brothers ran. The place where he'd paid his dues and earned his first nest egg. The place that had stifled him until he'd fled its restrictions and sought instead a wider field in which to attain independence and a reputation that owed nothing to the family name.

He smiled to himself. Now he was thinking long thoughts about returning home. That's what marriage does to a man, he decided. Makes him think about home and hearth, about settling down with a family. And Lily was just the woman he could envision himself waking up to every morning for the rest of his life.

She sang on stage now, her gaze remaining distant from his, as if she put him from her mind when she performed. Would she be content, should he offer her the sort of existence he had in mind? He listened to the confidence she exuded as her voice rose to harmonize with May's, saw the flash of a dimple in her cheek as she smiled at the men who sat almost literally at her feet.

And knew a moment of jealousy so stark it took his breath. *She's mine.* The words were alive in his head, resounding from his heart and piercing his soul. He would not, could not, ever give up the happiness she brought to him.

As one, the audience rose, clapping and whistling as the two women bowed before the crowd. The song was finished and with its final note Lily and May left the stage. "That's my cue," Morgan said softly, then rose and tilted his hat at an aggressive angle. He meandered carefully toward the side of the room, where three steps fed into the saloon, watching for the door to open, searching for Lily's slender form to appear in the dim light.

She was not long in coming, flashing a smile over her shoulder to something May said, then lifting her blue skirts to descend the stairs. Her eyes took a slow survey of the room and he thought they flickered when she settled her gaze on him. Looking neither right nor left, she wove her way between the tables to where he stood, speaking a word to men who sought her attention, offering a gentle smile that did not encourage her audience to encroach on her person.

"Nice," Morgan said, his gaze sweeping over her as she stood before him.

"Nice music?" she asked, tilting her head, looking up at him through long eyelashes.

"Nice everything," he murmured, taking her hand and lifting it to his lips.

She flushed, a wash of color that spoke of her pleasure, yet her words were teasing. "You're playing the gentleman tonight, Morgan. What brought this on?"

"You seem to bring out the best in me," he said, leading her to the door and out onto the wide porch. "Or the worst, maybe," he added. "I know I'm having a hard time keeping my hands to myself. And I was silently daring every man in that room to wiggle one finger in your direction."

"I've never asked for that sort of attention from men," she told him, waiting for his direction before she stepped off the wooden porch. "I think they look at me differently with this yellow hair on my head."

"I like your own better," he told her sharply. "I'll be glad to be shed of that wig."

She grinned at him. "Me, too. It itches my head. But it seems to give me leave to sing with more…" Her pause was thoughtful and then she spoke slowly. "It's as if I'm a different person up there. Not the Lily Devereaux I was on the riverboat. Certainly not the woman I was when I left home." She looked up at him and her eyes were soft, as if she asked his understanding.

"I'm not that same woman, Morgan. I've been reborn."

"I know that." His arm slid around her waist and he led her toward the hotel. The lights were dim in the lobby, the desk clerk's position empty and only the guard who watched the place at night to wave a hand in their direction as they entered through the wide doors. Morgan nodded a silent greeting and then held Lily's elbow as they crossed the carpeted lobby, then made their way up the stairs to the second floor.

"How much longer, Morgan?" she asked as he unlocked their door.

He would not insult her by a pretense. "Maybe tomorrow," he said. "The sheriff thinks our man may be here on the early boat."

She stepped into the room ahead of him and as he would have lit the candle beside the bed, she halted him, one hand touching his arm. "No light," she whispered. "Just you and me and the darkness for tonight. Please?"

He covered her hand with his and then turned her from him, the better to unbutton her dress and rid her of the clothing she wore. "I aim to please, Miss Lily," he said with a smile, and heard her answering laughter at his words.

The morning boat indeed slowed as it neared Brightmoor, and as the sheriff watched, a small skiff was lowered to the water and two men stepped into it. One of them carried a small valise, the other wore a cap that designated him as an employee of the boat. With steady strokes, he moved the small skiff toward the dock, and in minutes the passenger was discharged and the ferry was on its way back.

Tall, dark-haired and erect, the man looked to be military in his bearing. He adjusted his hat, then picked up his valise and strode from the dock in the direction of the center of town. The sheriff watched the visitor, and then pushed away from the post he'd been leaning on near the dock, and followed at a stroll.

From the hotel another tall figure left the porch and crossed the road and the three men converged in front of the jailhouse. The visitor looked at Morgan, assessing him. "Are you the law here?" he asked, his words crisp, with the twang of New York touching each syllable.

Morgan shook his head. "He's behind you, mister." And had the pleasure of watching as the Yankee turned abruptly to face the sheriff. As if he felt himself surrounded, the stranger glanced back at Morgan and his jaw set in a pugnacious arrangement of bone and flesh. His eyes darkened and his spine assumed an even stiffer position.

"I fear you have me at a disadvantage," he said to Morgan. "Do I know you?"

Morgan shook his head. "You haven't had that pleasure."

His nostrils flared as the visitor recognized the intended jab. And yet he held his temper well, Morgan decided. His hand extended, he introduced himself. "My name is Stanley Weston, of New York City."

Morgan ignored the outstretched hand, unwilling to touch the flesh that had caused Lily's hurt.

With an uplifted brow, Weston turned back to the sheriff. "I think you're the man who sent the wire, aren't you? I've come with a warrant for Yvonne Devereaux's arrest."

"Have you, now?" Rocking on his heels, his thumbs thrust in his trouser's pockets, the sheriff smiled. "How about letting me take a gander at it?"

With suave assurance, Weston reached into the inside pocket of his suit coat, drawing forth an official appearing document. "It's all there in black and white," he said smugly. "The woman tried to kill me, and then she stole some of my mother's jewels."

"Did she, now?" The lawman glanced over the warrant with a cursory look and leveled a sardonic grin in Weston's direction. "You got any proof?"

Stanley Weston lifted a wave of hair from his forehead, revealing an angry-looking scar. "There's where she hit me with a weapon. If it had been a gun, she'd have killed me. Came damn close to it as it was."

"What'd she hit you with?" the sheriff asked, leaning closer to examine the scar.

"A poker." As if he felt chagrined by the revelation, Weston's mouth drew up and he slanted an angry look in Morgan's direction. "Who is this man?" he asked, his tone belligerent, as if he resented the third man's presence. "What does he have to do with this? I thought you would have Miss Devereaux in custody, sir. And now I'm having to assume she's still on the loose.''

''What makes you think she's not sitting in a cell right this minute?'' the lawman asked.

Weston ignored his query. ''You don't seem very concerned with the seriousness of these charges,'' he retorted. ''She tried to kill me. Attempted murder is a serious offense in New York City.''

''Yeah, it is out here, too.'' With a shrug, the lawman glanced at Morgan. ''You know where your wife is, Mr. Morgan?''

''What does his wife have to do with this?'' Weston asked sharply. And then his eyes narrowed as he gave Morgan his full attention. ''Don't tell me you married her?'' His head tipped back and he laughed, an ugly sound if ever Morgan had heard one.

''Well, I hate to tell you this, Mr. Morgan, but you're about to see your wife led away in shackles.'' His smug satisfaction was about all Morgan could stomach.

''And where would you like to lead her off to?'' he asked, aware that his words were adding fuel to the flame of the other man's ire.

''They have a very nice jailhouse in New York,'' Weston said. ''The company isn't much, I understand, but then Yvonne should feel at home there. A lot of women of her caliber live in those cells.''

The sheriff moved, placing himself between the two men, his eyebrows almost meeting over his nose as he pushed the newcomer against the wall of the jailhouse. ''I think you're asking for a whole lot of trouble, mister,'' he said sharply. ''Morgan is a man you don't want to mess with. If you take my advice you'll watch your step.''

''If I hadn't given the sheriff my word to behave myself, you'd be spread-eagled in the middle of the street right now,'' Morgan said, the anger in his voice spelling out the words distinctly. "One of these days, Weston, you'll find yourself—"

"That's enough," the sheriff said harshly. "I think we need to go inside my office and talk about this."

"There's nothing to talk about," Stanley Weston said, his words charged with disdain. "The woman will be leaving here in shackles aboard the next boat heading north. I have the paperwork that gives me the authority to find an escort and see to it she faces a judge."

"An escort?" the sheriff asked, sitting down in his chair and shooting a warning look in Morgan's direction. "What sort of an escort are you talkin' about?"

"I'm sure I can hire a man willing to guard her. There must be a slew of gunmen in a town like this."

"Not one of them would go with you," the sheriff said firmly. "The lady is highly thought of here, and you'd better realize that she's not going anywhere until our judge shows up in a couple of days and takes a look at the paperwork you're so proud of."

"What judge?" Weston asked, his cocky attitude giving way to a frown that drew his mouth down. One hand shoved deeply into his pocket as he eyed the sheriff intently.

"Even a little town like this gets occasional visits from the law, Mr. Weston. Our particular judge is pretty much a country boy at heart. He don't take to city folk much."

Morgan hid a grin as the sheriff expounded in a droll, satirical fashion. The judge for this part of the country was as citified as a man could be. He'd heard much about the man, the most important item being that he was known to be fair and just.

"Well," Weston said, his jaw set, his face reddened with anger. "I want the woman put in a cell until your judge shows up. She'll run if she gets a chance."

"Not while she's got a job to do," Morgan said. "She

doesn't have a need to run from you, Yankee. She's an upstanding citizen of this town.''

''For how long?'' Weston asked suspiciously.

''Long enough,'' the sheriff said quickly. ''And in the meantime, I'd like to see some proof of your claims against Mrs. Morgan. I'm not about to ship her off upriver without having good reason.''

''If you know what's good for you, you'll turn her over to me today,'' Weston told him. He thrust the documents he'd brought with him across the scarred surface of the lawman's desk. ''She pawned my mother's brooch. She was seen leaving the house where she'd tried to kill me, and a friend of mine followed her. He figured she was acting suspiciously and took it on himself to find out what was going on.''

''She pawned jewelry belonging to your mother?'' Morgan spoke the words as a statement of fact, and noted the other man's firm nod.

''Exactly.''

''You have a picture of the jewelry? Proof of some sort?'' the sheriff asked.

''Better than that, I have the brooch itself.'' With a triumphant flourish, Weston drew forth a tissue-wrapped package from his valise and placed it before the sheriff. ''Take a look for yourself,'' he said smugly. ''My friend went into the pawn shop and redeemed it as soon as he decided that Yvonne was up to something suspicious.''

The sheriff unwrapped the piece of jewelry and picked it up, turning it over and examining it closely. ''Looks like real gold to me.''

Weston preened. ''It certainly is. Our family is well-known in New York. My mother has a large collection of precious gems.''

The sheriff looked up, his gaze piercing. ''You sure this

came from your mother's home? What was Mrs. Morgan doing in your mother's house?''

Weston stepped back a bit. ''She wasn't in my mother's home at the time.''

Morgan cleared his throat. ''Maybe we'd better get Lily over here and have her take a look at this thing,'' he said.

''I'll walk over to the hotel with you,'' the sheriff said, snatching his hat from a peg on the wall and guiding his charge toward the door. As if he were a shepherd steering his bellwether ram from danger, he politely removed Morgan from temptation.

''He's lying through his teeth,'' Morgan said grimly as the sheriff took long strides to keep up with his pace.

''Probably. But he's got all the signatures and everything looks official.''

''She's not going anywhere.'' And if he had to, he'd see to it that the scalawag met his end in the peaceful town of Brightmoor, Morgan decided. ''Sending Lily off on a boat with that man is not gonna happen, Sheriff. Not while I own a gun.''

''We're not having a gunfight on the main street. I won't have it.''

''It won't be a fight,'' Morgan asserted, stepping into the hotel lobby. ''He'll be the one stretched out full-length with a hole in him. I'll be the one with the smoking gun.''

''I'd have to arrest you,'' the lawman said with a shake of his head. ''Now, go on up and get your wife, Morgan. I'll wait here.''

Lily pressed the cool cloth against her face, then leaned her head back to wipe it the length of her throat and down her arms. She sighed with pleasure as the damp residue cooled her flesh. Getting dressed for the day was not something she was looking forward to. It was hotter than the dickens, Morgan had said early on this morning. And he'd been right. The dust rose from the street as horses rode past, and Lily thought longingly of rain that would settle the dust and refresh her spirits.

"Lily?" Behind her, Morgan opened the door and stepped inside the room. "I need you to get dressed and come with me, sweetheart."

She turned to him and felt a heavy weight settle on her chest. As if she could scarcely draw breath, she knew a moment of terror such as had never visited her before now. Even the horror of the long trip to New York five years ago had not overwhelmed her to this extent.

"What's wrong?" The words were barely audible, and she felt a chill touch her bare arms and shoulders. The heat of the morning was a thing of the past, as if a cloud had paused over her head, dropping the temperature abruptly.

"Stanley Weston is in town."

She searched Morgan's face for some hint of what she could expect, and found no answers in the unyielding force he exuded. "I see."

"Hell, no you don't," he blurted out. "You look like a woman facing the gallows, Lily. I thought we had this straight last night. I'm with you in this, remember? And that scummy Yankee isn't going to lay a hand on you."

It wasn't an absence of compassion she found in Morgan's gaze but a grim determination that seemed to ooze from his very pores.

"All right. I'll be right with you." She turned to the simple dress she'd pressed yesterday afternoon and slipped it over her head. "Can you button it up for me?"

He moved closer and his hands were warm against her skin, his fingers agile as he matched buttons and button-holes. "All set?" he asked.

"Almost." She picked up her brush and swept her hair back, catching it up in a twisting arrangement atop her head. Six pins held it in place within seconds and she turned to face him. "I'm ready."

They walked together down the wide staircase and Lily got a glimpse of sorrow on the sheriff's face as he looked up at her. It did not bode well for her, she decided, and silently cursed the man who was seeking his revenge. *Damn you.* Almost, she spoke the words aloud, but her upbringing would not allow them to pass her lips in front of the men who accompanied her out the door and across the street.

The man who watched her approach appeared to be seething with impatience as she walked to face him, his mouth thinning as his gaze encompassed her modestly dressed form. "You've come down in the world, Yvonne," he said, as if he jeered her appearance.

"I suspect that depends on your point of view," she answered, even as Morgan touched her arm and drew her close to his side. "I'd say I've improved my living conditions considerably since I was given the position of mistress in your shabby little love nest."

He flushed an unbecoming shade and his hands clenched into fists at her words. "You'll be singing a different tune once I have you under guard and on your way back to face your crimes," Weston said, his tone hateful in Lily's ears.

"Is it a crime for a woman to protect herself?" she asked boldly.

"It's a crime to murder a man in cold blood," he retorted hotly.

"Ah, but you seem very much alive to me."

"Not because you didn't try hard enough to split my head open with that damned poker." His hand swept the covering hair aside for the second time and Yvonne stared mutely at the scar he exhibited.

Not for the world would she admit to the cringing fear that swept her soul as she heard his words of condemnation. "You installed me as a slave," she told him. "You lied to me and abused me, Colonel. It took a long while, but when the time came I realized I had no choice but to escape."

"I never lied," he said, denying her charge. "I took you with me, away from that hellhole you called home, and you thanked me for it more than once."

"The only thing I thanked you for was the fact that you didn't burn my family's house and all of our belongings in it. You and your drunken men," she said, spitting the words in his face. "You told me you wanted to marry me and then tried to—"

"That's enough," Morgan said sharply, bending his head to speak the words beneath his breath, holding her close to his side.

"Ah, I'll warrant she didn't tell you about her stint as a camp follower, did she?" the Yankee asked. "And then the fool expected me to wed her in front of my family, ignoring the fact that I was already affianced to a lovely woman in New York City."

"A fact I was totally unaware of," Lily answered, and felt Morgan's fingers digging into her waist as she spoke.

"Show Lily the piece of jewelry," Morgan said.

"Why are you calling her by that name?" Weston asked, bringing out the tissue-wrapped package from his pocket.

"It's her name." As if he refused to elaborate on the issue, Morgan spoke the reply in sharp, clipped tones. And then watched Lily closely as she peered at the jeweled brooch Weston held before her.

"My mother's—" she began, only to cut off abruptly by Weston's sharp denial of her words.

"The hell it is," he said. "You stole it and a number of other pieces when you hit me with that poker and left me for dead. I don't know what you did with the rest, but my lieutenant followed you to the pawn shop where you sold this and bought it back for me.''

"There was no *rest*," she said. "That brooch was my mother's. She gave it to me for my eighteenth birthday. It's a family heirloom.''

"Prove it," Weston said, his voice harsh, his features contorted with anger.

"If my mother were here, she'd tell you," Lily said, her frustration riding high. "As it is, there's not much I can do to dispute your lies.''

"Well, now," the sheriff said slowly, as if an idea had come to roost and he was mulling it over. "Maybe we can't reach Lily's mama real easy, but I know, sure as shootin', that a wire can be sent to New York City, and we can have an answer in a day or so.''

He looked at Lily with a reassuring smile. "Do you know this gentleman's mother, Lily? Or where we might be able to reach her, should we send out a wire?''

"I don't know her. I wasn't fit company for his exalted family once he'd decided to set me up in a house. And it certainly wasn't his mother's house he took me to, either.''

"Oh? Then how did his mother's jewelry come to be there?" Morgan asked, and his eyes narrowed as he turned to Weston and awaited an answer.

"She'd been there to visit and left some things behind," Weston blustered, his face turning crimson as he offered his glib reply.

"You told me your family didn't know about the house," Lily said flatly. Then she turned to the sheriff. "I know where his mother lives. Her name is Edith Weston and she can likely be found in the family home near Central Park. I'll bet anyone in that area would know how to reach her.''

"Well…" The sheriff rocked back on his heels, his eyebrow quirking as he shot a seeking look at Weston. "You want to tell us the address or should I just go fishing on my own? It seems to me like we can clear this up right quick. We'll ask your mama about this piece of jewelry and find out just how many other things she's missing. How about that, Mr. Weston?''

The Yankee glared at Lily, then turned his attention to the sheriff. "I'll wire my mother today and ask her to describe the brooch for you."

"I don't think that's a wise idea," Morgan said, interrupting without apology. "The law is involved in this, Weston. We need to let the sheriff do his job. He can get to the bottom of this without any trouble, I'd think."

"The jewelry aside, Yvonne is still wanted for attempted murder," Weston said loudly. "I've got the scar to prove it, and she's already admitted it to the law. That's enough to put her in a jail cell for a good long time."

"And when the reason for her anger and the attack on you are made public?" Morgan suggested a scenario that made Lily inhale sharply. To have her name spread over the scandal sheets in New York would be a disgrace, and the family name must be protected, no matter that she had dragged it in the mud herself.

"Who'd believe her?" Weston scoffed. "She's a down-on-her-luck female, trying to make trouble for a man who is prominent in society. She'd swear to anything to gain what she wants."

"And what do you suppose that is?" Morgan asked quietly. "What would a woman in her position want in life?"

"Money," Weston said quickly. "Someone to buy her what she can't afford for herself—fancy things to cover up the soiled woman she's become."

"That doesn't sound like Lily to me," Morgan told him. "She's been taking care of herself for some time now, and she sure doesn't seem greedy to me. I'd give her all I've got and she knows it. Yet she asks for nothing."

"You probably don't have that much to offer," Weston said, looking askance at Morgan's dusty boots and the denim pants he wore.

"My daddy down in Texas would be downright upset to hear that," Morgan said, exaggerating his drawl. "He owns a spread that covers a couple thousand acres, and a third of it will be mine some day. A good bit of money connected to it is mine already."

Lily's eyes closed as she drank in the casual statement of wealth he offered. She'd wondered, as had May, where Morgan's funds came from. And had decided that he was, indeed, a very good gambler. Now the answer stared her in the face and she wasn't sure how she felt about the revelation.

"That's easy enough to claim," Weston said scoffingly.

"Easy enough to prove, too," Morgan returned. "But the argument seems to be getting off track here." He turned to the lawman, nudging him into action. "Let's send out a wire to the police department in New York City asking them to locate Edith Weston, and requesting that she describe jewelry stolen from her a number of years ago. In particular a brooch."

"I won't have my mother involved in this mess," Weston said, cutting in sharply.

"Your mother is *already* involved in this," Morgan told him. "You brought her into it when you lied about the brooch to begin with."

Weston tossed the brooch into the air and Lily reached for it, her fingers closing around the circle of precious stones and holding it tightly. "It's all yours, Yvonne," he said with a scathing glare. "I expect you earned it after all."

"That does it," Morgan said, breathing the words as if they were a curse. His first blow was a direct hit to Weston's nose, and blood spurted with a force Lily could not have believed possible. His left fist connected with a solid hit to the man's right eye, and from there it was a one-sided assault. Weston's hands rose to protect his face and Morgan blithely ignored their presence.

By the time the man was on his knees, the sheriff obviously had decided to intervene, and his hand on Morgan's arm held that particular weapon in a tight grip. "That'll do for now," he said, looking down at the defeated man who knelt at his feet. "I don't think our gentleman friend here is going to cause any more trouble to your wife, Morgan. And if he does, we'll know just how to deal with it."

"You'll pay for this," Weston blustered weakly, his voice trembling as he struggled to rise. A slit in his left eye allowed him to peer in Lily's direction. "And you, too, Yvonne. Morgan will never look at you from now on without thinking about the time you spent with me. You're damaged goods."

Barely on his feet, he was met with a final blow, an undercut that lifted him from the ground and left him spread-eagled in the dirt.

Lily ran. With every breath, she cursed the man who'd soiled her name. The man who'd dragged her through the dirt as surely as if he'd literally hauled her through a mud swamp in Louisiana. Running through the hotel lobby, she climbed the stairs at breakneck speed and sought the safety of her room. The key trembled in her fingers as she unlocked the door, and then she closed it behind her, leaning against its solid surface.

Her tears ran unchecked, her heart ached with a knowledge she could not deny.

She would never be clean, never be worthy of a man like Morgan.

Chapter Fifteen

"Just where do you think you're going?" Morgan's confusion matched her own, Lily decided, but at least he wasn't dealing with tears that refused to cease. As quickly as she could, she was stuffing her belongings into her valise, jamming her brush in one corner, her extra pair of shoes into another.

"I'm leaving," she managed to whisper, in between sobs that required the use of a large handkerchief. Morgan supplied her with his and she accepted it with a murmured thanks. "I'm going home, Morgan. I've got almost enough money to get me there, and as much as I hate to ask you, I'd like to borrow a few dollars. I'll pay you back as soon as I can, if you'll give me an address where I can write."

"The hell you are," he said, his tone of voice deadly. She looked up at him then, her gaze encompassing the long, lean lines of his body as he stood before the door. She didn't stand a chance of getting past him. Should he decide to hold her here, she was his prisoner. But there wasn't much chance of that. Morgan was too proud to attempt to hang on to a woman bent on moving on with her life.

"Things will never be the same for us," she said, forcing her eyes to meet his, refusing to back away from this confrontation. "This was bound to happen sometime," she told him. "We had an agreement, and we've reached the final stage. It's time for us to tie things up and for me to go home."

"The agreement included my *taking* you home, Lily. But not today. We have to give a statement to the sheriff and wait for word from New York before either of us will be able to leave."

"And if I walk away before all that happens? What then?"

"You'll be tossed in jail until this whole thing is cleared up."

Somehow, she doubted his words. In fact, her practical mind told her that Morgan was grasping at straws right now, talking off the top of his head in order to keep her under his thumb until he was ready to leave.

"I thought this whole thing was about keeping me *out* of jail," she said shortly. Her chin jutted and she jerked her valise from the bed. It was heavy and she almost rued the gesture.

"Give me that thing," Morgan snarled. Long steps carried him across the room to where she stood.

She released the bag into his hand. Indeed, she had no choice. Morgan on the warpath was a sight to behold. "You're a bully," she muttered, watching as he dropped the offending piece of luggage to the floor and then turned back to her.

"I'll be whatever it takes to keep you where you belong." His eyes silvered as he spoke the words, as if the threat was fueled by the icy depths of his anger. From between dark lashes, he viewed her with an all encompassing survey. "If I have to, I'll tie you to the bed, Lily. Don't push me."

"Why do you want me?" The words were a cry from

her heart, that throbbing bit of flesh that pumped blood through her veins and, at this moment, felt as though it were being torn asunder. "I'm no good for you. What Weston said was true. Every time you look at me, you'll think of his hands on me. I couldn't stand your disgust. One day you'd turn away from me, and I couldn't bear that. It's better that I leave now."

"You don't know what you're talking about," he said harshly. "You're my wife, Lily. I married you for better or for worse. This is the *worse* part, but it's going to get better. We're going to get past this and work things out. I won't let you leave me."

"That man forced me into his bed, Morgan." As if the words were torn from her, she cried them aloud, and tears flowed again as her memory traced the horror of her past. "He tossed me on the ground in the woods. I wore bruises from his hands clutching at me. He hurt me, Morgan, and I was too dumb to know what being with a man should be. Not until you paid five dollars for a night in my company did I realize that all men weren't alike."

"I don't want to hear what he did to you," Morgan said, his jaw clenching. "I should have killed the bastard while I had the chance."

"And spend your life in jail for that worthless piece of humanity?" She shook her head in despair. "If you can't stand to hear about this now, how can we ever get past it? This isn't a happily-ever-after story, Gage Morgan. This is real life, and so long as you're not willing to face up to what I am—"

"Stop it!" His hands reached for her and his mouth stifled her words. His lips pressed against hers with a fiercely bruising pressure, as if by that means alone he would suppress the aching pain that overflowed in harsh words. Words that spelled out the reality of their relationship.

"*This* is what you are, Lily. My wife, the woman I wanted so badly, I was willing to ignore all my own rules. The woman I'm willing to change my future to include."

She broke from his hold and her voice trembled as she accused him. "Your future? Ranching in Texas? A part of your life you never bothered to tell me about? I wasn't even worthy enough to know where you came from, not fit, I suppose, to introduce to your family."

"Damn it, Lily. That's not true. We've never truly talked about our families. You wouldn't even tell me where your home is." His hands were rough against her skin as he snatched her off balance and dragged her against himself again. The heat of his mouth against her flesh brought shivers to her skin, and he groaned at her response.

His kisses were scattered over her face, the words he spoke muffled by the brush of flesh against flesh, visiting her brow, then her throat and all the tender places between. His breath blended with hers, his kiss one of desperation, as if he could hold her to himself with the force of his desire. And then they were on the bed and her clothing was stripped from her body, his hands rough as he dealt with buttons and tapes. She lay beneath him wearing only stockings and he knelt between her thighs, reaching to loosen his fly, allowing the burgeoning arousal to be free from its confinement.

"I won't let you go, Lily," he said harshly. "I need you as I've never needed another person in my life." He leaned over her and his mouth opened against her breast, his lips drawing the puckered crest into contact with his teeth and tongue. Lavishing that small bit of flesh with his tongue, he suckled her, drawing forth a cry she could not contain.

His hands touched her breasts, long fingers encircling the round firmness, offering each equal attention. And as he rained kisses and caresses upon them, arousing touches that brought her to the brink of ecstasy, she closed her eyes. She would never again find someone like Morgan. No other man would ever take his place in her heart.

He would not force this mating. That was a given, and she had no intention of denying either of them this time together. She lifted her face to him, seeking his lips. The invitation was explicit, and with a groan that spoke of agony and desperation, his mouth moved against hers.

His full length covered her slender form, his weight alone holding her in place for his loving as, with long strokes of his tongue, he explored anew the soft tissues of her mouth. He thrust against the tender places there that brought pleasure to her, imitating the act he seemed driven to complete. And then he buried his face against her shoulder and spoke her name.

"Lily." It was a groan, drawn from the depths of his spirit, a simple plea for her understanding. "I wouldn't ever hurt you, Lily. I'd never force you, no matter how badly I want you, or how angry I am," he murmured. "Forgive me."

She reached for him once more, sliding her hands between their bodies, seeking that male part of him that even now sought entry to her warmth, and with ease, she guided him into position. Lifting her hips, she captured him— holding him fast within the narrow passage that seized and claimed the gift of his manhood. Her arms encircled him, lifting to his movement as she seduced him to her will, and in so doing found a quick, aching release.

Her grip on him tightened as he spoke her name again and his flesh warmed her, moving against her with each stroke—searing her with the pleasure of male textures against her own softer, feminine body. She met his rhythm then, and moved as he bid her, until, with a spiraling tension that sought release, they found together the rare, soaring delight of lovers who are in one accord.

* * *

"Are you singing tonight?" May asked. She caught up with Lily in the lobby, her gaze searching out the other woman's face as if she looked for evidence of trouble. "What's going on with you and Morgan? I heard you fussing earlier today, and I almost knocked at your door. Are you all right?"

"We did fuss a bit," Lily said, thinking how poorly that phrase described the altercation she'd shared with Morgan. The quarrel that had ended up with his loving her almost into oblivion, so long did he strive to bring her pleasure in every way possible. "It's all right now, May. Morgan's being a gentleman about this whole thing, but he'll be better off with a woman he can take home to his family, without having to make explanations."

May guided her to a settee against the far wall of the lobby and drew her down to sit. "Do you really think he cares about what happened to you before you met?"

"I know he does," Lily said sadly, thinking of the words that still rang in her ears, remembering the stony countenance he'd offered as he spoke. *I don't want to hear what he did to you.*

"He can't face what I became in order to survive," she whispered, feeling once more the anger she'd thought deeply buried. Brought now to the surface as she recalled the day she'd left her home.

"Stanley Weston had a torch in his hand and was ready to toss it through my mama's parlor window. He would have burned River Bend to the ground that day. And then, as if he dangled a carrot in front of my nose, he turned to me and smiled. "Come away with me," he said, "and I'll leave your folks in one piece." She drew a shuddering breath and her whisper was harsh. "God help me, I went with him, May."

"Ah, Lily." May leaned over to clasp a trembling hand. "You did what you had to. That's something we all have to live with. One time or another we make a decision that comes back to haunt us, bringing regret when it doesn't work out for the best. Morgan won't hold that against you.''

''He'll never be able to forget it, though.''

As though there were no response she could utter as assurance, May rose and drew Lily from her seat. ''Let's go have some supper before it's time to change,'' May said. ''Where's Morgan? Will he be coming down?''

Lily shook her head. ''No, he's not here. There was business with the sheriff to be taken care of.''

They walked through the dining area to a table in the corner. May picked up her napkin, glancing with a shake of her head at the mended spots and then placed it on her lap. The flourish of that piece of linen was a gesture guaranteed to gain attention, and the waitress came to them immediately.

''What would you ladies like?'' she asked nicely. ''The special is fried chicken tonight.''

''Sounds good to me,'' May said and then with a quick glance at Lily, she added to the order. ''Make that two chicken dinners.''

''I don't know how much I can eat,'' Lily murmured. She lined up her silverware, spread her napkin in her lap and then looked up into May's candid gaze. ''The man who showed up in town this morning is the Yankee colonel who took me from home five years ago,'' she said quietly. ''Once he leaves town, I'll be free to go,'' Lily said.

''And you think Morgan will let you?''

''He says not,'' Lily answered.

''Then I wouldn't count on leaving him behind, if I were you. He's got it bad, Lily. I watched out the window and saw the fracas earlier. Morgan wouldn't have knocked that fella's block off in front of the sheriff's office if he wasn't up to taking care of you.'' May paused and then smiled knowingly. "And then when he followed you back to the hotel I just made myself scarce. Thought I'd best leave well enough alone."

The waitress appeared, two cups and saucers in hand and placed them on the table, then poured coffee from an enameled pot. As she moved on, May bent toward Lily. "You're wise to steer clear of that Weston fella. He's a scoundrel if ever I heard of one. He'll be out for your blood, Lily. I'd advise you to stick close to Morgan."

"It looks like Weston will be on the next northbound boat. Morgan is over with the sheriff right now, making sure that the threats the man made won't follow me home."

Two steaming plates of food arrived, and both the women leaned back to allow the waitress access. Lily felt her stomach revolt as she eyed the meal before her. "I don't know if I can eat this," she said quietly, and then reached for May's hand, clutching it in her own. "It'll be better for Morgan if I leave."

May shook her head, dropping Lily's hand to the table, then patting it as she might pacify a child. Picking up a chicken leg, she took a bite, savoring the flavor with a sound of enjoyment before she answered. She chose her words carefully, as if reluctant to interfere. "Don't you think that's Morgan's choice to make?"

"No, it's mine. Morgan won't walk away from me. He's an honorable man, May. He's promised to stand by me, and no matter how hard that pledge will be for him to fulfill, he'll do it. I'm going to take it out of his hands."

"That's up to you, I suppose," May said with a dubious look. "He'll follow you. And probably catch up with you," May said matter-of-factly. "Then what'll happen?"

"I know a bit about staying out of sight," Lily told her. "I won't be traveling on the river. And that's all I'm going to tell you. I don't want you to have to lie to the man, and you better believe he'll be grilling you for any little clue he can get.''

''I just hope you know what you're doing.'' May settled down to eat and Lily tried to follow her example, aware that her body required food in order for her to sustain her strength for the days ahead.

''Why don't you unpack that bag?'' Morgan asked her. Propped against the headboard, he watched as she sorted through her belongings for the nightgown he fully intended to remove as soon as she climbed into the bed with him.

Damn. She was ignoring him, just fiddling around with her hair, brushing it until it seemed to breathe with a life of its own, clinging to her hands, and flying as it would around her head. She tamed it with long strokes of the brush, then loosely braided it for the night.

''You know I like your hair down,'' Morgan said softly, stifling the urge to go to her. He'd handled her roughly the last two times they'd met on this bed, not that he'd bruised her or caused her pain. But he hadn't offered the choice of refusing him, not until he'd aroused her to a state of willingness, and for that he felt shame to have so used her. She'd clung to him, crying out softly, holding him and accepting the pleasure he brought to her. And now he resolved to make amends.

''It's messy in the morning when I leave it down.'' She slid her brush back in the valise and folded her dress and petticoat with care, placing them on the chair. In the light of the single candle, she approached the bed and sat on the edge.

She was a conundrum, he decided. He'd be willing to bet his bottom dollar that she'd found little joy with the men she'd known. As if she were an innocent, as though pleasure was a stranger to her, she'd clasped it to her and reveled in the delights they found together.

He shrank from thoughts of those men, feeling a coward as he pushed the knowledge to the back of his mind, determined that it not come between them.

Yet she was withdrawing from him, as if she built a wall between them, stone by stone, and he knew a surge of frustration at her willfulness, at her obvious turning away. With a sigh, she slipped her feet beneath the sheet and tugged it high across her breasts. Morgan looked down at her, watched as her eyes closed and a yawn was covered by slender fingers.

"You're tired?" he asked, rising to divest himself of his own clothing.

"It's been a long, hard day," she murmured. "Yes, I'm tired." Turning her back, she faced the other side of the bed and he grinned at her back.

"Why don't I rub your feet for you?" he offered, lying down beside her.

"They're all right," she said quickly, and then stiffened in his arms as he drew her back against his chest.

"Good night, Lily," he whispered against the crown of her head. The scent of clean hair and freshly bathed woman rose to tempt him and he strove determinedly to set aside his need. Not that a man who'd been on a regular diet of loving for the past few weeks should have any needs left to speak of.

This having a wife had spoiled him, he decided. And he couldn't fault her if she chose to give him her back tonight. If only... He frowned as he considered her actions. The valise was still packed and Lily was edgy, a combination he found worrisome.

His eyes closed as her breathing evened out and she became soft in his embrace. Wiggling a bit, she sighed, then leaned against him and his grip on her tightened. It was a sad state of affairs when a man found himself content with a little hugging and a stolen kiss or two, he thought with a grin.

Come tomorrow, when the next northbound boat came by, the sheriff planned to usher Stanley Weston down to the dock and see to it he was on board. With the threat of exposure to his family, the man appeared to have accepted defeat. The sheriff was sending wires to all law enforcement agencies to take Yvonne Devereaux's name from their list of wanted criminals, and the warrant had been torn into small pieces and burned into ashes.

In a couple of days, Morgan decided, he'd gather up his wife and their belongings and be on his way to Louisiana. There would be a showdown somewhere along the way. For, without a doubt, Lily would rebel and protest his protective involvement with her, but he looked forward to it, almost certain she was becoming entangled in his web.

He loved her. There was no getting around it. He loved her with a depth of emotion he hadn't thought himself capable of. Only one other woman had drawn forth this sort of affection and she had been off-limits, another man's wife. And even that well-remembered rare beauty and innocence paled when compared with Lily's vibrant features and the strength of character she'd exhibited over the past weeks.

He should have told Lily today. Sometime during those moments when he'd loved her with every fiber of his being, he should have murmured the words in her ear. Now, even though she could not hear him, he whispered the vow against her silken hair.

"I love you, Lily. I love you." And wondered at the pleasure he'd gained from speaking those simple phrases aloud. Now, if she would only reciprocate. If somehow he could win her love in return, he would find a way to make her happy for the rest of her life.

* * *

"What the hell is all this about?" Morgan held a crumpled piece of paper in his hand as he faced May through the open doorway of her room. "Where's she gone, May? And don't try to tell me you don't know anything about it."

"She ran out on you, Morgan. It was her choice." And then May's tough facade cracked just a bit and Morgan saw regret touch her gaze. "She didn't think you'd ever get beyond her past. She doesn't figure she's good enough for you. In fact, she said you wouldn't be able to take her to meet your family, because it would involve explanations that she couldn't stand."

"Hell, who cares about my family?" he said roughly. "Lily's my wife. Nothing's going to change that." He ran long fingers through his hair and then clapped his hat back on. "Where'd she go, May? And don't try to tell me you don't know."

May's shoulders lifted in a shrug. "It's the truth, Morgan. She wouldn't tell me anything. Said you'd be on me for answers and she didn't want me to lie to you."

"How long ago did she leave?" Frustration tore at him, setting aside the relief he'd felt when Weston was put on the boat and the sheriff had announced the whole situation taken care of. Answering wires from Washington had assured Morgan that Lily was no longer wanted for any crime, given the fact that she had only defended herself.

So, he'd come back in triumph to their room, certain he would find her still sleeping, only to realize that she'd trotted herself out of town while he'd been tending to business.

"She's in the clear, May. For all the good it does now. Hell, she doesn't even know that it's safe for her out there. I don't want her hiding out, thinking the law's on her trail."

"I told her you'd follow her," May offered. "She seems

to think you can't catch up with her, though. She said she was good at covering up her tracks."

"I'm better." His jaw clenched as Morgan thought of Lily facing the perils of the road by herself. "Is she on foot?" he asked.

May shrugged. "I don't know. I doubt she had money enough for a horse and buggy."

"Damn!" Morgan's thoughts spun toward the livery stable. "I'll bet you she took my buggy. That little—" His descriptive phrase was too acerbic to be spoken aloud, and he swallowed the words. "Thanks, May," he called back over his shoulder as he headed for the stairway.

She leaned from the room behind him, and her final words were a revelation to him. "River Bend, Morgan. That's where she's going. It must be the name of her family's plantation."

He skidded to a stop and turned on his heel, returning to her with long strides. His hands clasped her waist and he picked her up in the air, lowering her until his mouth found her cheek and left a kiss there. "I won't forget you for this," he murmured as he set her down again.

The livery stable was forthcoming with the information he sought. Indeed, his mare and the buggy he'd left there were gone. The man had assumed that Morgan's wife had the right to use the vehicle. Yes, she'd been gone over an hour now. And then the gentleman found himself in the midst of negotiations as Morgan dickered for the price of a gelding that was for sale.

He'd paid too much, Morgan thought as he placed his single piece of baggage behind the saddle and tied it in place. But when a man was over a barrel he did whatever he had to in order to survive. And finding Lily was a matter of survival, as far as he was concerned.

It was four miles or so down the road when the horse began to limp, and Morgan lifted himself from the saddle.

A shoe was loose, and the animal stood with that foot lifted, unable to go any farther. Four long miles to walk, and no time to spare, Morgan thought. Swallowing his frustration, he turned back to Brightmoor and led the horse to the livery stable.

"It'll be a bit," the man, who doubled as a blacksmith, told him. "I'm in the middle of a job."

Morgan resisted the urge to lift the husky fellow up by his shirt front, and pulled a two-dollar piece from his pocket instead. "This says my horse gets tended first," he said quietly. "Especially since you sold him to me with a loose shoe."

The coin was snatched from Morgan's hand and the gelding was tied in the doorway. Within thirty minutes, a new shoe was in place and the remaining three had been checked and double-checked with capable hands.

For the second time within three hours, Morgan left town, hoping against hope that he would be able to pick up the tracks Lily had surely left behind. The road was rutted and he rode to one side on the grass, keeping his mount free of the rough track. He rode at a steady pace, not willing to push the gelding too hard, lest he tire before the day was barely begun.

The sun was hot and he cherished the shade as he passed through a wooded area. He'd traveled at least six miles, he figured, a good way beyond his first journey on this road.

The wagon tracks were old, for the most part, but fresh droppings from a horse caught his eye as he watched for new hoofprints in the dirt. If they were from the mare, Lily could not be too far ahead of him, and he picked up the pace, nudging his gelding into a lope as he looked ahead, hoping for a glimpse of the buggy.

By the time he'd reached the next town, almost twenty miles south of Brightmoor, his temper was on a fine edge and he drew to a halt before the sheriff's office. A sturdy lawman watched him from the doorway, and Morgan nodded a silent greeting. Tilting his hat from his face and leaning on the saddle horn, he asked a question.

"Have you seen a woman alone, driving a buggy, come through here in the past little bit? I'm trying to catch up with my wife and I don't like the idea of her being by herself on the road. She's off to visit her folks and I decided I'd better tag along." Close enough to the truth, it rang with sincerity, Morgan decided, and he plastered a smile on his face for the other man's benefit.

"Can't say that I have," the fellow answered. "Nobody's gone past that I've noticed anyway. You might stop at the general store, see if they've caught sight of her."

Morgan nodded and directed his gelding to the building the lawman pointed to, walking inside quickly. His query was met by a blank stare and then a brisk shake of the storekeeper's head.

"Naw, I ain't seen anybody special. If it was a stranger, I'd have noticed. Don't miss much of what goes on around here."

Morgan nodded his thanks and led his horse to a watering trough before he mounted and rode from town. He began to feel some doubts as to the value of his plan, yet surely Lily had headed south. She'd have no reason to go back the way they'd come, and with the buggy it was unlikely she'd take off cross-country. It would be necessary to stick to the road.

By nightfall he was ready to call it a day. Tired and grumpy and more than a little worried, he staked his gelding by a stream and stretched out on the bank to sleep. The sun would waken him early on, he figured, and with the abundant grass available all around him, the horse would be well-fed for the day.

Finding Lily was turning out to be a more difficult task than he'd thought, and he recognized the fear he felt for her well-being. The evening had turned blessedly cool, and he was relieved to know she had her shawl with her. Whether she had sought shelter in the open or in someone's barn, he could only hope she was safe.

Old habits stood him in good stead and he tugged his hat brim over his eyes, aware that the horse would alert him should anyone approach. He'd do better to rest for a couple of hours and then go on.

Chapter Sixteen

A direct route would have been faster, but Lily chose instead to weave a trail Morgan would have difficulty in following. A flat-bottomed ferry boat provided her with a safe crossing of the big river, even though she clung in fear to the horse's harness for the whole of the journey. Traveling on the eastern route, she stayed for two nights at hotels along the way, slept in the open while curled on the buggy seat and finally reached Vicksburg, road-weary and aching in every joint.

The ferry there was a bit larger, carrying the horse and buggy on board with ease, and when they reached the far shore, she felt a lightening of her heartache as she neared River Bend. The sorrow she'd lived with over the past days seemed relieved as each mile brought her closer to the home she'd left behind five long years ago.

Surely Mama and Susanna would be busy in the house. Her father might be in the stable with his horses, and perhaps there were even now workers in the fields, tending the cotton. And yet, she thought with a tinge of sadness, the people of the plantation might no longer be there. They'd been freed, and many had chosen to strike out on their own. Only the promise of work and a living to sustain them would have tempted some of them to remain.

The small towns she traveled through were changed, indefinably, but with a sense of despair apparent on the faces of many. Life was not easy. It was the message she read in the eyes and countenances of both men and women going about their daily lives. The thought of River Bend having changed to that extent made her anxious to arrive at her destination, and when the long lane of live oak trees formed before her, she found tears spilling from her eyes.

Her mare sounded a loud whinny, and it was answered by several horses in the near pasture. A tall, black mare kept pace with the buggy, and Lily admired the lean, long-legged beauty, not recognizing it from the past. Things would have changed, she thought reluctantly. No matter how badly she wanted it to be the same, she might not receive a welcome from her family.

They'd not understood why she left, and she had not told them. The sacrifice she'd made had been her own choice, and she would not, even now, lay the burden of it on those she loved.

The house appeared to be the same, although it looked to be needing a fresh coat of paint. A young woman, vibrant chestnut-colored hair braided into a long pigtail, stood on the veranda as Lily approached, lifting a hand to shade her eyes as she inspected the buggy and its occupant.

"Hello," she called out, and stepped down to greet the mare with an uplifted hand. Her attention all on the horse, she patted the animal's nose and murmured soft words of approval. Then she looked up at Lily. "I don't believe I recognize you, although your face seems familiar. I'm Katherine Devereaux. Welcome to River Bend." From behind the screened door a small boy called a greeting.

"Mama? Is that Aunt Jenny?" he asked.

"No, sweetheart," Katherine Devereaux answered.

"I'm another aunt," Lily told him, fearful of the lack of welcome she might receive today.

Katherine turned back to her, eyes wide as her gaze scanned Lily's face. "Don't tell me. You're Yvonne, aren't you?" Her mouth turned up in a smile that Lily thought could have rivaled the sun. "Oh, my! Wait till Mama knows you've come home. And Roan, too." She reached up to touch Lily's hand. "Come on in, won't you?"

The buggy seat was high, but Lily slid down easily, only the aching of sore muscles a deterrent to her progress. "I didn't know if I'd be welcome," she murmured. "It's been a long time since I left."

Katherine smiled quickly and nodded assurance. "Roan worried about the same thing when we came home. And we've never left since." She gripped Lily's arm and hustled her toward the porch. "And you won't have heard about Shay and Jenny either."

"Shay?" The name was not a familiar one, and Lily was puzzled.

"Your brother, Gaeton. He's called Shay nowadays, and he's living a day's journey away with his wife and their brand-new baby daughter. Just wait till you meet Jenny. You'll love her."

A dark-skinned woman pushed the screened door open and Lily looked into the familiar face of the woman who had been a part of her life forever, it seemed.

"Susanna!" she cried aloud, and was welcomed with a warm smile and a firm arm around her waist in greeting. Susanna's other arm was filled with a baby, probably six months old or so, if Lily could be any judge of the matter.

"My second son, Jonathan," Katherine said by way of introduction, taking the wiggling infant from Susanna's embrace.

"Do we have callers?" another woman asked from beyond a wide doorway. Cultured, and containing the melodic sounds of this area, it was a familiar voice from her past and Lily's heart began to beat rapidly.

"Mama?" she whispered, and took the three steps necessary to reach the parlor doors. A slender, still-lovely Letitia Devereaux looked at her from across the room.

"Yvonne." Not a query, but a statement of fact, Letitia spoke her name, biting at her lip, and hesitating where she stood. "Have you come back to stay?" she asked softly.

"I'm home," Lily answered. And wanting to set things to rights, she spoke boldly. "I'm using my middle name now, Mama. I'm called Lily."

"It was your grandmama's name, child," Letitia said after a long moment. "It suits you. But I don't know if your papa will get used to it. He's kind of a creature of habit, you know."

The space between them measured about a dozen feet, but it seemed to be an insurmountable gap as Lily awaited her mother's pleasure. "Is there a place for me here?" she asked, hoping against hope that she had not come in vain.

"There's always room for my children…*Lily.*" The name slipped from Letitia's lips easily and then she moved forward, arms outstretched, eyes aglow with tears. "My dear child," she whispered, holding fast to the daughter she'd thought gone forever.

"What's going on?" The voice was gruff, deep, and belonged to her brother, Lily decided, wiping her eyes quickly before she turned to face him.

"Roan?" she said, reluctant to assume he would be happy to see her. "I've come home."

He watched her from dark eyes, his mouth a flat line, his manner forbidding. And then as Lily watched, Katherine's hand lifted to touch his arm, and she stepped closer to him, speaking softly. "Roan, I'm so pleased to have another sister. Give Lily a hug."

"Lily?" He turned the name over in his mouth and for

a moment Lily feared he would deny her the right of its use. "She's not Yvonne any longer?"

"She was named for your grandmama, Roan. It's Yvonne's middle name. She has a right to it," his mother said quickly. "You didn't squawk when Gaeton came riding up with everyone calling him Shay, did you?"

Lily felt the years as a heavy weight on her shoulders as Roan's eyes took her measure. "You've changed," he said. And then his mouth softened. "Welcome home, Lily." Katherine looked up into his face and her smile was brilliant, Lily decided. Definitely the best thing that could have happened to Roan Devereaux was marrying this woman who gazed at him with eyes of love.

"Do you want to talk about the Yankee now or later?" Roan said calmly. "Do I need to plan on getting my gun out? Will he be paying us a visit?"

"No, he's been here once, and that was enough, as far as I'm concerned," Lily told him. "He's long gone, and if you want to know about him, I'll tell all of you the whole story at one time."

"Did he hurt you?" Gone was the flash of condemnation in his eyes. Instead Lily caught a glimpse of the brother she'd loved and looked up to for so many years.

Lily shot him a scornful look and laughed. "I don't carry any scars," she said.

"Some wounds don't leave outward traces," Katherine told her, even as her frown sent a silent warning to Roan. "Some do."

Lily felt her legs tremble beneath her and she sought the security of the sofa. "I think I'm a little tired," she said with a smile that asked for understanding. "Do you think Susanna might have some tea I could drink, Mama?"

"I already got it for you, missy," the woman said, coming from the hallway with a pitcher in one hand and three glasses in the other. Lily took one of the glasses and watched as Susanna poured the tea, and then she took a long swallow.

"Now I know I'm home," she murmured, and to the astonishment of those watching, she settled the glass on the table in front of her—just before her eyes rolled back in her head and she slid limply to her side on the sofa.

"River Bend? That's the Devereaux place, inland just a bit," the farmer said politely. "You lookin' for the old man, LeRoy or his boy, Roan?"

"Actually, I'm looking for the daughter," Morgan answered.

The farmer scratched his head and then shook it mournfully. "You're likely out of luck then, mister. Yvonne left here a long time ago, before the war was done. Went off with some Yankee colonel. Hasn't been seen or heard from since, far as I know."

"I think she's headed this way," Morgan told him. "She's my wife."

"Your wife? You ain't no *Yankee,* boy."

"Nope, I'm surely not. I'm from Texas," Morgan answered.

"Well, if your woman's at River Bend, you'll know soon enough," the farmer said. "It's about three miles the other side of town, and town's about a mile or so down this road. You oughta make it by suppertime if you move right along." He waved a hand in farewell as Morgan touched his gelding with his heels. "Hope you find your wife there," the man called out.

"Yeah." The single word fell from his lips as Morgan waved in return, and he felt a moment of fear as he considered his next move, should Lily not be at River Bend. He'd counted deeply on tracing her to this place, and should she not be at the end of this trail, he was faced with a long journey back, tracking her with very little to go on.

How she would welcome him was another matter. In fact, whether she welcomed him at all was a question he'd rather put on the back burner. First came getting there. Then he'd deal with the woman who'd been causing him no end of trouble over the past few days.

The town was nondescript, already about closed up for the night, with the exception of a dingy saloon. He rode down the single main street quickly, aware that he was the subject of covert stares from a few folks. Others outright ignored him, but for one man who waved a hand in passing. Morgan returned the gesture and rode on.

He'd just about decided that he'd somehow missed a turnoff when a long line of live oak trees on either side of a lane took his interest. As he neared, he caught sight of a weather-beaten sign that designated the place as River Bend. The lane bore to the left and he followed it across flat land for a quarter of a mile and then, where it took a turn to the right, he halted his gelding and leaned forward for a more leisurely appraisal.

The plantation house was still standing, and beyond it were barns and outbuildings, with a large garden off to one side. A few chickens squawked loudly as a dog chased them toward a pen and Morgan smiled in spite of himself. A man in overalls stood in the wide barn doorway and watched his approach, his skin dark, his manner friendly.

"Evenin', mister," the fellow said politely. "You lookin' for Mr. LeRoy? Or maybe Mr. Roan?"

"Could be," Morgan told him, sliding from his horse. "Are they around?"

"In the house," the man told him. "I'm Jethro, the fella kinda in charge of the animals around here. I'll take that horse if you've a mind to stay for a spell."

"I don't know if the woman I'm looking for is here or not," Morgan told Jethro. "My wife is headed this way and I'm hoping to find her."

"Your wife?" Jethro looked puzzled. "Only women here are Miss Letitia and Miss Katherine." He grinned widely. "And I pert' near forgot. Miss Yvonne came riding up just yesterday. Haven't got used to the idea of her bein' back yet."

"That's the one I'm looking for," Morgan told him. "She's my wife."

The man's eyes widened. "I didn't hear from Susanna that the girl'd got herself married. Don't know if she's told anybody yet." He laughed softly. "I'd say you're about to toss a fox in the henhouse, mister."

Morgan dismounted and gave the reins to Jethro, fixed a smile on his face and turned toward the house. The veranda was wide, stretching the length of the back, then bending to enclose the east side of the white building. At the back door, a tall figure watched his approach, and Morgan felt the inkling of trouble about to break over his head. He stiffened his spine and strode across the yard.

"What can I do for you, stranger?" the man in the doorway asked.

Morgan hesitated, then plowed ahead. "I'm looking for my wife."

"What makes you think she's here?" Stepping out from the shadows next to the house, the man seemed more formidable, taller and broader of shoulder than Morgan had thought at first sight. "Who are you?"

"Gage Morgan." He halted at the foot of the shallow set of steps and waited.

"Don't recognize the name, Mr. Morgan. Tell me, who's your wife?"

"Her name's Lily. She was heading here, last I saw her. You might know her better as Yvonne, though she doesn't lay claim to the name any longer."

"She's my sister," the man told him. "I'm Roan Devereaux." He turned his head as a voice spoke behind him.

"It's a visitor for Yvonne, Pa," he said quietly. "You want to go get her?"

"Ask the man in, Roan." Spoken with the natural courtesy of a Southern man, the words were a rebuke.

"All right." Roan stepped back and opened the screened door, watching as Morgan stepped onto the porch and faced the man who stood in the shadows of the room beyond the doorway. White-haired, with dark piercing eyes, he looked long and hard at his visitor.

"You'd better be Yvonne's husband." he said bluntly. "'Cause if you're not—if you're some fella who's been messing with my girl, you'd do well to turn tail and run, mister. Fact is, you're damn lucky you ain't the man who took her away from here. He's a dead man if ever I catch sight of him."

"I'm her husband," Morgan said, feeling his hackles rise at the challenge he'd been offered. "Where is she? Didn't she tell you about me?"

"Nope, she surely didn't. But that makes no never mind. Come on in anyway." The older man offered his hand. "I'm LeRoy, the girl's pa. This here's her brother, Roan."

"We've met," Morgan said shortly. He reached for LeRoy's hand and clasped it firmly. "Where's my wife?"

"Kinda in a hurry, ain't you, young fella?" LeRoy asked. "I don't know as Yvonne wants to see you, to tell the truth. She's been feeling a bit poorly since yesterday when she showed up here."

"She's ill?" Morgan felt his heart pick up in rhythm at the thought of Lily arriving at her parent's doorstep, alone and sickly.

"No, I reckon there's nothing wrong with her that time won't cure," LeRoy said flatly. "But I suspect you'd better take a look for yourself. Come on in." He led the way into a wide hallway and across it to parlor doors. One slid open at the touch of his hand and he entered the room, Morgan fast on his heels, Roan bringing up the rear.

If he'd ever felt surrounded in his life, it was at this moment, Morgan thought. And there, sitting on a couch, holding a glass of tea, looking every bit the Southern lady, sat his wife. Anger was his first reaction. Next came relief. If Lily was ill, it sure didn't show. She was rosy-cheeked, and her eyes shone with a dark glow as she smiled toward her father.

Her dress was one Morgan had never seen before, and he wondered if it had come from days past. Worn a bit, it nevertheless fit her well. She looked past her father then and spotted Morgan behind him. Her face paled and the color leached from her eyes.

"Morgan?" The single word was spoken quietly, even as Lily rose to her feet.

"Now, don't you be upsetting my girl," a woman said firmly. Morgan turned toward the voice and found a woman watching him. "I'm Letitia Devereaux, and *Lily* is my daughter." So focused on Lily, he'd not noticed the older woman's presence. And then with a longer look, he found a second woman sitting across the room, a slender female with red hair and what appeared to be a fairly young infant on her lap.

He ignored the other two women then, as Lily made a sound of despair, a whispered sob that clutched at his heart. He strode toward her, pushing past LeRoy, totally ignoring the men who followed in his tracks. His hands reached for her and in mere seconds she was clasped in his embrace.

His face rested against her hair, and he inhaled the familiar scent of her, once in a long, shuddering breath, then again, before he spoke her name, repeating it aloud as if he could not believe he held her in his arms.

"Lily. Are you all right?" he asked, and then held her

shoulders, removing her from himself far enough to look down more intently into her face.

She nodded and he felt the latent anger sweep through him, consuming the moment of anguish he'd felt. His words became harsh, his eyes glaring as he pronounced his fury aloud. "I've been worried sick about you, you foolish female." Almost, he was tempted to shake her, only the silent threat offered by the two men behind him holding him immobile.

"I'm fine," Lily said, tilting her chin defiantly. "You didn't need to follow me, Morgan. You've got things to do, folks in Texas to see, and your job is finished. You needn't be concerned about me anymore."

"*Concerned?* Damn it, Lily. I've been tracking you for days, hitting every town and talking to every lawman between here and Brightmoor. Where did you think you could hide without me finding you?"

She offered him a glare, and her words were sharp and piercing. "I'm not hiding. I'm right here, Morgan. Here at home where I belong. I told you I was coming back."

"And I told you I was going to bring you," he countered. "Why the hell couldn't you wait for me to finish up with the business we had in Brightmoor first? Why'd you go off half-cocked without me?"

"You fulfilled your part of the agreement," she said. "You don't owe me anything."

"I'd say he does," the older of the women said with simplicity, as though her claim was the final word.

"Never mind, Mama," Lily whispered. "Morgan's off the hook. He did everything he said he would."

"Including marrying you and promising to take care of you for the rest of your life," he told her bluntly. "And you didn't even stick around long enough to give me a chance."

''Does that include giving her your child?'' Letitia asked softly, and Morgan swung fully in her direction.

''What are you talking about?'' He looked back at Lily, his gaze taking in the stark expression she wore. ''What's going on, Lily?''

''*Lily* is going to have your baby,'' Letitia said. ''At least I'm assuming you're the father. Am I right?''

''Damn right,'' Morgan told her plainly. ''She can't be very far along, if my knowledge of these things is accurate.'' And then he did a bit of hasty arithmetic. ''About long enough for her to know for sure, though,'' he amended.

''Long enough for her to faint dead away on us yesterday right after she arrived, and then lose her breakfast this morning,'' her mother said stiffly.

''Mama!'' Lily's wail of anguish brought the russet-haired woman from her chair, baby and all, flying to Lily's side. She hugged Lily with one arm, the baby reaching instinctively toward his mother's neck.

''Just look what the pair of you have done,'' she said, shooting equally dismissive looks at Morgan and Lily's mother, bouncing the baby for comfort. ''Lily's crying, and that's not good for her.'' And as if to commiserate, the baby boy joined in with the chorus.

''Well, damn.'' In a frustrated gesture, Morgan snatched the hat from his head and slapped it against his thigh. ''Can we start this whole conversation over?'' He looked at the other occupants of the room and stated his case, pitching his voice above that of the wailing infant, speaking simply and to the point.

''I need to talk to Lily, and I'd like to do it with a bit of privacy. If the rest of you wouldn't mind leaving us alone, I'd appreciate it. If that won't work, then I'll pick her up and take her somewhere else.'' His gaze hardened as he awaited a reply, a reply not long in coming.

"Skedaddle, every one of you," the younger woman said, casting Morgan a look of understanding as she cuddled the child closer and released Lily from her embrace.

"Katherine…" It was a word of warning from the man called Roan, a warning blithely ignored by the small woman who seemed to have no fear of riling the man who stood over her in a threatening manner. She shoved the infant in his direction and then turned him forcibly toward the doorway.

"Go make yourself useful," she said, her words pithy and to the point. "Mama, come on with me. We need to see about helping Susanna with supper." Marching to the wide doorway, she turned and cast a long look at LeRoy. "Do you need a special invitation?" she asked sweetly, and was met by a grin from that austere gentleman.

After ushering the rest from the room, she paused in the doorway, her arms widespread as she began closing the sliding doors. "I can hold them off for about ten minutes, I figure," she told Morgan. "After that, you're on your own."

"Yes, ma'am." It was all he could think to say to her, this veritable whirlwind who apparently belonged to Roan Devereaux.

The door closed with an almost silent snick and he turned back to Lily. "For starters, it's gonna take me a good ten minutes just to tell you how mad I am." His gaze relented then as he regarded the sadness evident in her dark eyes. He reached for her again, this time holding her gently, as if he feared she might shatter into a million pieces if not handled with care. His mouth found hers and he kissed her, a gentle, tender whisper, a meeting of lips that bid her response.

She lifted her arms to encircle his neck then. "Don't be angry with me," she whispered. "I didn't know what to do, Morgan. I really thought it was for the best if I let you go home to your family. They must be missing you, and I knew my folks would come around once I got here.''

''*You're* my family,'' he told her. ''Plain and simple, Lily. We're married, and we're gonna be a real family before long. You, me and that baby of ours.'' A thrill, an aching joy he could barely contain swept through him as he considered the thought of a child such as the one Roan claimed as his own.

''I don't know if it will work,'' Lily said. ''I've thought and thought, and I'm not sure you'll ever be able to face my past without trying to hide from it. And that won't cut it, Morgan. You have to take me like I am, warts and all.''

He kissed her again, his fingers making runnels through her hair, scattering pins on the floor surrounding her and bringing a quick flush to her cheeks. His hands ran swiftly over her body, caressing the firm lines of her breasts, cupping the rounding of her hips and pressing her against himself in a surge of need he could barely suppress.

And then he took a deep breath, aware that his actions were those of a desperate man, and he still had a point to prove before he could set his marriage to rights in a way that would solidify their relationship beyond a doubt. ''I'm not pure as the driven snow myself,'' he told her, gaining control with an effort.

She nodded. ''I suppose not. But there are things you need to know. Things you haven't been willing to hear.''

''I'm ready to listen to anything you want to tell me, Lily. And I'll answer any questions you have to ask. That's about all I can offer you. If it's not enough, then I'm not sure what's next for us.'' But if he had anything to say about it at all, it was going to involve a private place and a bed, he decided grimly.

''All right,'' she said softly. ''Come and sit here beside me.'' And then as he glanced once at the door, she laughed. ''Don't worry. Katherine will keep them at bay. She's like a terrier at their heels. Keeps them in line as if she were born to the job."

"Katherine?" he asked, putting a name to Roan's wife.

"Katherine," Lily said firmly. "Everyone loves her. I don't know how anyone could help it. She's Mama's right hand, next to Susanna. My father thinks his daughter-in-law walks on water. She's given him his first two grandsons, and he's totally besotted with her."

"And Roan?" It was a foolish query, he thought. The big man was obviously smitten with the woman he'd married. And Lily confirmed his thoughts.

"He's a changed man since he married Katherine," Lily told him. "He and Shay are back to being brothers again, and Shay's wife, Jenny, is part of the reason. She drew them together, I understand. I haven't met her, or seen Shay yet, for that matter, but Papa sent a letter out this morning, asking them to come."

"Is there room here for me?" Morgan asked, sensing the family ties were well in place. Wishing his own were so sturdy.

"Of course there is," Lily said quickly. "If you want there to be."

"I won't go off and leave you, Lily. Not now, no matter what you say. I'm in this for the long ride, whether you like it or not. I told you before, I keep my promises. An agreement with Gage Morgan is worth blood, sweat and tears on his part."

"Even a marriage agreement?" she asked, her smile a bit unsteady.

"Especially a marriage agreement," he told her firmly.

Chapter Seventeen

It might not be the time or the place for her revelation, but she might not have another private moment with him. Lily forged ahead. "I have to tell you something, Gage," she said, choosing her words with care. "I love you."

One hand flew up, palm outward in warning, as he would have spoken. "Just listen. I know those are words you'll have trouble speaking aloud to me, but it doesn't matter. I've loved you I think since the first night you took me in your bed. I didn't recognize it for a while, but it goes back to the time when you offered me your protection and then kept your word."

"Now can I say something?" he asked, his smile tentative, as if he were trying to accept the words she spoke as fact. "I whispered those words to you the last night we were together. I told you then that I love you, Lily. You were asleep, but I guess I hoped you'd hear me in your dreams. You're the woman I've looked for, long and hard. I've only met a couple of women I'd want to bring home to my folks, and you top the list, sweetheart. The other is one I've already told you about, a woman I never loved as I love you."

"She must be wonderful," Lily said wistfully. "But I'm glad she's in your past."

"She didn't even know I cared about her," he admitted ruefully. "And you're right on that angle. She's in my past. You're my future, Lily."

A brisk knock on the door announced a visitor just before Katherine slid it open a bit and stuck her head through the gap. "Supper's on the table. Y'all had better finish this later. Mama doesn't like it if the food gets cold."

"We're coming along directly," Lily said, and then slid from Morgan's embrace, tidying her hair quickly and straightening her dress.

"You look fine," Katherine said, opening the doors wider. "You can get all gussied up later, Lily."

They followed her to the dining room where the table held a platter of fried chicken and bowls of steaming vegetables. "Nothing fancy," LeRoy told Morgan. "Just good Southern cookin'."

"Suits me," Morgan told him. And as heads bowed around the table, he followed their example and reached his hand to grasp Lily's. The words spoken were brief, but he felt honored when his name was included in the list of blessings LeRoy mentioned aloud.

"Now, pass the chicken," Roan said, casting one last, long look in Morgan's direction, his dark gaze settling on Lily's rumpled appearance. And in that look gave warning that the two of them would have a discussion before very many days had passed.

He couldn't blame the man, Morgan decided. He seemed to have taken on the responsibility for this place, and that included Lily's welfare over the past two days. He would be a formidable foe, he sensed, but a strong, loyal man to have at your back should the need arise.

Shay and Jenny showed up on the third day, Jenny climbing down from the buggy in haste, meeting Katherine with a squeal of delight and then looking up to where Lily awaited her turn. Shay followed behind, their son in tow, his arm bearing an infant. An older man brought up the rear, and LeRoy took him in hand, leading the way to the barn.

"I'm so glad you're here," Jenny said breathlessly, and then she turned to her husband. "Let me take Mattie. She needs to meet her new aunt."

Shay was silent, a darkly tanned man with a puckered scar on one cheek, but the small boy who held his hand seemed not to pay any mind to it.

The family was close, Morgan decided, the women hugging, the children in the midst of it all. With orders flying here and there, they were shepherded into the dining room and settled around the table.

The meal was finished in short order and Lily drew the attention of her family as she rose, glancing from one to another, as if trying to gauge their degree of acceptance before she began. It was time, Morgan thought, somehow aware that Lily had not confided in her family yet. Her words proved him right.

"I need to tell you all about why I left here," she said, her voice faltering.

"No need," LeRoy stated firmly. "You're back and that's all that matters."

She shook her head. "It matters to me. Gage already knows most of this, but the rest of you don't, and I can't live with you thinking I left for the wrong reasons."

"I know why you left," her mother said quietly. "I saw the torch in that colonel's hand, and I watched when he whispered in your ear, Lily."

Lily felt a flush climb her cheeks and she looked with gratitude at the woman who spoke. "Then you haven't hated me for the past years, Mama?"

Letitia shook her head. "You're my daughter, Lily. I never hated you. Only myself for allowing you to sacrifice yourself for the rest of us."

"He threatened to burn the house, didn't he?" Jenny asked, her face pale, her voice strained. As Lily watched, Shay reached to take his wife's hand and bent his head to whisper in her ear.

"I've been where you were," Jenny said frankly. "And I made the same choice as you, Lily. I'd do it again if I had to."

"Jenny—" Shay cut in and his wife held up her hand in a swift movement, halting his protest.

"I don't mind if they know, Shay. They're family, and I can't help but stand by Lily and let her know that I understand her motives. I'm only thankful that I was left behind to clear up the mess after those horrid men rode off."

"I wish it had been that simple for me," Lily said. "Instead I was bundled up and taken on the longest trip of my life. The ragtag end of the colonel's unit headed for home, and I was forced to live in the woods and sleep on the ground for more days and weeks than I want to remember. All along the way, he promised we'd be married once we got to his family home."

She paused as if the words were too painful to speak aloud, and Morgan's hand reached for hers, his fingers squeezing gently in comfort. "Instead I was taken to a house in the city and stayed there, almost a prisoner, wondering all the time when this wonderful wedding was going to take place. I had no place to go and no money to get there. It seemed hopeless to try to escape him by then. I had nowhere to go.

"Then the colonel came in one night and told me he was getting married. The ceremony wasn't going to include me. He'd been affianced to a society woman before he went off to war and the wedding date had been set." She paused and wet her lips, fearful of her family's scorn when she revealed the climax of the story.

"I picked up a fireplace poker and smacked him with it."

"Good for you," Roan muttered beneath his breath, and Lily gave him a trembling smile.

"He fell on the floor and there was blood all over. I thought he was dead."

"And was he?" Katherine asked, leaning forward in her chair.

Lily shook her head. "But I didn't know that for two years. Until just a few weeks ago, in fact."

"Where'd you go?" Jenny watched with tears running down her cheeks, and her hands were clenched now on the table.

"I headed out of the city." Lily turned to her mother then. "I pawned your brooch, Mama, the one you gave me for my eighteenth birthday. I had to have money, and that was the only thing of value I owned."

"Should have cleaned out the bastard's pockets before you left," her father said. And then grimaced as his wife cleared her throat. "I'm sorry, Letty. Shouldn't have said that."

"I saved the money and found a job tending children. After that I traveled as far west as I could afford to go on my earnings and worked in a restaurant at a hotel. Next came another job with a woman who was having a baby and needed help with her children. Her husband paid me well and I stayed there for almost a year."

"I might have known you'd head for home, first chance you got," her mother murmured. "I just wish it hadn't taken so long to get here."

"I discovered that I could earn more by using my voice," Lily told them. "All that Sunday morning choir singing came in handy when I found an ad in the paper in Chicago for singers for a fancy restaurant. They hired me and I stayed there for another year, till I earned enough to head South again. I still had the money from the brooch. I think I had dreams of redeeming it one day. But in the meantime it was my nest egg, insurance against the day when I'd be dead broke.

"That day came when I continued on to the Mississippi River and my funds were gone," she said.

"I met her on a riverboat," Morgan said, cutting in abruptly. "I knew from the first that Lily wasn't the sort of woman to work her way down the river."

"What sort of work?" Shay asked, even as his smile spoke of his trust in Lily's integrity. "I'll warrant she sang, didn't she?"

"Yeah, she did," Morgan said, and Lily knew he would not reveal more.

"I was on a job for the government, and Lily and I made an agreement. She wanted to come home and I needed a good cover for the work I was in the midst of. We got married as soon as we left the boat, and then traveled into Arkansas. We were there for a while, setting up the plan I'd hatched with the local lawman, and then Lily apparently thought…"

His pause was long and he glanced at the woman beside him. "I think Lily thought I didn't love her enough to be married to her. She left me and went to Brightmoor. Found an old friend there and began singing again." He looked around at her family and his silvered gaze was a warning.

"You'd have been proud of her. She looked like an angel up there in front of the crowds. But when I found her, I determined never to let her leave me again." He grimaced as he began to tell the rest of the story.

"Lily had been featured on Wanted posters along the river." At her mother's gasp of horror, Morgan quickly gave the pertinent details of the encounter with Colonel Stanley Weston. "She got away from me again." His words sounded harsh, his frustration with her evident. "And so I followed her," he finished firmly.

From outside the open windows, a chorus of insects chirped and made themselves known, a mockingbird sang its repertoire into the stillness, and then LeRoy rose to his feet. "I suspect all of this will go no farther than this room," he said firmly. "Lily's home with us, her husband is here with her, and this is a family visit."

"We won't argue that story," Shay said firmly. His arm had slid across the top of Jenny's chair to enclose her shoulders in his embrace and she glanced up at him with a damp smile.

"You'll get no quarrel with us," Roan said, and Katherine nodded her agreement.

Lily sat down, feeling that her legs could no longer hold her erect. That they had accepted her, recognized the woman she'd been forced to become, and loved her still, was almost too much for her to absorb.

That Morgan had spoken up and glossed over the trip on the riverboat, not exposing her depths of despair to the family, only served to deepen her love for him.

At Katherine's nudging, Morgan was sent to the veranda with Lily in tow as the rest of the women cleared table and joined Susanna in the kitchen. "I think she wants us to have some time alone," he whispered as Lily preceded him out the door.

She led him to a swing that hung at the end of the long porch and he sat beside her. "Do you truly mean to stay on here?" Lily asked forthrightly, as if the query burned to be spoken aloud. "I don't know what your plans are, Gage. I only trust they include me."

"I'll do whatever you want," he told her. "I'd like to

see my family one day, but I'm not in any hurry. They've gone this long without me hanging around. A while longer won't hurt anything.''

''How long are we talking about? A year? Five or ten? Or maybe a month or so?''

''You tell me,'' he said flatly. ''I'll stay here until the baby comes if that's what you'd like, Lily. I don't know if I want to haul you around the country right now. Or if you'd rather, we'll take our time and go to Texas for a visit while you're still able to travel, and see how the wind blows.''

''I've missed my mama,'' Lily said in a small voice. ''I think I'm going to need her over the next months.''

''That settles it then,'' Morgan said firmly. ''We'll stay until you want to move on.''

Lily smiled at his words. ''I think we need to be here long enough for you to get to know Shay, and I'd like to spend more time with Jenny.'' She sobered as she thought of the man who'd been her eldest brother, had borne the name of Gaeton and exchanged it for Shay. It was a story she would hear one day, she decided.

''He's been terribly scarred, hasn't he? But Jenny doesn't seem to give it a second thought. Did you know that the boy, Marshall, is Jenny's child. He seems to consider Shay his private property, I noticed,'' Lily said. ''You'd think he was Shay's own flesh and blood. And Jenny is so pretty. She really loves my brother, I think.''

''She's not as pretty as you,'' Morgan said with emphasis.

''How can you say that?'' Lily scoffed. ''She's beautiful.''

''You're the most beautiful woman I've ever known,'' he said. ''Not just your face or hair or the body that makes me feel like a randy schoolboy.'' His grin seemed a bit sheepish, but he plunged ahead, determined to finish the tribute he'd begun.

"It's the woman who lives inside that form that means the most to me, Lily. You're beautiful from the inside out. I know that sounds sort of old hat, but I mean it. It's the woman who stood up to adversity and dared to make it on her own who holds my admiration."

He watched as tears formed in her dark eyes, and his heart melted as her lips trembled. "Don't cry, sweetheart. I can't stand it if you cry."

"Then don't let me," she said. "But know this, once and for all, Gage Morgan. I never knew another man but the one who took me away from my home. There's been no one else for me but you. I swear it, as God is my witness."

Morgan's eyes closed for a moment, then he looked deeply into her gaze and murmured words of repentance. "I refused to face the facts, Lily, and I'm sorry. I think I knew all along that you were as close to innocent as a woman could be. I only wish I could claim the same. Will you forgive me?"

She nodded, her smile trembling at his words. "Kiss my tears away, Gage Morgan. Just love me with all your heart. For all the years to come."

It was still a bit early for bedtime, but no one spoke a word as the two of them walked through the door and toward the wide staircase that rose to the second floor. They climbed it slowly, his arm encircling her waist, her head tilted upward, the better to meet his gaze. And then they made their way to the last bedroom at the end of the hall. "This is the beginning. The two of us making a fresh start," Morgan said, unbuttoning her dress and sliding it to the floor.

"No," she said with a quick shake of her head, resting

her hand on the rise of her stomach. "*This* is the beginning. From now on it's the three of us, Gage."

"However you want to slice it, lady, this is bound to be the happiest night of my life. Guaranteed."

Epilogue

Christmas Eve

The house seemed to have shrunk over the past two days. The appearance of a huge pine tree in the parlor made shifting furniture a necessity, and the subsequent clutter involved in readying the whole house for Christmas had taken every available hand to clean up.

Shay and Jenny had arrived yesterday, with her father and their son, Marshall, in the back of the surrey while Mattie slept on her mother's lap. The bedrooms on the second floor were full, almost to overflowing, with Marshall ensconced in Jeremy's bed, a fact that delighted both small boys.

Celebrating a holiday was more fun with family, and this Christmas was bound to be the best Lily had ever known. For if she was any judge, there might be a new family member joining the clan before Christmas morning.

She'd wakened early on, restless and vaguely aware of a backache. Susanna had noticed right off, as soon as Lily made an appearance in the kitchen to help with preparing breakfast. It was a fact that didn't surprise Lily, and she only smiled as Katherine cast her a long look.

"It's the baby coming, isn't it?" she'd whispered as they prepared to carry breakfast into the big dining room table. And then she'd smiled, that blinding, brilliant smile that transfixed those who saw its appearance, no matter how long they knew the woman. And Lily was no exception. Katherine was all she'd ever wished for as a sister. Jenny had been a bonus, each visit bringing them closer to forming the same kind of union as she shared with Roan's wife.

Now Lily sat beside Morgan at the table and spoke brightly of holiday excitement, teasing Roan because he hadn't wrapped Katherine's gift as yet, and agreeing with Letitia that certainly turkey was holiday fare. Privately, LeRoy had confided that he was rather partial to ham, but no one was about to tell Letitia that her menu was less than perfect.

Morgan was quiet, and then in the midst of the gaiety that filled the room, he reached for her, enclosing her fingers in his palm. "Are you all right?" he asked softly, lifting her hand to his lips, and looking at her from beneath lowered lids. "You didn't sleep well, Lily. Are you hurting somewhere?"

Morgan had spent the past months watching her like a hawk, a situation that Katherine assured her was normal. Menfolk fussed over their wives during the long months of pregnancy, she'd said, though Lily privately thought that not all men fit that criteria.

"I'm just a little queasy this morning," she answered lightly. "My back aches a bit, but I'll be fine."

"Is it time, do you think?" he asked, his gaze sharpening on her, the silver-gray of his eyes warming as he seemed to consider the possibility of becoming a father today.

"I hadn't planned on spending Christmas in bed," she murmured ruefully, "but I think it's a distinct possibility."

Her free hand moved to rub fretfully at the lowest area of her belly as a niggling cramp settled there. "I don't think I'd better eat much more," she said thoughtfully. "Susanna said that once I began this process I'd do well to stick to tea and toast." She'd kept her voice to a whisper, but her tension seemed to draw attention.

From the foot of the table, Letitia eyed her daughter with concern. "I declare, you don't look a bit well this morning, Lily. Are you under the weather?" It was a phrase that had been a synonym for many conditions in Letitia's vocabulary, and Lily smiled a bit, aware that her mother was honing in for a private word with her daughter.

"I'm fine, Mama," she said quickly. "Just a little tired. I didn't sleep well."

"Well, maybe you'd best go up and take a rest this morning," Letitia said firmly. "We want you to be in good form tomorrow."

"You'll no doubt feel better by morning," Katherine said in a low voice from Lily's other side. "You'd might as well tell Mama," she told Lily with a grin. "She's persistent as all get-out."

Lily sighed. "You're probably right." She looked at her mother again and tossed a verbal firecracker into the middle of the general conversation that seemed to have come to a sudden halt. "I believe I'll just go up and get ready to have a baby."

Bedlam struck. LeRoy pushed his chair back and rose hastily. Lily thought he hadn't been so quick to move in years. His steps carried him to her side, and he frowned down at Morgan. "Why is this girl sitting here at the breakfast table when she's about ready to give birth?" he asked sternly.

Morgan merely shrugged. "I only do as she tells me, sir. You ought to know by now that Lily rules the roost where I'm concerned."

Almost choking on her laughter, Lily pushed her plate away and got to her feet, a rather lengthy process involving levering herself up on the table edge. "I believe I'll take my leave now," she said. "Now that we've all had a good laugh." Her look toward Morgan was clearly of the *wait-till-I-get-you-alone* variety and Katherine hooted with a total lack of dignity.

Yet, it was Katherine and Jenny who settled Lily in her bed several hours later. They'd walked for a time, up and down the long hallway on the first floor, then moving their arena to the bedroom area. "I'm worn out," Jenny said with a yawn, "and I'm not even the one having this baby."

"Well, you'd better stay awake for the big event," Lily told her. "I'm hoping for some support from the both of you."

"You'll have it," Katherine said. "If Morgan lets us stay in the room."

"Morgan? He won't want to get too close to this production," Lily predicted.

And found her words to be contrary to Morgan's own expectations.

"I'm going to be with you," he said firmly. "Shay was with Jenny when she had Mattie. Just ask him."

Shay had just poked his head in the door, announcing himself a delegation for the men who waited belowstairs, to get a progress report. Now he shrugged his shoulders, and smiled, nodding his agreement with Morgan's announcement. Lily considered that argument lost, and knew a sense of relief that Morgan would not forsake her today.

She shot a look at the dark, strangely handsome man who, like herself, had chosen a new name for himself. "I'll just go back downstairs," Shay said, as if relieved to be excused from the proceedings. "Letitia's on her way up, by the way."

Lily felt surrounded by her family, including the sisters

gained through marriage, not to mention having added a niece and three nephews in one fell swoop. It had been no accident that they'd met and things had come to pass in good order, Morgan had told her. All things work according to a plan, he'd said, including their meeting and the events that led them both to this place.

She settled in the bed, laughing as Susanna shooed everyone aside while she made up the proper arrangement for a birthing. Draw sheets must be stretched just so, and thick pads she'd sewn over the past weeks kept handy for the event. Two ropes were looped over the posts at the foot of the bed and Jenny explained their use, waving a hand as though the labor was of little import, and only the results were worth discussing.

And then the aching back and the clenching of muscles beneath her belly began to mesh into a form of pain designed to bring her child into the world, and Lily was caught up in the process. She did as Susanna bade her, allowed Morgan to rub her back, drank the tea Katherine and Letitia offered as a panacea for the pain, and clutched Jenny's poor hands until they both decided the ropes would bear up under bruises better than Jenny's fingers.

It was after midnight when a lusty wail rose from the bed as Morgan's wife was delivered of a son. Dark hair that appeared to have a tendency to curl covered his head, and eyes of slate-blue peered at his father as if he heard a familiar voice when Morgan spoke his name.

He took the baby from Susanna and turned to Lily, his voice deep, but trembling with emotion as the baby's name was spoken in their hearing for the first time. "Lily and I are going to call him Joshua Devereaux Morgan," he said, looking down at Lily, with a dubious frown. "That's an awful mouthful for such a little fellow, don't you think?" he asked, barely able to contain his pride.

And then he knelt beside the bed, the babe in his arms

as he bent to kiss Lily's forehead. She was tired, but filled with an exhilaration that far surpassed any happiness she'd ever experienced.

"We'll call him something else if you like," she offered, reaching to touch the dark hair, then opening her arms as Morgan delivered him to her embrace. He was sweet, small, but sturdy, Susanna had said. His head smelled like nothing she'd ever inhaled in her life, and his mouth was making urgent sucking movements, as if notifying his mother of his needs.

"I think you'd better put him to breast," Katherine said. "It'll help with the afterbirth if you nurse right away."

Morgan stood, his eyes damp, his smile tremulous. "I think I'll go on down and tell the others," he said. "I'll be back a bit later." And then he bent once more to Lily, his mouth taking hers with a kiss of promise, a fresh sealing of their vows in a blending that never failed to bring joy to her heart.

"I love you," he whispered. "And I'm the most fortunate man alive. We made it, sweetheart." He paused and then reminded her of a day long months ago. "Remember when I told you that first night on the porch that it was the happiest night of my life?"

She nodded, already aware of what he would say.

"I was wrong, Lily. This surpasses even that night, when I thought all my dreams had come true and Christmas had come early." He kissed her again, uncaring of those who watched in silence.

"Christmas is truly here, finally. It's past midnight, sweetheart," he whispered. "Happy Christmas, Lily, my love."

*   *   *   *   *

FALL IN LOVE WITH
FOUR HANDSOME HEROES
FROM HARLEQUIN HISTORICALS.

On sale May 2004

THE ENGAGEMENT
by Kate Bridges

Inspector Zack Bullock
North-West Mounted Police officer

HIGH COUNTRY HERO
by Lynna Banning

Cordell Lawson
Bounty hunter, loner

On sale June 2004

THE UNEXPECTED WIFE
by Mary Burton

Matthias Barrington
Widowed ranch owner

THE COURTING OF WIDOW SHAW
by Charlene Sands

Steven Harding
Nevada rancher

Visit us at www.eHarlequin.com

HARLEQUIN HISTORICALS®

From *USA TODAY* bestselling author

CANDACE CAMP

Lady Kyria Moreland is beautiful and rich, but when she receives a strange package she is confronted by danger and murder—not things that she can dispatch with her beauty or wealth....

Rafe McIntyre has enough charm to seduce any woman, but behind his smooth facade hides a bitter past that leads him to believe Kyria is in danger. He refuses to let her solve this riddle alone.

But who sent her this treasure steeped in legend? And who is willing to murder to claim its secrets and its glory for themselves?

BEYOND COMPARE

"Readers looking for a good 19th-century ghost story need look no further than this latest charmer...A truly enjoyable read."
—*Publishers Weekly* on *Mesmerized*

Available the first week of April 2004
wherever paperbacks are sold.

COMING NEXT MONTH FROM

HARLEQUIN HISTORICALS®

- **THE LAST CHAMPION**
  by **Deborah Hale,** author of BEAUTY AND THE BARON
  Though once betrothed, Armand Flambard and
  Dominie De Montford were now on opposite sides of the
  civil war raging in England. But when Dominie found herself
  in dire straits, Armand was the only man who could help her.
  Would they be able to put aside the pain of the past and find
  a love worth waiting for?
  HH #703 ISBN# 29303-8 $5.25 U.S./$6.25 CAN.

- **THE ENGAGEMENT**
  by **Kate Bridges,** author of THE SURGEON
  After his brother jilted Dr. Virginia Waters at the altar, mounted
  police officer Zack Bullock did the decent thing and offered a marriage of convenience…but then broke off the engagement when vil-
  lains threatened Virginia's life. And to make matters worse, Zack's
  commanding officer ordered him to act as the tempestuous beauty's
  bodyguard.…
  HH #704 ISBN# 29304-6 $5.25 U.S./$6.25 CAN.

- **THE DUKE'S MISTRESS**
  by **Ann Elizabeth Cree,** author of MY LADY'S PRISONER
  Three years ago Lady Isabelle Milborne had participated in
  a wager that had ruined Justin, the Duke of Westmore. Now Justin
  would stop at nothing to see justice served, but would he be content
  to have Belle as his mistress for just the Season, or would he need
  her in his life forever?
  HH #705 ISBN# 29305-4 $5.25 U.S./$6.25 CAN.

- **HIGH COUNTRY HERO**
  by **Lynna Banning,** author of THE SCOUT
  Bounty hunter Cordell Lawson needed a doctor to treat a wounded
  person stranded in an isolated cabin, and Sage Martin West was
  his only hope. As Sage and Cordell traveled to the victim, their
  attraction was nearly impossible to deny. Could the impulsive bounty
  hunter and the sensible, cautious doctor overcome their differences
  and find a lasting love?
  HH #706 ISBN# 29306-2 $5.25 U.S./$6.25 CAN.

**KEEP AN EYE OUT FOR ALL FOUR
OF THESE TERRIFIC NEW TITLES**

HHCNM0404